Devon Pulled Her Roughly to Him and for the First Time His Mouth Touched Hers.

His kiss was fire, a startling sensation that started at her mouth and seared its way down her body. Her arms went around his neck to draw him closer, his skin touching hers at the torn shoulder of her dress, sending tremors to the depths of her.

Linnet pressed her body against him. Devon lowered her to the ground and she felt his weight on top of her. She was burning. He ran his lips along her neck and she arched to give him access to any part of her he desired. His hands tore away part of her dress and he touched the beginning curve of her breast.

"Oh, Devon," she whispered.

Dear Reader,

We, the editors of Tapestry Romances, are committed to bringing you two outstanding original romantic historical novels each and every month.

From Kentucky in the 1850s to the court of Louis XIII, from the deck of a pirate ship within sight of Gibraltar to a mining camp high in the Sierra Nevadas, our heroines experience life and love, romance and adventure.

Our aim is to give you the kind of historical romances that you want to read. We would enjoy hearing your thoughts about this book and all future Tapestry Romances. Please write to us at the address below.

The Editors
Tapestry Romances
POCKET BOOKS
1230 Avenue of the Americas
Box TAP
New York, N.Y. 10020

Sweetbriar

Jude Deveraux

A TAPESTRY BOOK
PUBLISHED BY POCKET BOOKS NEW YORK

Books by Jude Deveraux

Highland Velvet
Sweetbriar
The Velvet Promise
Velvet Song

Published by POCKET BOOKS/TAPESTRY BOOKS

This novel is a work of historical fiction. Names, characters, places and incidents relating to non-historical figures are either the product of the author's imagination or are used fictitiously. Any resemblance of such non-historical incidents, places or figures to actual events or locales or persons, living or dead, is entirely coincidental.

An *Original* publication of TAPESTRY BOOKS

 A Tapestry Book published by
POCKET BOOKS, a Simon & Schuster division of
GULF & WESTERN CORPORATION
1230 Avenue of the Americas, New York, N.Y. 10020

Copyright © 1983 by Deveraux Inc.

ISBN: 0-671-45035-2

First Tapestry Books printing May, 1983

10 9 8 7 6 5 4 3 2 1

Printed in the U.S.A.

Chapter One

Kentucky Wilderness—October, 1784

THE FOREST CLOSED AROUND THE MOTLEY ARRAY of wagons, horses and people. Four wagons, in good repair, stood to one side, oxen grazing nearby, while two carriages, once pretty things, were barely standing on their high wheels. Tired women went about the chore of preparing supper while the men looked after the animals. A group of children was playing within sight of the adults.

"I can't tell you how glad I am to be rid of some of this heat. It's the sea I miss." Mrs. Watson stood, putting a hand on the small of her back to ease her stomach and the child that would soon be born. "Where's Linnet, Miranda?" she asked the woman across the fire from her.

"She's playing with the children again." The smaller woman's voice had a clear, En-

1

glish accent, so different from her companion's slurred words.

"Oh, I see her now." Mrs. Watson shielded her eyes from the glare of the setting sun. "If a body didn't know better, you wouldn't be able to tell which was the children and which was Linnet." She watched the girl, holding hands in a circle, no taller than the half-grown children for all her twenty years, a loose dress covering the young curves of her body, the same curves that had sent Mrs. Watson's oldest boy to the Tyler wagon so many times. "You know, Miranda, you and Amos ought to talk to Linnet. It's high time she had some young'uns of her own, 'stead of takin' on everybody else's."

Miranda Tyler smiled. "You're welcome to try, but Linnet has her own mind. Besides, to be honest, I'm not so sure young men are ready to take on the responsibility of my daughter."

Mrs. Watson looked away and gave an embarrassed little laugh. "I'm afraid you're right. Not that there's anything wrong with Linnet, she's certainly pretty enough, but it's just the way she looks at a man, something about the way she stares at him and the way she always seems to be able to take care of herself. Mind if I sit a spell? My back hurts more every minute."

"Certainly, Ellen. Amos set a stool out for me."

The heavy woman sat, knees apart, as she tried to balance her huge stomach. "Now where was I?" She either didn't see or pretended not to see Miranda's frown. "Oh yes, I was talking about Linnet, the way she unnerves men. I did try to talk to her once, tried to explain how men like to feel they're somethin' special. Now look over yonder to Prudie James."

Miranda did as she was told before returning her attention to the pot of beans.

"Now there isn't a time of the day when Prudie isn't surrounded by young men," Ellen continued. "She's not near as much to look at as your Linnet, but she always has the boys. Remember last week when Prudie was stung by a wasp? Four boys ran to help her."

Miranda Tyler looked across the clearing to her daughter, her lips curving in a fond smile. She had her own memories, such as the time the little Parker boy had left the camp alone. Linnet had been the one who found him and had risked her own life to wedge herself under those loose rocks and bring the terrified boy to safety. Mrs. Watson could have all her Prudies she wanted.

"Of course, I'm not sayin' anything against Linnet, she's shore been a big help to me, it's just that I . . . well, I want to see her happy, with a man of her own."

"I'm grateful for your concern, Ellen, but I'm sure Linnet will find a husband someday and I'm sure he'll be to her liking. Would you excuse me, please?"

The only warning they had was a dog's yip, cut off in the middle, but even that wasn't heard since the children were laughing in glee as they waited excitedly for the thimble to be secretly placed in their waiting hands.

The Indian raiders had long ago learned the benefit of surprise, attacking when the tired men and women were most relaxed, least vigilant. The men on guard had been easy to kill, their throats slashed in one clean, silent stroke. All that remained were the women, a few young adults, and the children. The children were what was of most interest to them, and two young braves were sent to tie and secure them.

Linnet, like the others, was paralyzed with shock. Her head turned sharply at a muffled cry, and she saw Prudie James fall to a heap on the ground. People began running then, trying hopelessly to escape the Indian men who seemed to be everywhere.

Linnet saw her mother take a step forward. Linnet put out her arms and began to run. If she could catch her mother, hold her, everything would be all right. "Mother!" she screamed.

Something hit her foot, and she slammed forward, the hard ground knocking the breath from her. Dazed, she tried to recover herself, feeling a moment of panic when her breath did not return right away. She blinked her eyes, seeing everything spin. As she turned her head, she tasted blood in her mouth from where her teeth had sunk into her lip when she'd fallen. Her mother lay quietly on the ground, near the fire, close to Mrs. Watson. They might have been napping, so ordinary did they seem, except the ground around them was a growing pool of a thick, red substance.

"Linnet! Linnet!" Screams came from behind her as a hand roughly pulled her to her feet and pushed her toward the children. Little Ulysses Johnson ran to her, his arms wrapped about her legs, his tears wetting her skirt and his little body shaking horribly. He was pulled from her by one of the Indians. When the child fell, the man jerked the boy's arm so that he cried out in pain.

"No!" Linnet ran to the boy, knelt before him and smoothed the dirt from his face. "I think they mean to take us with them. You'll be brave, Uly? We'll all be together, whatever happens. I don't think they'll hurt us if we obey them. Do you understand, Uly?"

"Yes," came his jerky reply. "My Ma . . ."

"I know . . ." One of the Indians pushed her, pulling her hands behind her back, tying them tightly with the cutting, rawhide rope. She tried not to look at the carnage to her right, to the body of her mother, or to think of her father who had been on guard duty. She faced her eyes ahead to the six children in front of her.

It had been only minutes, yet their lives were forever changed. Patsy Gallagher fell, dragging Uly with her, and screamed when the Indian pulled her by her ties to her feet, the thin leather cutting her wrists. Ulysses began to cry again, and all the children stared at the fires the Indians had started and the bloody messes that had been their parents.

Linnet began to sing. Quietly at first, but with a slow, steady persistence that first one child and then another began to join: "Rock of Ages, cleft for me, Let me hide myself in Thee."

They began walking, stumbling, falling often, as they marched slowly into the wilderness, tied together in a single, awkward line.

Linnet held Ulysses in her arms, the child's limp body as much unconscious as asleep. They'd been traveling for three days with little rest and less food. The two younger children looked as if they couldn't last much longer, and Linnet had persuaded one of the Indians, the leader, to allow her to carry the boy on her back. She moved her toes now, aware of the blisters, the many cuts. She was hungry, but she'd given half her cornmeal to Ulysses, and still he had whimpered for more. She stroked his forehead, aware that he was becoming feverish.

There were five Indians, sullen men, who demanded what they wanted and always got their demands. When Linnet had slowed her step because of the added weight of the heavy five-year-old on her back, they had prodded her with sharp sticks, forcing her to keep pace. Now she was too weary to sleep, her body hurting in too many places.

One of the Indians turned toward her and she

hastily closed her eyes. Several times she had seen them pointing at her and talking, and she knew they discussed her.

It wasn't light yet when the seven captives were pulled to their feet and made to begin another day's journey. Near sunset, the Indians led them to a stream, waist deep, and pulled them into it.

"I'm scared, Linnet. I don't like the water," Uly said.

"I'll carry him." Linnet gestured to the man at the end of the line. He cut the connecting leather, and Ulysses climbed onto her back.

The other children were already on the far side when Linnet slipped and fell into the water. Instantly, one of the men cut the line that connected her to the others—they would not risk losing all their prisoners if one should chance to drown. Linnet had a difficult time pulling the hysterical, fighting Ulysses to shore, and when she did, she lay back on the ground panting from her exertions.

"Linnet! What are they saying?" Patsy Gallagher demanded.

Linnet looked up to see two of the men pointing at her and gesturing wildly. He called another man, the leader, and she saw the anger on this man's face. Still dazed by her struggle in the water, she took a long time to realize that they pointed at her chest. The wet garment clung to her, emphasizing her full breasts. She crossed her hands to cover herself.

"Linnet!" Patsy screamed as one of the Indians advanced on her angrily.

She moved her arms quickly to cover her face from the first blow, but could not shield herself from the hard kicks to her ribs. She doubled in pain as more blows fell.

The Indians spewed angry words at her, and one hand turned her to her back, her bruised, maybe broken, ribs causing her to catch her breath sharply. The man tore her dress away to the waist, exposing her to him. What he saw seemed to make him even more angry. He doubled his fist, but Linnet never saw it land across her jaw.

"Linnet, wake up!"

She stirred slightly, wondering where she was.

"Linnet, they let me take care of you. Here, sit up and put this on. It's Johnnie's shirt."

"Patsy?" she whispered.

"Oh, Linnet, you look awful! Your face is all swollen and . . ." The girl sniffed and pulled her friend to a sitting position as she shoved her arms into the coarse linsey-woolsey shirt. "Linnet, talk to me. Are you all right?"

"I think so. They let you come? I thought they would leave me. Why were they so angry?"

"Well, me and Johnnie figure they thought you was a kid and when they found out you wasn't . . ."

8

"Oh, but why have they let you come to me?"

"I don't know, but if it wasn't for you, we all know we couldn't have made it. Maybe the Indians know that, too. Oh, Linnet, I'm so scared." The girl threw her arms around Linnet's neck and she had to clench her teeth to keep her pain from showing.

"I'm scared, too," Linnet whispered through her teeth.

"You! You're never scared. Johnnie says you're the bravest person in the world."

She smiled at the girl, although it hurt her to do so. "I may look brave, but I'm all apple jelly inside."

"Me, too."

Patsy helped Linnet back to the Indians' camp, the woman no larger than the twelve-year-old girl. All the children welcomed her with half-smiles, the first time they had even tried to overcome their terror.

Early the next morning, they reached the more permanent camp of the Indians. Women, dirty, ragged, ran to greet their men and run hands over the children. The Indian leader pushed Linnet toward a group of women, pointing and gesturing from his chest to hers.

One of the women yelled and tore the shirt open, striking her on the breasts. Linnet bent forward and covered herself with her arms, and the women laughed. She looked up to see the children being led away, their cries for help making her try to go to them, but the women stopped her, laughing, pinching her. One of them pulled her braids.

The Indian man spoke again, and the women took their hands from her, grumbling. One pushed her forward until Linnet realized she was to crawl into a crude grass-and-stick shelter. There wasn't room to stand in the shelter, just room for two people to sleep. The woman followed her, holding a pottery bowl in her hands.

The contents of the bowl smelled horribly of rancid grease, and the Indian woman began to smear the paste all over Linnet's face, and the upper part of her body, working it into her hair. She sat still, trying not to cry out or give way to her tears when the woman's rough hands pressed on a particularly bruised area.

She was left alone then, alone to listen to the noises outside, the frantic yells of the men as they celebrated their successful raid.

"Here, drink this." A strong arm supported Linnet and a metal cup was pressed to her lips. "Not so fast or you'll choke."

She blinked several times, not aware that she had fallen asleep. The man's wide shoulders seemed to fill the little shelter. The flickering light from a fire outside caught the ivory gleam of a necklace tight around his throat, his body barely clad. He gently leaned back against a supporting pole and took her wrist, studying her hands before rubbing salve into the cuts.

"I can see why they thought you were a child," he said in a deep low voice.

"You speak English," Linnet said in her quiet accent.

He cocked one eyebrow at her. "Not the same sort as you, but I reckon it'll pass for English."

"I saw you. I thought you were an Indian, but you're not. I think your eyes are blue, aren't they?"

He looked at her in surprise, wondering at her apparent calm.

"Where are the children? Why are we here? They . . . killed the others."

He looked away from her for a moment, not wanting to see the grief in her eyes, yet amazed that she could even think of someone besides herself. "This is a group of renegades, a mixture of outcasts from several tribes. They capture children and sell them to other tribes to replace lost sons and daughters. They thought you were one of the children and weren't too happy when they found you weren't." His eyes went involuntarily to her breasts. Crazy Bear had had a lot to say about her womanliness.

"What . . . what do they plan to do with us now?"

He watched her carefully, his blue eyes intense. "The children will be cared for, but you . . ."

Linnet swallowed and met his gaze. "I'd like to know the truth."

"The men gamble now to see who gets you. After that . . ."

"Gets me? I am to marry one of these men?"

His voice was very soft. "No, they don't intend marriage."

"Oh." Linnet's lower lip trembled and she caught it between her teeth to still the motion. "Why are you here?"

"My grandmother was a Shawnee and one of these men is my cousin. They tolerate me, but that's about all. I've been in the north, trapping."

"I don't guess there's anything you can do to help us?"

"No, I'm afraid not. I must go now. More water?"

She shook her head. "Thank you, Mr. . . . ?"

"Mac." He wanted to get away. She was so young and it was obvious she had been beaten.

"Thank you, Mr. Mac."

"No, just Mac."

"Mac? Is that your surname or your Christian name?"

He gaped at her in bewilderment. "What?"

"Is Mac your last name or your first name?"

He was astonished. "You are the beatinest woman. What the hell difference does it make?"

She blinked at him, looking as if his harsh words might make her cry, even when all the blows had failed.

He shook his head at her. "My name's Devon Macalister, but I've always been called Mac."

"I thank you for the water and the company, Mr. Macalister."

"Not Mr. Macalister, just plain Mac!" The girl was making him angry. "Look, I didn't mean . . ." He stopped as he heard a step just outside the low doorway.

"You must go," she whispered. "I don't think they will like finding you here."

He looked at her again in astonishment and left the shelter.

Mac walked alone into the woods. She was the strangest girl he'd ever met, and in spite of what Crazy Bear said, he could only think of her as a girl. The Indians talked about her courage on the trail, how she'd carried the youngest child most of the way. Mac had seen the boy and he was certainly no light burden.

How calm she'd been! Last time he'd seen a girl in her situation, the girl'd been hysterical. He'd tried to help her, too, but she'd screamed so loud, he'd hardly escaped being found out. He didn't like to remember what these men were like when they'd had too much whiskey. The last girl had bled to death.

He thought of the girl who waited so patiently in the shelter now. Instead of screaming, she'd asked him about the others and thanked him, as if they'd been sitting in some rich woman's fancy parlor.

He remembered her big, luminous eyes and

wondered what color they were, remembered holding her little hand in his. Damn! he thought, then sighed in resignation. He'd probably just declared his own death.

He saw her again when he reentered the shelter. She was sitting quietly, hands folded in her lap.

"Why, Mr. Macalister, I don't think you should be here again."

He grinned, white teeth showing, and shook his head at her. "Tell me, can you read?"

"Why, yes, certainly."

"If I take you away from here, would you teach me to read?"

"Of course," she whispered and her trembling voice betrayed how frightened she really was.

His admiration for her increased. "All right then, try to stay calm. It will take me a while and then I might not win."

"Win? What do you mean?"

"You'll just have to trust me. Now try and sleep, nothing will happen before morning. But tomorrow, just be silent and trust me. Will you do that?"

"I will, Mr. Macalister."

"Not Mr. Macalister!"

She gave him a weak smile. "I will trust you . . . Devon."

He started to protest but knew it would be useless. "I'm sure this is all a dream, and I'll wake up soon. You are truly the beatinest woman I have ever seen." He gave her one last look and left.

Linnet could not sleep. She had resigned herself to whatever the future held for her, but now this big man had given her new hope, and she almost wished he hadn't. It was easier before. Dawn came, and one of the Indian women entered the shelter and motioned for Linnet to follow her, pinching her several times.

Other women waited for them outside, laughing, hitting her when her wobbly knees threatened to collapse. They half-dragged her to a tree and pulled her arms to the back of it, tying them securely. There was no sign of the children anywhere.

Two Indian men walked toward her, each clad in the small breech cloth, their bodies lightly oiled. Her eyes were drawn to the taller man with the blue eyes, and she saw Devon clearly for the first time. He walked solidly, as if completely assured of his place on the earth, the lean muscles of his body playing under his dark skin.

Devon was also seeing the woman he was about to risk his life for and he was not so well pleased. Her delicate features were distorted by a swollen cheek, deep hollows under her eyes, and her skin and hair reeked of rancid bear grease. But the eyes that looked up at him were clear and oddly colored, like mahogany.

Before he could reach her, one of the women tore her shirt away, revealing Linnet's breasts and the girl bent her head forward in an effort to cover herself. She knew Devon stood before her and she made a great effort to look at him. She looked instead to the woman beside her, laughing and pointing from Devon to Linnet.

She looked toward his face then, saw he nodded at the laughing woman before meeting Linnet's eyes. She immediately felt her strength returning, as if it flowed from him to her.

"Don't be frightened," he said as he put his hand on her shoulder. "The Indians already talk of your courage." He moved his hand downward, and she was startled when he cupped her breast, her breath catching in her throat, but his eyes never left hers.

His hand left her body and he grinned at her. "I hope you clean up better than you are now. I don't think I could stand a teacher that smells like you do."

She managed a slight smile, but his hand on her body had stunned her, as much from her reaction to it as anything else.

He pulled Linnet's shirt together, nodded to the old woman, and walked away to stand beside the other Indian. The woman cackled and pointed from Linnet to the Indian but his eyes were angry, and he spat on the ground at Linnet's feet, turning his back to her.

Linnet still wasn't sure what was to happen until the two men faced one another in the grassy clearing before her. A piece of rawhide was tied to their ankles so that they were never more than a yard apart. Linnet drew her breath in sharply when they were each given a knife.

They circled one another, and a knife flashed in the sun as the Indian drew first blood, cutting Devon's arm from shoulder to elbow. The man didn't seem to notice the cut, but quickly grazed the Indian's stomach with his own knife.

Linnet watched the animal grace, the strength of the man who risked his life for her. He was neither a white man nor an Indian, but a combination of the white's cunning and the Indian's oneness with nature.

Devon slashed the man's shoulder, barely missing the vulnerable neck, all the while his left arm dripping blood onto the thick grass. The Indian lunged and Devon sidestepped, jerking his foot back sharply. They both sprawled in the grass, rolling together. Both knives disappeared between their bodies, Devon on bottom, then they stopped, neither moving.

There was a hush in the camp; even in the forest, the stillness seemed to penetrate. Linnet didn't dare breathe and wondered if her heart still beat.

The Indian moved, and she could feel the triumph of the women near her. It seemed ages before the Indian was gone from Devon's body, and she had trouble realizing that Devon had thrown the other man's lifeless body off. She watched, still unbelieving, as Devon cut the

17

rope about his ankle, sprang to his feet and came to her. He cut the leather binding her wrists and freed her.

"Follow me," he said in a cold, steely voice.

She clutched her buttonless shirt together and used all the strength she could muster to keep up with his rapid pace. He practically threw her onto the saddle of a big sorrel and mounted behind her in one fluid motion. His arms encircled her; one took the reins, the other held her waist. She tried to see the bloody cut on his arm, glad it was not too deep.

They rode hard, as hard as the horse could stand carrying two people and Linnet sat as straight as possible, trying not to add an extra burden to the man behind her. They came to a stream when it was well past noon and finally stopped. He lifted her from the horse and set her to the ground as she tied the tails of the shirt across her stomach.

"You think they're following us?"

He bent over the stream and splashed cold water on his arm. "I'm not sure, but I'd rather not take the chance. These aren't like a tribe of Indians, they have no honor. If the Shawnee made a bargain, they'd keep it, but not these men. At least, I'm not certain of them."

"Here, I'll do that." She tore away half of her petticoat and dipped it in the water, then began washing his wound. As she bound it, she looked up at him, and only then did she realize he was looking at her breasts, at the shirt pulled tight in a knot, bare skin showing from throat to the top of her stomach. Instinctively, she clutched it together.

He looked away. "Don't worry. I haven't sunk to Crazy Bear's level yet, although I may look like one of his tribe."

She was glad to change the subject. "You do, Devon, except for your blue eyes. I imagine that when you're asleep, you look just like an Indian."

He still wasn't used to the name Devon since, to his knowledge, no one had ever called him that in his life. "I'll remember that next time I'm sleeping on the trail. Let's go now and see if we can put some more miles between us and them before dark."

He stopped beside the horse and removed several pieces of jerky from a pack, handing her some. "The Indians called you Little Bird. The name fits you, because I'm sure your bones aren't much bigger than a bird's."

"Little Bird," she said, as if amused at some private joke.

"It was an honor that they named you," he said as he lifted her onto the horse. "They don't often do that with captives." He put his arms around her to take the reins. "What is your name?"

"Linnet. And I am sure you'll not believe this, but a linnet is an English finch."

"You mean . . ."

"I'm afraid so—a little bird."

Devon laughed, a rich, deep sound that she could feel where his chest pressed into her back. "You are . . ."

"May I guess? The beatinest woman, whatever that term means."

"I should say it's exactly what you are, the oddest woman I've ever met."

She didn't know why the statement pleased her so much, but it did.

Chapter Two

THEY RODE UNTIL DUSK, NOT TALKING, UNTIL they finally halted by a stream. "We'll camp here for the night," Devon said as he put his arms up to help her from the horse.

Linnet briefly wondered at the way she took for granted that he would help her.

"Stay here. I'll go back a ways and see if we're being followed. You'll be all right here alone?" He grinned at her, knowing how ridiculous his question was.

Linnet sat alone for a while, resting. Her head itched and she scratched it, giving a look of disgust to the black filth under her nails. Sighing, she began to look about for firewood to set up a camp.

Devon returned and saw she had unsaddled the horse and made a comfortable camp.

"I wasn't certain if I should light the fire yet, in case you didn't want to be seen."

"Good, but I think Crazy Bear's people are too lazy to follow us. They got their children and that's all they wanted."

"Crazy Bear. Was he the man you . . . ?"

"No, that was Spotted Wolf." He looked at her intently as he fed the new fire.

"I'm sorry you had to . . ."

"Let's not talk about it again. It's done. Now come over here and let me look at that cut on your mouth."

She moved across the few feet separating them and sat down before him as he took her face in his large, strong hands and gently probed the bones.

"Open your mouth."

She obeyed, looking at his forehead as he studied her teeth.

"Good. They didn't seem to break anything. What about the rest of you? Hurt anywhere else?"

"My ribs, but they're only bruised."

"Here, let me look. I imagine they could all be broken and you'd not say a word." He lifted the tail of her dirty shirt and ran his hands firmly along her delicate ribs and, when he finished, he took his hands from her and sat back on his haunches. "Doesn't seem to be anything broken there, either, but if I didn't know for sure, I'd say you were no more than a kid. I brought a couple of birds back with me. Let's get 'em cooked and some meat on you."

"Birds?" she said as she tied her shirt again. "I didn't hear a shot."

"There are other ways of trappin' game besides using a rifle. While you start cookin' I'm gonna wash some of the dirt off me."

Linnet looked toward the water wistfully. "I'd like to bathe also."

He shook his head at her. "It's my guess it's going to take more than just water to get that grease off you."

She looked down at her torn, ragged skirt, the knotted shirt, her dark, greasy skin. "Do I really look so awful?"

"I've seen better lookin' scarecrows."

She frowned up at him. "I can't understand why you risked so much to save me. You could have been killed, Devon."

"I don't understand either," he replied in all honesty as he tossed the dead birds to her. "You know how to cook, don't you?"

She smiled at him for the first time, showing perfect, pretty little teeth. "Yes, I am glad to say that I can."

The smile made Devon remember her femininity, well hidden under the dirt. He turned away quickly, took his saddle bags and went to the creek.

When he returned, Linnet was startled by Devon's transformation. He wore dark blue cotton trousers and a heavy blue homespun shirt, gathered about his broad shoulders. A great deal of his Indian looks had gone with the scant breech cloth and bone necklace, but he still had the aquiline nose, the almost straight profile, and dark hair. Sitting across the fire from her, he grinned. "I'm civilized again."

She touched her hair, plastered to her scalp. "That's more than I can say for myself."

"If I can stand the stench, you'll have to."

They ate the birds greedily, so delicious after all the jerky and dried cornmeal. Devon gathered leaves and made two beds a few feet apart. He handed her a blanket.

"It will probably be ruined after touching me," she laughed.

Devon stared at her, the moonlight making the dirt on her face less obvious. "I doubt that," he said quietly.

Linnet looked into his eyes and had a momentary feeling of fear of the man she owed so much to. She looked away as she settled into the bed, and she was asleep before she had time to consider her fear more fully.

When Linnet awoke, she saw she was alone, but a twig snapping made her turn. Devon came from the trees carrying a dead rabbit by the ears. "Breakfast." He grinned. "This time, I'll cook."

She smiled at him and walked to the stream, determined to try and wash. After several minutes, she decided she was doing little good, merely rearranging the grease rather than removing it. Giving up, she returned to the camp.

Devon turned a smile to her that soon changed to laughter, but he stopped when he saw her almost tearful expression. He went to stand in front of her, pulled his shirt from the inside of his pants and began to wipe at her face. "It's hard to believe, but I think you've made it worse. I hope the people of Sweetbriar realize you're human."

She looked at her feet. "I'm sorry I'm so offensive."

"Come on, sit down and eat. I'm gettin' used to you."

She sat, bit into a rabbit leg, and as she wiped the juice from her chin, she grinned at him. "Maybe I should just run after the animals and scare them to death."

Devon laughed. "You just might be able to do that."

They rode hard the next day and Linnet had to concentrate to stay awake.

"I guess you're pretty tired," he said in the afternoon.

She shrugged. "I've been worse."

"Well then, maybe it's good we rode so long last night. We'll reach Sweetbriar tonight."

"Sweetbriar?"

"That's where I live. One hundred of the most beautiful acres you ever saw, right along the Cumberland." He handed her a piece of jerky.

"Do you live there alone?"

"No, it's practically a city," he said, laughter in his voice. "There's the Emersons, the Starks, the Tuckers. Nice folks, you'll like them."

"Then I'm to live there too?"

"Sure, how else you gonna teach me to read? You didn't forget our bargain, did you?"

She smiled because actually she had. "Well, that should be an easy matter."

They reached the place Devon called Sweetbriar late at night, and Linnet was beyond exhaustion. She had a brief glimpse of several cabins in a clearing before Devon put his arms up for her and she practically fell into them. He caught and carried her easily.

"Devon, please, I can walk. I'm just a bit tired."

"After what you've been through, I wonder you can open your eyes. Gaylon!" he bellowed above her head. "Unlock this door and let me in."

The door opened, and an old man stood there frowning. "What you doin' comin' here this time o' night and what you got there?"

"It's not a what, but a who."

The thick old man raised a lamp to Linnet's face and she closed her eyes against the glare. "Don't look like much," he declared.

"I am Linnet Blanche Tyler, Mr. Gaylon, and I am very happy to meet you." She held out her hand to him.

The old man looked in astonishment at her: a

filthy girl, lying in a man's arms and acting as if she were being presented to the president. He looked at Devon incredulously and Devon grinned back at him.

"Ain't she somethin'? She was like that when I found her—Crazy Bear's prisoner."

"Crazy Bear! He didn't let her go just for the askin'!"

"Sure didn't and I got a sore arm to prove it."

"Devon, would you set me down, please?"

Gaylon stared at her. "Who's she talkin' to?"

"Me." Devon was embarrassed. "Calls me Devon."

"How come?"

"Because, you old coot, that's my name— Devon Macalister."

"Hmph! Didn't know you was anythin' 'cept Mac."

"You argue with her," Devon said as he set Linnet to her feet. "Run over and fetch Agnes. She'll like the girl, her bein' English and all."

"That why she talk so funny?"

"Yes, it is. Now go get Agnes and hurry up."

He led Linnet to a chair in front of the fireplace, and she sat down gratefully. She didn't think she'd ever been so tired in all her life.

"Agnes'll be here in a minute and she'll take care of you," Devon reassured her as he brought the fire to life.

Almost instantly a woman appeared—at least it seemed so to Linnet as she stirred from her drowsy state. The woman was tall, pink-cheeked, with a man's coat thrown over her nightgown. Her cleanness made Linnet feel even dirtier.

"Mac, what is Gaylon trying to tell me?"

Linnet rose. "I'm afraid I'm the cause of all the problems. Devon rescued me from some Indians, and now I fear I'm to be a burden on all of you."

Agnes smiled fondly at the dirty girl while Devon and Gaylon exchanged looks.

"She hasn't had much sleep or food in the last few days and she's been through a pretty rough time," Devon explained.

"From the looks of her, I'd say you was makin' light of what's happened to her. I'll just take her home with me. What's your name?"

"It's Linnet Blanche Tyler," Devon said and grinned. "Watch her or she'll be runnin' your whole house before too long."

Linnet looked down at her feet in confusion.

"Come along, Linnet, and pay no mind to these men. Would you rather sleep first or eat?"

"I'd like to bathe."

"I can understand why." Agnes laughed.

Hours later Linnet slipped beneath the bed covers, her hair and body finally clean, scoured until Agnes had made her stop. She'd eaten four fried eggs and two huge pieces of toasted bread, coated with sweet, creamy butter. Now she lay in a clean nightgown, miles too long for her, and slept.

When Linnet woke, the house was still, but she knew it was late in the morning. Stretching, she touched her hair to reassure herself it was still clean and left the bed to crawl to the edge of the loft and look down. The door opened and Agnes came in.

"So, you're awake. All of Sweetbriar's dying to see what Mac brought home. I been to the Tuckers', and their Caroline lent me a clean dress for you. Come down and we'll see how it fits."

Linnet backed down the ladder, holding the long gown up.

Agnes held the dress up to her. "Just as I thought, I'll have to let it out in the bosom. You sit there and eat while I take a few stitches. Won't take me but a minute."

Linnet ate cornmeal cakes, bacon and honey while Agnes sewed on the calico dress.

"There now. All done. Let's see what we have." After she'd helped Linnet dress, she smiled at her. "I think Mac's gonna be real surprised when he sees what he brought home."

"Do I really look so different?"

"Honey, a doll made out of tar—a tar baby— wasn't any uglier or blacker than what Mac showed me last night. Let me brush your hair."

"Agnes, you don't have to do all this. Please, let me help you in some way."

"You done said your thanks too many times last night. I've never had a daughter, and so it pleasures me to be able to do this." She stepped back, admiring her handiwork. Linnet's hair cascaded in heavy locks down her back, a deep gold color with streaks of lighter hair, even a hint of red. Thick, dark lashes over big, odd-colored eyes made a person want to stare and stare just to try and find out what color they were.

Agnes looked at Linnet's trim, shapely figure in the snug dress. "You're sure gonna give Corinne a run for her money."

"Corinne?"

"She's the Starks' oldest daughter, been after Mac since she was twelve, and now that she's about to get him, somethin' like you comes along."

"Mac? Oh, Devon. Didn't he tell you that he brought me here to teach him to read?"

"Devon, is it? Well, I could have taught him . . . Never mind. Let's get goin'. I can't wait to see Mac's face."

Agnes Emerson's house was about a mile from the clearing that contained Devon's trading post and the other buildings, and there were people, mostly children, every few yards, all anxious to look at the girl Mac had brought with him. They'd heard his stories all morning, greatly colored by Gaylon's exaggerations.

"She don't look like what Mac said," a voice came from behind Linnet.

She turned to see a boy, about seven, with a dirty face and a long piece of string trailing from his pocket. "And what did he say?" she asked.

30

"Said you was the bravest woman he'd ever seen."

Linnet smiled. "He doesn't know me very well. I was just too scared to make any noise. I imagine you'd like to hear about his fight with Spotted Wolf."

"Mac fought an Indian?"

"He certainly did."

"How come you talk so funny?"

"I'm from England."

"Oh, well, I gotta go. See ya."

Agnes put her arm around Linnet. "Let's go, and you all stop starin' at her like she was some kind of freak," she said to the children who still watched. "Let's go show you to Mac."

The log house was large, L-shaped, and Linnet wondered that she hadn't realized that it was some sort of store when she had seen it before. Devon was standing with his back to her, talking to a pretty, dark-haired girl with an incredibly voluptuous figure.

The girl stopped in mid-sentence and stared at Agnes and Linnet in the doorway. Devon turned and looked at her, his eyes widening.

"Well, ain't you gonna say somethin'? Some difference from that smelly heap of rags you gave me last night." Agnes' eyes sparkled.

Devon couldn't speak. Linnet was pretty, very, very pretty with a delicate little face that held enormous eyes, a tiny nose and soft lips that curved now into a slight smile. He didn't know why he felt betrayed, but he did. Why didn't she

31

tell him she was so damned good-looking? he thought in an unjust burst of anger. Maybe not tell, but at least warn him.

"I think you've knocked his voice out. This here's Corinne Stark and she's often here at Mac's store." Agnes' voice told everyone what she thought of Corinne's forwardness.

Devon looked away from the women to a big table piled high with furs. "Agnes, why don't you take her over to Old Luke's cabin? I figure she can stay there after it's cleaned."

Linnet looked in question to Agnes, wondering what she had done to cause Devon to shun her as he was doing, but Agnes kept her eyes on Devon's back.

"I got too much work to do at my own place. You take her and show her Old Luke's place."

Corinne smiled, turning to look at Devon. "I'll go with you, Mac."

Agnes gave a cool smile to Corinne. "To tell the truth, Corinne, honey, I been needin' help with a new quilt pattern your ma lent me, and she said you'd be the very one to help me."

"I can do that anytime." The girl's eyes were cold.

Agnes gave her a piercing look. "Well, I ain't as free as you with my time, and I need you this mornin'."

Corinne gave a pouty look of defeat, cast one more glance at Devon and followed Agnes out of the store, avoiding Linnet altogether.

They were alone together, silent, Devon still

with his back to her. She walked closer to him. "Devon?"

He turned and glared at a spot somewhere above her head. "If we're gonna see the cabin we'd best go now. I got work to do." He left the store, walking quickly, ignoring Linnet as she tried hard to keep pace with his long strides.

Chapter Three

THE CABIN WAS A MESS. IT STOOD A FEW YARDS from Devon's store, sunlight pouring through a hole in the roof, chickens roosting on the stones of the fireplace, flying squirrels scurrying out the open windows. Devon shooed the chickens out, their wings raising the dust. "Here it is. It ain't much, but it could be livable with a little hard work. You ain't afraid of a little hard work, are you, English lady that you are?"

She smiled up at him and he thought of their two nights alone on the trail. It's a good thing she didn't look like she does now, he thought. He looked away.

"Devon, are you angry with me?"

"Why should I be 'angry' with you? What reason could you give me for being mad at you? I hear even Jessie Tucker likes you, and that kid don't like any women. No, there couldn't be any reason for being mad at you." He sat on a bench, dust flying.

She blinked at him several times. "How's your arm?"

"My arm's just perfect."

"Would you like me to look at it?"

"I don't need any motherin', especially from . . ."

She looked away from him, unable to see any reason for his anger and not a little hurt by it.

Devon studied the toe of one boot, mad at himself for acting the way he was, which made him even madder at her for making him mad. "Damn!" he said aloud.

"Pardon?"

He looked around the filthy cabin. "What you plannin' to eat here? Did you think of that?"

"No, I haven't. I really haven't had time to think of anything. It seems everyone has taken care of me for so long. First you and then Agnes. Of course, you told Agnes—"

He interrupted her. "Well, as I recall, our deal was that if I took you away from Crazy Bear's men, you'd teach me to read, and now I've thrown in this cabin, but I ain't gonna feed and clothe you, too."

"I don't expect you to. You've done far too much already."

He watched the sunlight coming through the open window, dust-filled, circling around her, those big eyes gazing at him, accepting that he just might let her starve, never asking for more from him or anyone else than they were prepared to give.

She smiled, eyes sparkling through the sunlit halo. "Who cooks for you, Devon?"

He was startled back to the present reality. "Gaylon, if you can call it that. Sometimes the women around here take pity on me and invite me to supper."

"I'll make a bargain with you."

"What do you have to bargain with? Even the dress you're wearing is borrowed." Involuntarily, his eyes went downward and he knew that dress had never looked like that on anyone else.

"I can cook. If you furnish the food, I'll cook for you, and if you supply cloth and thread, I'll make you new shirts and myself two dresses. Does that seem fair?"

More than fair, he thought. "Who's gonna take care of your firewood?"

"I can. I'm strong."

She looked anything but strong. Shaking his head, he grinned at her. "I'll bet you could walk through a pile of manure and come out smelling like roses."

She returned his smile. "From what everyone said of how I looked the last few days, I think I've done just that." She put both hands to her head. "It feels wonderful to be clean again, with clean clothes." She smoothed the faded cotton skirt. "You didn't say, Devon. Do I look all right? Were you surprised that I didn't look like a tar baby anymore? That's what Agnes said I was."

She was standing a few feet from him, and as

she pulled a fat strand of hair away from her head, little flyaway pieces glittered in the sun. "It's so nice to touch my hair and not get my hands dirty."

He couldn't help himself as he extended a brown hand and touched her hair, rubbing it between his fingers. "I never would have thought it was yellow. It was so black before." He dropped the silken stuff immediately, but looking at her face, he saw she smiled at him and he wasn't angry anymore. "Linnet, I never would of guessed you were the same girl as that smelly, black lump I found in that grass shack. Now that that's all done, let's get this place clean."

"Oh no!" she said quickly. "Now that we have all the business settled we can go after the children."

Mac wasn't sure he heard her correctly. "Children?"

"The children Crazy Bear took, of course. We can't just leave them there."

"Now wait a minute! You don't know what you're talkin' about. We've learned here that we let the Indians alone and they leave us in peace."

"Peace!" she gasped. "They killed my parents and now they have the children. I can't possibly leave them there. They have to be returned to their people."

"You! *You* can't leave them there? Have you forgotten what they were plannin' to do to you?"

37

"No," she said softly, swallowing. "But I also remember seeing my parents' blood. The children can't be raised like that!"

He stepped closer to her. "Listen to me, woman! Those children will be given good homes and there's nothing wrong with bein' raised an Indian. As for you, our bargain was for you to teach me how to read. I've risked my life for one stranger and I won't risk it again for a bunch of strangers' kids." He turned to leave.

"If you'll lend me a rifle and a horse, I'll go. I'm an excellent shot. I've hunted game in Scotland and—"

He looked at her as if she'd lost her mind and left the cabin.

Linnet stood still for a moment, not sure what to do, but with a sigh she started cleaning. This was an argument she meant to win, but perhaps it would take a while. She didn't believe the Indians would harm the children, but she knew the children *must* go back to their own people.

"I see the dress fits," a young girl said from the doorway. She was about fourteen, small like Linnet, freckle-faced and plain.

Linnet smiled at her. "Thank you for the loan, but I'm afraid it's going to get dirty today. I'm Linnet Tyler." She held out her hand to the girl, who blinked in surprise for a moment, then grinned and shook the offered hand.

"I'm Caroline Tucker."

"Tucker? I think I met your brother this morning."

"You must mean Jessie. He's been talkin' about you. Can I help?"

"Oh no. I'm just going to clean this place a bit. This is my home," she added proudly.

Caroline looked past to her to the ramshackle cabin and doubted if it could ever be made livable. "Well, I ain't got nothin' else to do," she said as she grabbed one end of the bench Linnet was trying to push outside.

The next people to appear were the eight-year-old Stark twins, Eubrown and Lissie, their identical brown braids flying, their pug noses twitching in curiosity to meet Mac's girl. Mac's girl she was if Mrs. Emerson was to be believed. Corinne was fit to be tied!

Word spread about Sweetbriar that Linnet was pretty, and soon most of the young men found excuses to drop by the workers at Old Luke's place. Linnet left them to fetch another bucket of water from the spring about a hundred yards from the cabins. She halted in her crouched position when she saw two feet near her and hadn't heard anyone approach. Swift memories of the Indians, the last sight of her mother that she had buried so deep, made her heart race. She looked up but could see little of the man's face, the sun behind his shoulder blocking her view.

She stood. "Hello, I'm Linnet Tyler." She put out her hand as he gaped at her, speechless, his mouth open a bit. He was hardly more than a boy, thick, well-muscled, coarse brown hair that stood out around his head, a mouth too wide to make his face handsome, but, still, a pleasant looking young man.

"You're the girl Mac brought back," he stated flatly, a nice voice.

"Yes, I am and you are?" She still had her hand extended.

"Worth, ma'am, Worth Jamieson. I live on a farm about five miles out. I just came to the store today."

She took his right hand from where it lay at his side and shook it. "I am happy to meet you, Mr. Jamieson."

"Just Worth, ma'am."

Linnet had a difficult time adjusting to the way all Americans insisted upon using Christian names immediately.

"You living in Old Luke's cabin?"

"Yes, I am."

"Here, let me take that. You're too little to carry anything so heavy." He took the full bucket of water from her.

She smiled at him. "Thank you. I don't know why everyone seems to think I'm so helpless but I have to admit I find it a pleasure."

"Miss Linnet, you are the prettiest thing I have ever seen."

She laughed. "I thank you not only for your kind help but your flattery also. Now, let me take that. I have a floor that needs scouring."

Worth wouldn't relinquish the bucket but took it inside with him and set it on the floor, looked about for a minute, then went outside. Moments later, Linnet looked in astonishment to see him on the roof repairing the hole. Smiling, she waved at him before returning to the filthy floor.

"Hey, Mac. You seen what's goin' on over at that little girl's cabin? She's got the whole town over there helpin' her," Doll Stark called from his favorite seat in front of the now-empty fireplace.

"Yeah, I seen it," Devon's reluctant answer came from across the store.

Gaylon stopped his knife from the stick he was slowly reducing to nothing. "She's even got Worth Jamieson up on the roof."

"Worth?" Doll asked. "Why, that boy's skittish as a three-day-old colt. How'd she get him to even look at her, much less get him to work?"

Gaylon resumed whittling. "She's got a way with her all right. Even ol' Mac here fought one of Crazy Bear's renegades to save her from the Indians, and I can tell you what he saw then weren't no sweet-smelling thing like she is this mornin'."

"Can't you two find nothin' else to talk about 'cept Linnet?" Mac asked from behind the counter, an open ledger before him.

Gaylon and Doll exchanged looks, eyebrows raised, mouths pulled down.

"We could always talk about the weather, but ain't half so interestin' as that little gal you brung home," Gaylon continued.

41

"Hey, Mac, you better put your brand on her afore Cord comes back."

"Cord?" Devon asked, stupidly.

"Yeah, Cord," Gaylon said. "You heard of him, ain't you? That boy that took the little Trulock gal from you last winter."

"That ain't the way I remember it, and just because I brought Linnet back here, don't mean she belongs to me."

Doll's mouth twitched at the corners. "Sure don't. Not the way she's got every man from seven to seventy sniffing around her."

Devon slammed the book shut. "Since you two don't seem to have anythin' else to do, why don't you join them?"

"I would but I'm afraid she'd put me to work like them other fools. I outgrew my courtin' days long ago, and any time I can escape work, I do." Doll gave a sideways look to Gaylon.

Mac walked toward the door. "I think I'll go outside myself then, get some fresh air and some peace and quiet for a change."

"You do that, boy. Better take some nails. I hear tell they're needin' nails," Doll yelled as the door slammed.

Devon took a length of string from his pocket, smiling at the two old men's words. It was close to sunset and he'd need game for supper. The thought of supper alone with Linnet broadened his smile.

Two hours later, Devon held the two rabbits as he stood before Linnet's door and knocked. She opened it and smiled at him, a smudge of dirt across her cheek.

"We've just finished," she said as she reached for the rabbits, her hand shaking slightly.

He pulled them back from her reach, put his hand on her shoulder and guided her to a bench before the fire. "Sit down and rest. I'll cook these."

"Devon, that wasn't our bargain."

"What'd they do? Work you all day, ask you hundreds of questions, then leave you to go home to their own suppers?"

She gave him a weak smile.

"Don't worry. They didn't mean anythin'. It's just that ever'body is used to takin' care of themselves."

"Except me. I'm a burden on you always, aren't I, Devon?"

"None at all. You'll make it up. Wait till you try to knock letters in this thick skull."

"Oh!" She sat up straighter. "Your reading lesson!"

"You think I want a teacher as tired as you?"

"No, look on the mantel."

He stood and saw a piece of wood with letters charcoaled on it.

"It says Devon. At least I think that's the proper spelling of your name."

"You don't know?" He was incredulous, as if very disappointed in her.

"There are always several ways to spell a word, especially a name. I can only guess at yours. Do you possibly have a certificate of birth?"

"A what?" He carefully slipped the wood into his pocket.

"A piece of paper that the doctor wrote when you were born."

He tested the roasting rabbits, the juices dripping into the fire. "'Tweren't no doctor there when I was born, just Ma and a neighbor woman, but I do have a Bible and it has some writin' in it."

"That could be what we need. Could you bring it tomorrow, that is, if you want to postpone the first lesson?"

"I'd hate to see you fall asleep right in the middle of Macalister. Now let's eat some of this rabbit."

Linnet stood, yawned slightly and stretched, easing her sore shoulders. Devon looked away as she threatened to pop the buttons down the front of her dress. Sometimes he wondered if she even knew she was a grown woman. "Tell me what you think of Sweetbriar," he said.

"Everyone has been so good to me, I'm not sure as to how to repay them. Do you know Worth Jamieson?"

"Sure." He bit into a succulent piece of rabbit.

"Tell me about him."

"He stays by himself, quiet, a real hard worker. He come here about two years ago, staked out a claim and works all day, all by hisself. Comes in about once a month to the store, trades for what he needs." Devon frowned at her. "Why you so interested in him?"

"Because he asked me to marry him."

Devon nearly choked on the mouthful of rabbit. "What!" he sputtered.

"I said I was interested in Worth Jamieson because he asked me to marry him."

Devon clenched his teeth several times. "You just set there, calm as anythin', lickin' your fingers, and tell me some boy's asked you to marry him. You so used to marriage proposals you don't even notice 'em anymore?"

"No," she said seriously. "I don't think so. There haven't been too many."

"Too many! Well, just what do you call too many?"

"Only two, really, besides Worth's, a man in England, but he was very old, and a man on board the ship coming to America. He's in Boston now, I believe."

"Damn! You are somethin'!"

"The beatinest woman, perhaps?" Linnet asked innocently. They stared at one another and then laughed together.

"There ain't many women in Kentucky yet, so I imagine lots a' men'll propose." He gave her an appraising look. "I can tell you're goin' t' set this community upside down. You finished with that? I'll take the bones outside. I got to be goin' anyway." He paused at the door. "What'd you tell Worth?"

"Thank you."

He turned back to face her, his anger returning. "Thank you! That's all?"

"It's an honor for a man to ask you to marry him. It means he is willing to spend his whole life with you."

"I don't want to hear a speech about what marriage is. What answer besides 'Thank you' did you give Jamieson?"

"Do you mean whether I said I'd marry him or not?"

He glared at her in answer.

Slowly, she picked a piece of lint from her hair. "I told him I didn't know him well enough to give him an answer yet." She smiled up at him. "May I come to your store in the morning and get some cloth? I'd like to return Caroline's dress."

"Sure." He felt sheepish after his outburst. "Good night, Linnet."

"Maybe tomorrow we can discuss going after the children," she said tiredly.

His eyes turned angry. "*You* discuss it. I got more important things to do." He slammed the door behind him.

Chapter Four

"GOOD MORNING, DEVON."

He looked up from a ledger to smile at Linnet.

"That her?" a whisper came from one of two men by the fireplace.

"Linnet, girl, you come over here," Gaylon called.

"You two leave her alone?" Devon said. "She's got more to do than waste her time with the likes of you."

"What's eatin' you, boy?" Gaylon asked. "You get up on the wrong side of the bed?"

Doll leaned over and whispered something to Gaylon that caused both men to lean back in their chairs and bellow with laughter, slapping their thighs.

Devon scowled at both of them and turned back to Linnet, but she was already walking toward the laughing men.

"May I introduce myself? I am Linnet Blanche Tyler at your service." She gave them a deep curtsy.

They stared for a moment, speechless.

"Don't that beat all?" Doll said. "What's that you jest did?"

"It's a curtsy, the deeper the curtsy, the higher the personage. Here," she demonstrated, "a baron; lower, a duke; and here, a king."

"Well, well, that's real purty. You from England, you say?"

"Yes, I am."

"They sure raise 'em purty in England," Doll said. "No wonder you're bringin' all the boys out of the fields."

She politely ignored him and studied a carved wooden figure on the mantelpiece. It was about four inches tall, incredibly detailed, a statue of an old man, his shoulders drooped, every line emphasizing his weariness. "Did you carve this?" she asked Gaylon.

"Naw, that's Mac's. He's the whittler around here."

"Devon did this?" She looked across the room to where he was hidden amid several bags of flour.

"She means Mac," Gaylon told the man beside him. "It's his, all right."

"It's beautiful." She missed the exchanged looks between the men. "Would you excuse me? I need some fabric." She set the wooden man back on the mantel reluctantly.

"You through tellin' them all about England?" Devon said angrily.

"Devon, I don't know why, but I always seem to be making you angry."

He faced her. "I don't know why either. Somethin' just comes over me. Now," he said hurriedly, "what is it you wanted?"

"Just some dress goods and something for a new shirt for you."

"I don't need a shirt."

"I think you do. Besides, I can't just take cloth for myself because of our bargain, and I need to return Caroline's dress; so I have to make you a shirt."

"I don't know about you, Gaylon," Doll's voice came to them, "but I'm beginning to feel like another left foot, yes sir, another left foot."

Gaylon cleared his throat. "I see what you mean. How about takin' a gander at the Tuckers' new pigs?"

"I feel a mighty urge to do just that." The two men left the store.

Devon glared at the closed door.

"Why ever are you looking like that, Devon?"

"Can't you see nothin'?" he demanded. "Just because I brung you back from a bunch a' murderin' Indians, this whole town's got us wedded and bedded. They probably even got names for our kids picked out."

"What do you think they are?"

He whirled around to face her, his eyes bright with anger. "What!"

"I just wondered what names they had chosen for our children."

He realized she was laughing at him and then he, too, saw the humor. Relaxing, he shook his head at her.

"Devon, people always react the same way. It doesn't matter. You shouldn't let it bother you so."

"Specially since you seem to be so attached to Worth Jamieson."

She was silent for a moment. "Do you think Worth knows anything about Indians? Perhaps he'd be willing to help me go after the children."

"Jamieson!" Mac sputtered. "That boy grew up on a farm in Pennsylvania. He couldn't follow a trail of oxen, much less a bunch of renegade Indians."

"Then who do you know who could help me?"

"Ain't nobody gonna help you!" Devon fairly shouted. The way she was looking at him, as if he could easily produce six captured children, was making him furious. "You gotta get this idea out of your head. Now come over here and take whatever cloth you need."

With a gracious smile, she stepped behind the counter. "Thank you."

"Mornin', Mac," a woman's voice came to Linnet. She couldn't see who it was from her place near the floor.

"Mornin', Wilma. How're you today?"

"I'm feelin' fine, but I hear you're havin' some troubles with Corinne."

Devon cast a sideways look at Linnet behind him but she didn't look up. "What can I get for you?"

"Oh, nothin' really, I just come by to look at this here green ribbon again. I saw your little English girl yesterday and she's just as pretty as you said, although Corinne had some other things to say about her. How do you think my Mary Lynn would like this green ribbon?"

"I think she'd like it real fine." Devon stepped from behind the counter and took Wilma Tucker's arm and began pulling her toward the door. "It'd match her eyes perfect."

"Mary Lynn's eyes are brown," she said indignantly.

"Well, you think on it. Brown and green look good together." He practically shoved her out the door and closed it.

"I think I've chosen these two." Linnet put two rolls of cloth on the counter. "Do you like the blue for a shirt, Devon?"

"Just fine." He moved away from the door.

"Now, if I may measure you."

"What for?"

"Your new shirt."

He sighed in resignation and watched as she tore some strips from a rag stuffed under the counter.

"Come over here." She beckoned him to the fireplace. "Stand right there." She climbed on a stool to tear the strips to the correct lengths for

51

the broadness of his shoulders and the length of him.

"Are you sure you know what you're doin'?"

"Certainly. That's all I need," she said.

He turned to her, their faces inches apart on a level plane.

"Mac."

Devon whirled at Corinne's voice. "Mornin', Corinne."

"Hello, Corinne." Linnet stepped down from the stool. "I must be going. I'll see you at supper, Devon." She closed the door on Corinne's words, "What she mean by 'see you at supper'?"

"Lynna! Lynna! You up yet?"

Linnet opened the door to Jessie Tucker, grinning up at her with his pug nose and freckles, and she noticed, distastefully, that something seemed to be alive in his pocket and was trying to find its way out. "Good morning, Jessie."

"Mmm. You even talk funny when you first get up."

"So do you, and I have been out of bed quite some time."

He ignored her as he walked inside.

"What do you think of my house?"

"It's a house," he said in dismissal as he sat down on the bench. "You wanta have a look-see at Sweetbriar?"

"I'd love to, but I can't stay long. I need to sew today and make a shirt for Devon."

52

"How come you call him Devon when his name is Mac?"

"Why do you call me Lynna when my name is Linnet?"

He shrugged. "Sometimes I like you, but then sometimes you're a girl."

"I think there's a compliment somewhere in that. Let me eat something and then we'll go."

"My ma made me bring you a whole basket of food. She said it was the least she could do since I was gonna visit you. What'd she mean by that?"

"She meant that you are an incredibly lively young man. Jessie, when we're outside, would you please release that monster that wiggles in your pocket?"

He grinned impishly. "Sure. You gonna scream when I show it to you?"

"I should hope not. I am sure the anticipation is much worse than the reality."

"Huh?"

"Let's go see what your mother sent. I'm starved."

Jessie showed her what he considered the important parts of Sweetbriar, a hidden spring, deer tracks, two birds' nests he had hidden, and an abandoned lair of a wildcat. Toward noon she left him to return to her own cabin and work on her sewing. She smiled as she entered the one-room house because someone had been there while she was out, and she knew it was Devon.

There were bags of cornmeal, dried apples, a bucket of lard, bacon, dried fish and a little barrel of pickles. Four rabbits hung inside the wall of the fireplace, and a huge pile of chopped wood stood near the fire that had been renewed. She touched each item before setting to work on Devon's shirt.

There was a knock on the door and she called, "Come in," from her place by the fire.

Devon walked inside the cabin. "How come you told me to come in when you didn't even know who I was? You should keep this door locked and don't let anybody in until you find out who it is. There are people who might take advantage of a pretty girl alone in a cabin."

"Thank you."

"What you thankin' me for?"

"For saying I'm pretty."

He shook his head at her. "I brung the Bible like you said. What smells so good?"

"Your supper. Do you want to study or eat first?"

"Both." He smiled. "If it tastes as good as it smells, I want to eat before and after."

"All right, you shall." She ladled a bowlful of thick, rich stew from the iron pot over the fire. A door in the side of the fireplace revealed a golden, crusty loaf of new-baked bread. She sliced a thick hunk of the bread and laved it in sweet, creamy, fresh butter. A mug of cool milk was added to the food.

"Where'd you get all this? I didn't send no butter or milk or these onions or potatoes." He poked at the stew.

"It's the strangest thing, Devon, but all afternoon I've been hearing knocks at the door and when I open it, no one's there, but some food has been left. It was such a mystery."

"Was?" he said through mouthfuls.

"Finally two of the donors stopped to talk, the Stark twins."

"Which ones?" he interrupted.

"How many are there?"

"Two sets, and Esther's about to have another young'un, and everybody says it'll be more twins. Twins seems to be the only thing Doll Stark can make. Go on about the food."

"Eubrown and Lissie told me it was all for you, that they knew I was cooking for you, and you'd done so much for them that they'd like to repay you in some way."

Devon looked down in embarrassment for a moment, then grinned at her. "If they owed me so much, why'd they let me eat so much of Gaylon's cookin'?"

"I'm sure generosity has its limits and, as I understand, it has something to do with the wrath of Corinne." She watched him intently, but he was silent as he concentrated on his eating. "I am going to have to become better acquainted with this young woman. Is she so formidable?"

He grinned as he broke off a large piece of the

bread. "If you're plannin' to have a fight with her over me, let me know. I'd sure love to watch."

She looked at him coolly. "I very much doubt that we shall. Now, if you are finished gorging yourself, may we proceed with your reading lesson?"

He lifted one eyebrow at her, containing his laughter. "I reckon I'm as ready as I'll ever be."

She took the Bible and opened it to the middle, engrossed for a moment in the family tree so meticulously recorded there. "Why, Devon, your whole family is listed here. Here's your father—Slade Rawlins Macalister; your mother, Georgina Symington Macalister."

"Georgina?"

"I think she has a pretty name."

"Had, she's dead," he said flatly.

"Oh, I'm sorry. Yes, the date's here. Only three years ago, the same year as your father." She looked at him, his profile to her, elbows on knees, hands clasped tightly. "Here you are— Devon Slade Macalister."

"Slade? That was my pa's name."

"And yours, too, it seems. Who's this? Kevin George Macalister."

"My brother."

"I didn't know you had a brother."

"Didn't hear you ask. Can we get on with this and stop goin' over my whole family?"

"Why, Devon! The birthdates are the same— January 10, 1758. He was your twin brother."

"Still is as far as I know. If I'd known there was so much told in that book, I'd a' left it at home."

"All right." She began to close the book, then another name caught her attention. "Cord Macalister. He's the man whose name I keep hearing. He must be your first cousin."

"Yeah, Cord's my cousin." She was startled at the emotion in his voice.

She closed the book, not wanting to pry any more into Devon's family history, obviously somehow painful to him, and turned her thoughts to the unfamiliar task of teaching. "How about your name first?"

He took the piece of charcoal from her and laboriously wrote "Devon" on a stone of the hearth, smiling triumphantly at his accomplishment. "I been practicin'."

"Devon, that's wonderful! You're going to be an easy pupil."

"It's not so good," he murmured.

She looked at him sternly. "When someone gives you a compliment, you say, 'Thank you.' You do not deny the person's words, even if you think them to be false."

"You really are goin' to be a teacher, ain't you?"

She waited patiently.

He finally smiled and said, "Thank you for the pretty words. Now teach me somethin' else."

"Gladly." She smiled back at him.

* * *

Linnet threw another log on the fire. She'd been at Sweetbriar for two weeks and was beginning to feel as if she'd always been there. The people had become her friends, and she loved them for their faults as well as their virtues. And they had accepted her, too. She poked viciously at the fire. Except Corinne Stark. That girl used every opportunity to say some sly remark about Linnet, had even started the rumor that what she and Devon did each night alone in her cabin had nothing to do with reading.

Linnet laughed in memory—she didn't know whom the people of Sweetbriar were trying to protect, her from Devon, or their precious Mac from a grasping female. For four nights she and Devon had been constantly interrupted by callers with the weakest excuses imaginable for their intrusions. Devon had finally gotten angry and given his opinion of their thoughts, along with his opinion as to their rights in the matter even if what they thought was going on was going on (that had made Linnet blush). But everyone finally left them alone, and Devon was progressing with his reading very rapidly.

Linnet smoothed the skirt of her new dress, one of two dresses, two aprons, a shawl, and a nightgown that she now owned. Devon laughed that he had more shirts than all the men of Sweetbriar combined, but she knew he was actually pleased.

A knock on the door brought her from her thoughts. Wilma Tucker stood outside, her look nervous, her hands wringing and pulling on one another.

"It's Jessie," she said. "Is he here?"

"No, he's not." Linnet frowned. "Come in and sit down. You seem to be very upset."

Wilma buried her face in her hands. "Jessie's gone. He's run off or been takin'. I don't know what. I thought he was in bed when I looked last night, but this mornin' it was only a heap of quilts. He ain't been home all night. Somebody's takin' my only boy," she wailed and began to cry.

Linnet tried to control her own fear. "All right, stay here and I'll get Devon. He'll know what to do."

"Mac ain't here. He went huntin' afore sunup. I went to him first 'fore I remembered, but then, you bein' his woman an' all, I come to you."

Linnet blinked a few times—Devon's woman —the first time she'd heard it stated so blatantly. "We'll look for him." She wrapped her shawl about her shoulders. "Go to the Starks', and then get Agnes. Agnes will know what to do. Do you understand, Wilma? Where's Floyd?" It was her first thought of Jessie's father.

"He went huntin' with Mac."

Linnet grabbed Wilma's arm, her fear no longer easy to control. "Could Jessie have gone with his father?"

"No. Jessie and Floyd had a terrible row. Floyd said Jessie was to stay and help Jonathan with the farm, but you know Jessie."

Linnet stared at the woman. Yes, she did know Jessie. He had wanted to go hunting with his father, and when he wasn't allowed to go, he had decided to run away, fixing his bed so no one would know he'd gone. "Wilma, go to Agnes now, and we'll start looking." Linnet felt her fear growing, remembering the children who had been captured by Crazy Bear. Involuntarily, she remembered her mother lying by the fire, the growing red stain by her head. A feeling of panic began to seize her. Jessie, for all his bravado, was just a little boy and was in grave danger.

She nearly pushed Wilma out the door. "Go to Agnes, and she'll help to get the people to search," she repeated.

"Where you goin'?"

"I'm going to look for Jessie. I think I know some places where he might be." She stepped into the cold November air and walked toward the forest, her heart beating rapidly.

Chapter Five

IT WAS SUNSET WHEN DEVON RODE INTO THE clearing, and he smiled in the direction of Linnet's cabin and wondered what she had for supper. Pausing for a moment, he thought about how much he enjoyed the evenings alone with her, how quick she was to laugh, how her pretty little mouth . . . He told himself to stop that line of thought, grinned, and went into the trading post.

"You back, boy?" Gaylon asked.

"Yeah, Floyd and me brought back a buck. I got half of him outside."

"You hear about the excitement today?" Gaylon asked him.

"What excitement?"

"Little Jessie Tucker got hisself lost."

Devon stared at the old man. "Lost? He been found yet?"

"Oh yeah. He slept in the woodshed, and that's just where his ma wanted him. I 'spect Floyd'll have a few more words with him."

"He deserves them," Devon commented, aware of the dangers that the woods held.

"Shore does. He had everybody in Sweetbriar lookin' for him. Lost a whole mornin's work."

"Well, I'm glad he's not hurt. Go out and get that buck and dress 'im, would you? I'm starved."

"Goin' to your little gal's agin', huh?" Gaylon grinned. "When you gonna hitch up with her and spend all your time over there? She must be able to do somethin' besides just read and cook."

"Linnet's my own business, and I don't need you or anybody else to tell me what to do." He gave Gaylon a stern look before breaking into a wide grin. "I'm just takin' my time, enjoyin' the wrappin' afore the sweet."

"That's all well and good," Gaylon said seriously, "but if I was you . . ."

"Well, you ain't me," Devon snapped, "and ain't likely to be. Now go get that deer like I said and leave me to my own courtin'."

"All I was goin' ta say was she's too pretty to leave unattached. Somethin' might happen to her. I hear tell Worth Jamieson's after her."

Devon glared at him.

"No need to get riled," Gaylon protested. "I'm just givin' you some advice, but I know you young bucks. I was the same at your age, thought I knew ever'thin'." He closed the door behind him.

Devon went outside to the barrel of rain water behind the store and washed some of the grime off himself from the day's hunt. As he dried his strong forearms, he thought how Gaylon was right. But just what did Linnet mean to him? He knew how much he liked being near her, how sometimes her shoulder brushed his and his immediate reaction startled and embarrassed him. Damn! he thought, even now he could feel his body's reaction just to the memory of her nearness. He grinned, white teeth gleaming in the moonlight. Worth Jamieson. He was a boy while he, Mac, was a full-grown man. He wasn't worried about Jamieson.

He looked up at the stars, saw it was getting late. Rubbing his palms on his thighs, he walked toward her cabin and was surprised when she didn't answer right away; she was usually waiting for him. He pushed the unlatched door open. "Linnet?" He instantly saw that she wasn't there. Damn! he cursed and was startled by how awful he felt when he realized he wasn't going to see her right away. As he walked back to the store, he saw no sign of her. He went to the back of the store.

Gaylon knelt, knife in hand, over the deer carcass.

"You seen Linnet?"

"Not all day, but there's lots of times I don't

see her. Try over 't the Emersons'. Maybe she thought you wasn't comin' back tonight."

"But I told her—"

"She could forget, boy. You ain't the only one in her life."

Devon gave him a quelling look but Gaylon just laughed and returned to the deer. Devon slipped a bridle on his already tired horse and led it from the stall. Silently gliding onto the animal's bare back, he rode toward the Emersons' cabin.

She wasn't there and no one had seen her all day. He rode toward the Tuckers'.

An hour later he left the Tuckers' place cursing. Wilma had gone to Linnet for help in finding Jessie, but nobody'd thought to tell her Jessie'd been found. He'd talked to Jessie for a few minutes and had some ideas where Linnet might have looked for the boy. Devon was so mad at all of them that he didn't trust what he might say or do and had to leave, but he figured they knew his thoughts.

The moon was gone and it was very dark and very cold. He'd called her for so many hours, his voice was almost gone, but still no response. His stomach hurt with the fear that he might never find her, that Crazy Bear had gotten his revenge on Devon by taking the girl from him. Cocking his head to one side, listening, he heard a faint sound from far away. It was an unusual sound, not part of the forest, but he was already about fifteen miles from Sweetbriar. Surely she hadn't come this far!

He kicked his horse ahead and when she appeared as a dark shape huddled by a tree, he silently swung off the horse and knelt beside her. "Linnet?" he whispered, and his voice held all the worry, the agony he'd felt when he hadn't been able to find her.

She turned a pale, tear-ravaged face up to him. Her crying had been what he heard. Without a word, she fell against him and he held her in his arms, crushing her in his relief. "Jessie," she cried. "Jessie's lost."

"Linnet." He lifted her face to his. "Jessie is safe. He was just mad at his pa and hid. He's fine now, just fine." But not so the girl he held, he thought, his anger at the Tuckers increasing.

Her tears didn't stop, but began afresh. "It was like . . . It was like . . ."

"When Crazy Bear took you and the children?" he asked quietly.

She choked on her words, but nodded her head against his chest.

He leaned against the tree and drew her into his lap, realizing again how small she was, how delicate. Damn Wilma Tucker for putting her burden on the frail little shoulders he held! They'd all been doing that lately, knowing she would listen to their troubles, always be a friend, never thinking what they were doing to her. "Tell me, Linnet, talk to me about that time."

She shook her head, wanting to keep the memories buried.

He touched her cheek. "I'll share it with you. Tell me."

The words began to come out, slowly at first and then tumbling over one another in their hurry to be released. She told of her terror at the Indian attack, seeing her mother lying in her own blood, of not knowing of her father, the long march with the children. She told how afraid she was when the Indians beat her and she thought they'd leave her to starve alone. She felt Devon's arms tighten about her, the wondrous safety of them. "I was so horribly, horribly frightened, Devon."

He stroked her arm. "You don't have to be frightened any longer. I'm here and you're safe now."

"I'm always safe when you're near. You have always come to me, always been near when I needed you." She moved back and looked up at him as he smoothed her tear-dampened hair away from her face. The sky was growing lighter in the early morning and her mouth was so near his, so soft, her breasts against his chest. He moved his head to kiss her.

But Linnet pulled away. "I was afraid Jessie'd been taken, that he'd have to live away from his own family like the other children are. Devon, you should have seen little Ulysses. He was a pretty boy, so sweet. Jessie is like him."

66

Devon released her in disgust. "You can't leave nothin' alone, can you? You gonna drive me to my grave naggin' me about those damn kids that don't mean nothin' to me."

"What's this, a lovers' quarrel?" came a voice above them.

They both turned to see Cord Macalister looming above them. Only one word could describe Cord Macalister—dazzling. He was a powerfully built man, standing with legs apart, hands on hips, dressed in white buckskins with two-foot-long fringe from every seam. Across his broad chest was an intricate design of tiny glass beads that caught and reflected the early morning light. His thick, wavy hair was the color of sunlight, his eyes like the bluest of lakes. He watched Linnet's face, sure of the reaction he would get, the way all women looked when they first saw him, or saw him for the hundredth time for that matter, and when he saw the same look on Linnet's face, he rewarded her with his best smile, the smile that many women said rivaled the stars in beauty.

Devon also saw the expression on Linnet's face and looked at her in disgust. He set her from his lap and helped her to stand, and when she glanced at him in question, he looked away. "Cord," he said flatly. "I didn't expect to see you this early."

"Didn't expect to see me this early this year or to see anybody this early in the mornin'?" He grinned at Linnet.

Devon clenched his teeth together. How come Linnet isn't sticking her hand out and introducin' herself like all the other times? he thought. "This is Linnet Tyler. Linnet, this is Cord Macalister."

"Tyler, is it? From the looks of you two I expected her to be a Macalister. Glad to know she ain't." His eyes swept her body, her tangled hair full of leaves. "Real glad to know she ain't took yet."

Devon felt the hostility that always surfaced when Cord was near, hostility based on years of being together, of seeing and knowing women's reactions to him. "Come on." He jerked on Linnet's arm. "Let's get back to Sweetbriar and get you to bed. You look awful."

"Now that's a matter of opinion, little cousin. This little lady looks awful pretty to me. You have only the one horse?"

"Yeah, I just found Linnet." He briefly told of Jessie's disappearance and Linnet's search for him.

"Then you've got one tired horse." Cord watched Linnet, thinking that her relationship with Mac wasn't at all what he had thought at first. She stared up at him now with those big eyes. "What color are your eyes?"

"I . . . I don't know." Linnet found her voice nearly failed her.

Cord chuckled and threw an arrogant look to Devon. "Mac, ol' cousin o' mine, why don't I give the little lady a ride back to Sweetbriar on my horse? Wouldn't want to wear your only horse out, would you?"

"No," Linnet said emphatically. "Devon . . ."

"Devon?" Cord interrupted. "Now it does seem that I remember your other name was Devon. Ain't heard nobody call you that, though."

Devon glared at his cousin. "Take her if you want, I ain't got no claim on her."

Cord grinned. "Right glad to hear that, boy." Before she could protest, he picked up Linnet, put her into the saddle of his white horse, mounted behind her and nudged the horse ahead. "Well, little girl, tell me how you come to be at Sweetbriar."

She briefly told him of Devon's rescue of her.

He laughed, the sound vibrating the air. "Now if that ain't the way to impress a lady, I don't know what is. Ol' Mac killed Spotted Wolf. Crazy Bear ain't goin' ta forgive that too easy, what with Spotted Wolf bein' Crazy Bear's brother and all."

They arrived at Sweetbriar hours later, and the whole town awaited them in the clearing. They were somewhat startled to see Linnet riding in front of Cord, but they were nonetheless relieved to see she was unharmed.

Floyd Tucker lifted her from the horse. "Linnet, I'm real sorry about what happened."

"An' me," Wilma said, her eyes beginning to tear. "I was just so lost in my own problems, I didn't think of nobody else."

"It's all right, Wilma." She patted the woman's arm.

"No, it ain't all right." Devon slid from his horse. He had not ridden back beside Cord, but had gone another way, alone. "Linnet could have been killed while she was out lookin' for your boy!"

Wilma sniffed.

"Devon! It's all right. There's no harm done." Linnet insisted.

"No harm done! I ain't had any food since yesterday noon, lost a night's sleep, and you say there's no harm!"

She looked at him in anger, her mouth a firm line. "I am most sorry to inconvenience you to such an extent. I am sure I can find some food for you."

He matched her anger. "I wouldn't want to tear you away from any other duties you have—or interests. If you'll excuse me, I have my own business to attend to." He turned to the store and slammed the door behind him.

In the clearing, Gaylon poked Doll. "What you think brought that on?"

Doll spat out a mouthful of tobacco juice and nodded his head toward Cord's broad back. The trapper stood surrounded by women, from the seven-year-old Stark twins on up to Agnes Emerson. "I think that's Mac's problem, as it's always been his problem."

Gaylon looked on in disgust. "Why a woman would fancy him I don't know. He's got no more

70

to him than some fancy feathers I seen once atop a rich man's horse."

"Well, whatever it is, the women sure seem to like it."

Linnet sat quietly in her cabin for a while, glad to be away from the noise. She washed her face and hands, started to remove her dress, but she'd unbuttoned no more than a few buttons when she fell onto the bed, asleep almost before she settled.

A knock woke her. Hurriedly, she looked at the window, saw the light was fading. Devon had come for supper and reading, and she was still sleeping. Groggily, she waked herself. "Come in," she called before she remembered how Devon didn't like for her to do that.

Cord Macalister stood in the open doorway. "Well, if you ain't a sight for sore eyes." His eyes raked her sleep-flushed face, golden hair flowing across her shoulders, down her back, the unbuttoned dress revealing a full curve of her breast.

"Cord, I didn't expect . . ."

"You 'spectin' Mac? Well, he's luckier'n I thought."

Linnet hurriedly fastened her dress, pulled her hair back into a long, fat braid. "What can I do for you?"

He settled himself onto the bench by the table, long legs out in the floor. There was something demanding about Cord Macalister that made you pay attention to him, made you always aware of his presence. "I'm just bein' neighbor-ly. Thought we might like to get to know one another." His eyes held amusement as she had to step over his legs to get to the fireplace.

"I'm afraid you'll have to excuse me, but I have to prepare supper." He watched her as she hurriedly scraped potatoes and threw them into the pot.

"Seems like a lot of food for one so little as you," he commented.

"It's for Devon. He eats supper here."

"Well now, that's real cozy for him, ain't it?"

"It's little enough to repay him."

He lazily looked at her body, considering her without clothes, then brought his eyes back to hers. "I just reckon I could find another way to have a debt repaid, if you owed it to me."

A knock on the door made Cord shout, "Come in," before Linnet could get there to answer it.

Devon lost his smile when he saw Cord and turned cold eyes to Linnet.

"I didn't know you had company. I'll just go tend to my own business."

"Now, cousin, don't be that way. This little lady's cookin' a mighty fine supper. I'm sure there's enough for both of us."

Devon shot Linnet a look of contempt. "I wouldn't want to interrupt anythin'. Good night." He closed the door behind him.

Linnet started after him but Cord caught her arm. "Leave him be. He's always been like that.

Got the quickest temper you ever saw. Never could say nothin' to that boy without him gettin' riled."

Linnet's eyes caught Cord's and flashed anger at him. "And you knew this about him and deliberately provoked his anger."

Cord gave her an incredulous look. "Well now, you might say I did, but then when the game's a pretty little thing like you, I'd say any way of huntin' was all fair." He held her arm, running his hand over her from wrist to elbow.

She pulled away from him angrily. "Now that you've invited yourself to supper, you may as well eat it. . . ." She tossed half-raw stew into a wooden bowl, splattering the front of her dress.

Cord was fascinated. In thirty-six years, no woman had found his charm resistible—any woman he decided he wanted, that is. The reluctance of this one held him in awe. He ate slowly, unmindful of the food, but watching Linnet as she angrily stabbed a needle in and out of what looked to be a man's shirt. When he'd finished, he rose and stretched, white fringe whirling about him, beads glittering in the firelight, grinning when he saw Linnet watched him. "Miss Tyler, honey, it's been a real interestin' evenin', real interestin', but I got to be goin'."

She nodded. "Good night."

He flashed a smile at her, then paused at the door, thoughtfully. "Sweetbriar ain't never been one of my favorite stoppin' grounds, but I just may change my opinion of it real soon. Might be nice to stay around here this winter and just see what happens." He left her alone.

Cord walked into Devon's store, expecting the people who waited there for him. He was a good storyteller, and his visits were enjoyed. With a grin at the eager children before the fireplace, allowed to sit up late on Cord's first night in Sweetbriar, he went to where his cousin stood by the wide counter. "Real fine cook that little lady of yours."

Devon turned cold eyes up to the man, ten years older than he, but his rival most of his life. "I don't remember puttin' a brand on her."

"Just wanted to hear it again. Sweet words they is, too." He sauntered toward the fireplace, beginning a story already.

Chapter Six

LINNET STOOD QUIETLY IN THE DOORWAY FOR A moment, a cloth-covered basket under her arm. She watched Cord, surrounded by enraptured people, his big blondness, the white of his fringed buckskins, setting him apart from the others. Doll Stark caught her arm and silently motioned her to a door at the back of the store. No one noticed her as she opened it, thinking it led outside to the stables. She was momentarily startled when she found herself in another room, and it took a while to adjust to the darkness before she saw Devon lying on the narrow bed, his shirt and boots thrown onto a bench. His dark skin gleamed in the moonlight, his black hair thick, curling about his neck. She marveled at how young he looked, how like one of Crazy Bear's braves. She thought of the necklace he'd worn the night of her rescue.

She tiptoed to a bench by the bed. She should leave, she thought, she should leave the basket of food for him and go away. His fingers twitched in some dream. How much she wanted to touch him! His eyes were open, staring at her, the blue so incongruous with the dark skin.

"Brought your supper," she said quietly. "I wouldn't have come in here except Doll Stark pointed this way and I thought the door led outside," she explained too rapidly. Of course that didn't explain why she was sitting two feet from him or why she had put out her hand to touch his warm fingers.

He sat up, bare feet on the floor, and ran his hand through his thick hair, and she wondered if his hair was coarse or soft. There was no hair on his chest, just clean, dark skin, long, lean muscles.

"You didn't have to bring me anything."

She smiled, trying to keep her eyes on his face. "I know I didn't, but I wanted to. I couldn't let you go hungry, not after it was my fault that you hadn't eaten or slept."

He took the basket from her. "I get pretty mad sometimes and say things I don't mean. Oh, Lord! Don't tell me this is fried chicken."

"An entire chicken and a whole apple pie."

"I think I can eat it all."

"I thought you could." As Devon bit into a chicken leg, she looked around the room. There was a shelf on the far wall, and she went to look at the ornaments there. She couldn't see them very well in the darkness, but they were more of the wooden ornaments she had seen in the front of the store. She ran her hands over one of them, enjoying the smoothness of the carving, as Devon watched her. "You made these?"

He nodded, his mouth full.

"Devon, do you know that these are works of art? That if you were in the East they could be sold for high prices?"

He paused a moment before resuming eating. "Just whittlin'. My pa was a lot better'n me."

"I can't imagine that." She picked up another piece. "What was he like, your father, I mean?"

Devon smiled. "He was a good man. Ever'body liked him. Best pa a boy could have. Let me alone when I needed it, tanned me when I needed it."

"He wasn't very old when he died, was he?"

"No," Devon stated flatly.

"How did it happen?" she asked quietly.

"Bear." Devon seemed to put some of his grief in that one word, grief that he'd felt after he'd seen his beloved pa torn apart by that bear. Gaylon had held him and kept him from tearing into the animal with his bare hands. Devon wondered later how the old man had had the strength, since Devon was already a strong young man of twenty-three.

"Take some of 'em if you want," he motioned to the figures, "or all of 'em, I don't care."

77

"Devon, you should care. They're beautiful, and you can't just give them away indiscriminately."

"Whatever you mean, I don't know."

"You can't give them away to just anyone."

"Why not?" he demanded. "They're mine, and there's plenty more where they came from."

"Devon Macalister, don't you dare get angry with me again. I've had quite enough for one night."

Her words reminded him of Cord and he ate silently.

"I would like to have one of them, though, but it's too dark to see and I couldn't possibly decide which one I wanted." She walked toward Devon. "I'll take the basket now if you're finished."

"That was good, one of the best meals I ever had," he said sleepily as he put his feet on the bed. "Thank you."

"Good night, Devon," she said at the door.

"Good night, Lynna."

In the morning Linnet went to Devon's store, but Gaylon said he'd ridden out very early, his horse loaded down with food.

"He runs off most every time Cord shows up," Doll said. "Goes to see his great-grandfather, the Shawnee one."

"Don't worry, he'll be back," Gaylon said.

Linnet couldn't believe how lonely she grew in the next few days. She spent time with all the people of Sweetbriar, but they had their own lives and not much time to spend with her.

When Cord asked her to go riding, she hesitated but accepted. She wanted to know what caused the animosity between the two men.

Cord put his hands on his hips and looked down at her, a slight smile on his face. "You ain't afraid of me, are you?"

She studied him for a moment. "No, I'm not."

"Then there's no question about it. I got another horse from Floyd Tucker and if'n you're ready, we can leave anytime."

The idea of a ride and getting away from the settlement appealed to her very much. "I would like to go for a ride, Cord. Let me get my shawl."

Cord watched her enter the little cabin, then looked up at the gray sky. Yes sir, he thought, everythin' was goin' just like he planned.

Linnet knew the weather was unseasonably warm, and everyone said it couldn't last much longer, and today it was overcast and everything had the strangest feel to it, as if things were hollow and each sound echoed through the forest. Cord didn't say very much, just led her down a narrow path into the woods. It seemed they had gone miles.

"Cord, haven't we gone far enough from the settlement? Devon keeps warning me about the Indians."

He grinned back at her. "Just 'cause that cousin of mine sometimes lives with the Indians, don't mean he's the only one understands 'em. You can trust me, I'll not take you anywhere it ain't safe. Anyway, we're there."

She rode her horse up beside his and they sat together, looking out over the wide, blue expanse of the Cumberland River.

"Pretty, huh?" Cord broke the stillness.

"Yes, it's breathtaking."

He dismounted. "Got anythin' like that in England?"

"Everything in America seems so much larger, even the people seem bigger."

He stood beside her horse and put his arms up for her, the way Devon had done so many times. She put her hands on his shoulders as he lifted her to the ground, but he did not release her, holding her firmly about the waist. He gazed into her eyes for a moment, and Linnet found that her heart was beating rapidly. The knowledgeable way he held her, the confidence he emanated, made her breath catch. Slowly, he brought his face close to hers, his eyes searching hers all the while. His lips touched hers gently, then he forced her mouth open. She was startled at first, but she found the sensation not unpleasant at all; in fact, she quite liked being kissed. He moved his mouth from hers and pulled her to his chest, and she heard his heart pounding. Oddly enough her own had returned to normal.

"You're a sweet little thing, Linnet," he said as he stroked her hair. He pulled her from him to look at her face, but before either could say a

word, the skies broke apart, torn asunder by a
brilliant flash of lightning. Immediately, sheets
of bitter cold rain filled the air.

Linnet gasped as the first deluge soaked her to
the skin and she instantly began to shiver. "Get
your horse," Cord shouted over the downpour.
"Follow me."

She grabbed the reins and followed the big
man. Within minutes, he had led them to a deep,
dry cave. She wrung out her hair and wiped the
water from her face as Cord took the horses to
the back of the cave and unsaddled them.

"Here, this'll help until I get a fire going."
He put a blanket around her shoulders. She
watched as he took twigs from a rather large pile
of dry firewood along the wall and started a fire.
"Now, come over here and get warm. You look
froze to death." He rubbed her cold, wet shoulders, and soon some circulation came back into
them.

She held her hands over the fire. "That is
certainly the coldest rain I have ever experienced."

"It'll turn to snow 'fore too long," he said as he
threw some more wood on the fire. "I'm afraid
our Indian summer is over and winter is upon
us."

"It was good that you knew of this cave." She
looked at him when he was silent.

He turned laughing eyes toward her. "It sure
was a good thing." Stretching out on the sandy
floor, head propped on his bent arm, he put one

hand out to her. "Why don't you come over here and let's keep on where the rain stopped us?"

She stared at him for a moment. The cold rain was like a doorway that locked them inside the cave. She looked at the pile of firewood, then rose and went to the mouth of the cave to look at the rain, shivering at the cold, now that she was no longer near the fire. "You planned this, didn't you?" she asked quietly.

"Now how could I plan a storm like this?"

"You've lived in the woods a long time and you know what the weather in Kentucky is like."

He grinned at her slowly, taking in the wet, clinging dress, thinking of her skin, creamy, smooth. "You might say I had some ideas about what it could do today and I thought I might as well be prepared. What're you frettin' about? Ain't nothin' gonna happen that you ain't gonna enjoy as much as me."

"Tell me, Cord, what would happen if I said no to you?"

He looked genuinely surprised. "Well now, come to think on it, I don't rightly know. Ain't no woman ever said no to me before."

She continued to stare at him, and his expression changed to a harder look.

"Truth is, Linnet, I don't think I'd like a woman sayin' no to me."

She looked back at the rain.

"You ain't thinkin' about goin' out in that, are you? I wouldn't advise it. It's gettin' colder by the minute, and I doubt you know your way back to Sweetbriar. Now why don't you stop bein' so all-fired ornery and come back here by the fire?" He watched her a moment, then laughed. She looked back at him. "I reckon this must be your first time with a man, and you're scared. You don't have nothin' to be ascared of. I'll be real gentle, and there'll hardly be no pain a'tall."

She walked back to the fire and grabbed her shawl. Cord's grasping hand missed her skirt. He sat up, eyes flashing. "You ain't goin' out in that!"

"I fear you leave me no choice. It's either stay here and . . ." She sighed. "Or take my chances outside. I prefer the rain."

He stood, his face furious. "I don't force myself on no woman and I ain't about to start now."

She stopped tying her shawl. "Does that mean that if I stay here you'll leave me alone?" The incredible anger in his eyes answered her. "Then I truly have no choice whatever."

"Just don't you think I'm gonna come and rescue you like Mac done. You go out there and you go alone. I'll see you at your funeral." His eyes swept her body. "Such a waste," he sneered.

Linnet gave one last look at the warm fire and ducked her head as she stepped into the freezing rain.

Cord watched her for a moment, then turned and kicked at a loose rock on the cave floor. He sank down on the blanket by the fire. "Don't she beat all?" he said aloud, shaking his head a moment before grinning. He'd wait a few minutes and then go and get her. She'd be plenty willin' to come to him after a while in that cold. Stretching, he put his arms behind his head. The girl sure had courage, he thought, as he rubbed his hands over the fire and remembered kissing her. He'd never wanted anything so badly in his life as he wanted this little girl.

Linnet realized how right Cord's words were as soon as the cold rain turned to sleet. Ice formed on her hair, hanging off her shawl. Her feet were already numb, but she kept her head down against the driving sleet and kept walking. In one respect, Cord had been totally wrong: Linnet had an excellent sense of direction and now she unerringly headed for Agnes Emerson's house. Once she thought she heard someone near her and she glimpsed Cord's unmistakable white buckskins through the trees. She hid behind an enormous, rotten stump and waited until he was gone.

An hour later she was not so sure of her decision to leave the warm cave. How bad could Cord have been when you compared him with death? She was more than cold, her body too numb to even shiver. The sleet had turned to snow, and her wet dress was frozen on her, clinging and dragging her down.

It was strange how she didn't seem to feel the cold anymore, but she was incredibly sleepy. All she wanted to do was lie down somewhere and sleep. She heard a dog barking far away, but the sound came to her in a haze. If she could just sleep a while, then she could get up and walk some more. It couldn't be far to Agnes' house. A dead tree lay across her path, and the snow made such a fluffy, white, soft bed next to the log. She sank to her knees and touched the stuff. To her hands, past blue, turning to an ugly gray, the snow seemed almost warm. She stretched out; ah! the bliss of sleep. Something touched her face but it didn't wake her.

"Ma! She's over here. I found her!"

Agnes ran through the rapidly falling snow to her son. The eighteen-year-old Doyle knelt by Linnet's still form and brushed the snow from her face. His hands on her throat reassured him that she was alive. Bending forward, he lifted her into his arms, appalled at the stiff, frozen dress.

"She's alive, but just barely," he said when Agnes appeared.

"Let's get her home. She ain't too heavy for you?" Doyle cast a contemptuous look at his mother. Would she never realize he was a grown man? He held her close to him, trying to warm her with his own body. She was as cold and stiff as a piece of iron, only, thank God, not as heavy. They reached the cabin quickly, and his mother motioned him to put her on the bed that she pulled nearer the fire.

"Now go out and find Lonnie and your pa. I'll get her warmed." Doyle left quickly, wondering if anything as frozen as Linnet would ever be alive again. Agnes had to cut the dress from her, the cloth too cold to handle. Then she wrapped the girl in one of her own enormous flannel nightgowns, rubbing the little body all over with a coarse woolen blanket.

The door opened and Doyle, his father and the eight-year-old Lonnie entered. "She looks awful, Ma. She dead?" Lonnie asked.

"No," Agnes snapped. "She ain't dead and she ain't gonna be. Lyttle," she addressed her husband, "you rub her feet and, Doyle, you make some hot sassafras tea."

"What can I do?" Lonnie asked eagerly.

"You rub her hands. Think you can do that?"

"Sure, Ma." He began his job. "Look at 'em; they're so little and they're a funny color, ain't they?"

Agnes sat on the bed, Linnet's head cradled in her lap.

"Why don't she say somethin', Ma? How come she just keeps layin' there like she was dead?"

"Because she's cold, Lonnie, and we need to get her warm."

Lonnie held Linnet's hands in his and blew on them, then looked to his mother for encouragement.

Agnes gave her young son a faint smile, but everyone could see she was worried.

"I'm gonna wrap her feet up," Lyttle said. "Maybe we could put a lot of quilts on her and stoke up the fire." Before the words were out, Doyle threw another log on the fire.

"Ma," Lonnie said, and when he looked up, there were tears in his eyes. "I don't want her to die. She's nice, and Mac'd be real mad if she died."

"She won't die!" Agnes said with a force that startled even herself. "We won't let her die."

Lyttle held a stack of quilts and began spreading them over Linnet. Agnes stretched out and pulled the cold girl close to her and Lyttle covered them both. Lonnie lifted the edge of the quilts.

"Lonnie! What are you doing? We want to get her warm."

"I know," the boy said seriously. "I'm gonna get in front." He climbed under the covers and pressed the back of his little body to Linnet's. "She sure is cold, ain't she, Ma?"

"She sure is, Lonnie," Agnes whispered as she felt her heart swell in pride for her son.

Chapter Seven

LINNET OPENED HER EYES SLOWLY. AGNES BENT over the fire stirring something that smelled delicious in a big black pot. She turned and smiled at Linnet.

"It's good to have you back again."

Linnet tried to move one arm and found her muscles were incredibly sore. "What am I doing here?"

"You don't remember?" Agnes replaced the lid on the kettle and stood up. "Cord come to the house yesterday and said you was lost in the storm and could we help find you."

"Cord did that?" Linnet said with contempt, remembering all.

Agnes lifted one eyebrow. "Cord ain't all bad, just seems to be sometimes. Although I never heard no young girl complain about him afore."

"You have now." Linnet obviously did not want to discuss Cord.

"Here, I want you to drink this." Agnes held a steaming mug before her. "You're gonna be pretty weak and sore for a few days, I reckon, but we'll take good care of you."

"Agnes, I can't stay here." Linnet tried to sit up, but Agnes quickly came to give her some much-needed support.

"It seems to me I heard all this afore when you first come to Sweetbriar and I don't want to hear it again."

Linnet laughed but stopped because the gesture made her stomach muscles hurt.

Agnes smiled at her. "Now that that's done, let's get some food in you."

Linnet took another stitch in the stretched quilt. She'd been at Agnes' house for nearly a week, and each time she mentioned leaving, the whole family refused to listen to her. She'd heard that Devon had returned, but he'd not come to visit her. Agnes, on the other side of the frame, ran her hand over the work and eyed it critically.

"Rose of Sharon's always been one of my favorite patterns. It was Mrs. Macalister's?" Linnet asked as she paused in her sewing.

"Mac's ma, 'cept she wouldn't let her boys call her Ma. They had to say 'Mother.'"

Linnet looked back at the quilt. Devon hadn't

been to see her since she'd been ill, but then there was no reason for him to visit. "You knew his mother, then. What was she like?"

"Oh, she was a real fancy lady. Slade, that's Mac's pa, went north to see if he could get some money to open a tradin' post in the new Kentucky territory. All of us, the Tuckers, the Starks, and Lyttle and me lived in North Carolina then. None of us was even married, just friends and neighbors. Like I said, Slade went up north. Ah." Agnes paused and sighed. "Now Slade Macalister was a good-lookin' man, tall, handsome, dark hair, broad shoulders, walked as quiet as a cat."

"Like Devon," Linnet whispered to herself.

Agnes paused but gave no other sign she heard Linnet's comment. "When Slade come back from the north, he had hisself a bride, pretty little thing, talked all funny and had the funniest ways about her." She eyed Linnet again, noticing the way the English girl made the crude mug of tea seem like a piece of translucent porcelain. "She was expectin' already when they got back home and as soon as her twin boys was born, a whole passel of us lit out for the new land of Kentucky. Right off, Slade's wife had troubles. She complained all the time about the travel, about all the work; near drove us crazy, but Slade sure loved her. I never seen no man dote on a woman like he done." Agnes chuckled at some private joke. "At least that wife of his seemed to be good for somethin', 'cause many a mornin' Slade'd get up tireder'n when he went to bed."

Linnet kept her head bent, hiding her stained cheeks.

"I reckon you can't blame the woman too much. Slade told me she grew up in a house with ropes on the walls, and when you pulled one of those ropes, some man or woman came runnin' just to see what they could do fer you."

Linnet looked at Agnes, startled. She could very well say that her own life had been like that until her father's mines had been exhausted and the land sold to pay the debts. "What about Devon?" she asked quietly.

"Those boys! They might have been twins, but two more opposites there couldn't have been. Kevin looked just like his ma, yellow curly hair, white skin, while Mac was like his pa, dark but with them blue eyes. After a while, Slade began to stay away from Sweetbriar. I guess his wife's complainin' finally started to get to him, but then the real fights came with the Indians."

"What Indians?"

"Slade's ma was a pure Shawnee, some kind of higher-up in the tribe, and all the time her relatives was comin' to see the twins. The Indians frightened the boys' ma and she started to keep the boys in the house, never lettin' 'em outside. Slade and her had a big row about that, could hear it a mile away. But after the boys started walkin', they solved their own problems, at least Mac did." She laughed.

"How did Devon do that?"

"That young'un was slipperier'n a greased pig. Couldn't no room hold him inside. I 'member one time Slade nearly whaled the tar out of him when he found him on top of the roof. He was only four years old, and we never did figure out how he got up there." Agnes laughed to herself and continued sewing.

"But what happened to his mother, and where is Kevin?"

Agnes sighed. "That was a real sad story. When the boys were about five and Mrs. Macalister had long since quit tryin' to keep Mac inside the cabin, she found him hunkered down in the dirt with a young Indian boy, both dressed in those little leather breech cloths and the boy was teachin' Mac some Shawnee words. That pore woman started screamin' till she like to have lost her mind."

"But why?" Linnet asked honestly.

Agnes smiled at her fondly. Even after her time with the Indians, Linnet still didn't hate them as some folks did. "I reckoned it was 'cause you couldn't tell her son from the Indian babies runnin' around the store. Now with Kevin it was different; he always obeyed his ma. But not Mac. That night we heard her screechin' at Slade that she was goin' back east and takin' her boys with her. Two days later some missionaries come through, headin' east, and she took Kevin and went back. We never saw her again."

"But what about Devon? How could she leave her little boy?"

Agnes shook her head. "I don't rightly know, but she did. She hugged him and kissed him and told him over and over that she loved him, and then she got on a wagon and left."

"And Devon?" Linnet asked quietly.

"He was just five then, and he just stood there a minute and then went back in the store. We all thought he was too little to understand what was goin' on."

"But he wasn't," Linnet said flatly.

Agnes shook her head sadly. "He sure wasn't. A few hours later Slade missed him and began to search. We all searched. Two days later one of his Indian cousins brought him back, and the little boy looked like he hadn't slept or eaten in all that time. Slade just stood there, and we all thought he was gonna whup him, but he just knelt down and put his arms out and Mac ran to him." Agnes paused to wipe away a tear. "It was just awful. That little boy cried for so many hours Slade had to give him whiskey to make him sleep."

"And did he see his mother again?"

"Never, but three years ago when Slade died, I wrote his brother and sent one of Mac's carvin's. Kevin wrote back, said their mother'd died recently and sent Mac some carving tools all the way from Germany. I keep hopin' that Kevin will show up here someday."

They were quiet for a while, listening to the steady rhythm of Doyle chopping wood. The heavy snow outside made an unnatural quietness even in the house.

"Why does Devon hate Cord?" Linnet kept her head bowed. She wanted to know, needed to know, and she couldn't risk Agnes' censure.

Agnes seemed to be having the same thoughts. "Mac didn't meet Cord until he was eighteen, and they took one look at each other and become enemies, but for a while they was friendly enemies. Ever' summer we get a few batches of people travelin' west through here, and Cord and Mac always tried to see who could get the most girls to fall in love with 'em."

Linnet looked at Agnes incredulously, and Agnes grinned back. "I know. It was awful of 'em. I talked to Slade about it, but you could never reason with him about Mac. He thought the sun rose and set on that boy of his. I was just tired of seein' weepin' girls and Mac and Cord grinnin' at each other. But then last summer things was different. A little girl named Amy Trulock come through, and Mac fell in love with her real hard."

Agnes ignored Linnet's wide-eyed stare. "Cord wasn't around then, but when he come back he turned real charmin' to the girl, just like always, 'cept to Mac this was different. I wouldn't a' knowed what happened, 'cept Lyttle and Mac was out huntin', and they saw the girl together with Cord—swimmin' with no clothes on. Ever since then, Cord can't do nothin' 'cept it don't make Mac mad."

They didn't talk for a few minutes, and Agnes found herself watching Linnet's bent head. She wondered what the girl thought of Mac, what had happened between her and Cord. She knew that Mac hadn't visited because he felt sure he knew what had gone on between them. That time with Amy Trulock had hurt him more than he knew, and Agnes guessed he wasn't ready to even think about loving anybody again, especially after Linnet had spent so long in the woods with Cord. Mac wouldn't risk getting hurt again.

Early the next morning, Linnet walked the mile back to her own cabin. She had some difficulty convincing Agnes and the rest of the Emersons that she was perfectly well and did not need anyone to walk with her. Finally she had given an exasperated look to Agnes, and the older woman had understood that Linnet wanted to be alone.

Now, she stepped lightly through the rich, muddy earth, the cold air refreshing after the long week in the cabin. Little patches of snow showed in places, but it had nearly all melted. Linnet breathed deeply and set out at a brisk pace. Since Agnes' story of the day before, she had thought of nothing else but Devon's life, of the little boy crying for his mother and the grown man seeing the girl he loved swimming nude with his cousin. She realized now why

Devon hadn't visited her, hadn't inquired about her to her knowledge—he had judged her and found her guilty of the same crime as Amy Trulock. Of course what she could do was go directly to him and tell him the truth, the entire story of what had happened between her and Cord.

But why should she? Yes, why should she? If she went now and begged him to believe her, and she knew it would take a while to convince Devon of her innocence, she would set a pattern. Forever afterward, she would have to explain herself to him. Briefly she visualized the future: Devon fifty years old, coming to her cabin for his reading lesson and accusing her, a gray-haired lady, of being interested in another man. No! She wiped away the absurd vision. He must accept her as she was, and if he thought she spent nights with men, then he must do so. He had to see she was Linnet Tyler and not Amy Trulock. A brief moment of panic swept her as she realized what her decision meant. Devon could be so angry he could walk away from her. She tried to tell herself that if he was that shallow a man then she was well rid of him. She laughed aloud at the absurdity of that statement, because she knew what she'd do if it came to losing Devon.

The clearing came into view, and she realized there was smoke coming from the chimney of her little cabin. So short a time she had lived there, but how sweet a home it was. She picked up her skirts and ran to the door. She was out of breath when she entered, her back against the closed door, and she surveyed the little room. The fire burned brightly on the hearth, the floor had been swept and everything was tidy with none of the week's dust she had expected.

Four objects on the end of the table made her walk toward them. Her eyes blurred for a moment, both from relief and happiness, for they were four of Devon's carved figures. She held the first one, feeling the curves, the delicate lines. She stared for a time before she realized the figure was an exact likeness of Agnes Emerson. Agnes stood with her shoulders thrust back, her energy and vitality felt even in the four inches of wood.

Linnet quickly turned to the other carvings, curiosity eating her. The next figure was the four Stark twins in a circle, holding hands, their swirling skirts showing the motion of their bodies. The girls seemed to be identical, but Linnet knew instantly which girl was Sarah. She smiled, fascinated by the carving.

The next sculpture was easy to recognize. Doll and Gaylon sat on a bench, Gaylon bent over, whittling a stick, Doll with eyes alight, his mouth open in laughter.

The last work puzzled Linnet. It was a young girl looking down at Jessie Tucker, Jessie's pockets bulging, but Linnet did not recognize the girl and thought immediately of Amy Trulock. The girl had a slight smile on her face and looked as if nothing else in the world mattered except whatever Jessie was saying. Linnet didn't particularly care for a statue of Amy Trulock, but she loved the other three. She lovingly set them on the mantel, the one of Jessie and the girl a little apart, and all day, as she kneaded bread, peeled vegetables, filled the box with more firewood, she looked at them, was reassured by them.

The evening light was fading, and Linnet nervously smoothed her skirt and hair as she opened the door to the knock. Devon stood there and she stared up at him for a moment, unable to speak.

"You gonna let me freeze out here or you gonna let me in?" He smiled at her and she stepped back.

"Of course, please come in."

He walked past her and looked about the cabin. "You find ever'thin' all right when you got back?"

She went to stir the stew in the pot over the fire. Devon was acting as if she'd been visiting relatives. "Yes." She smiled. "Everything was perfect. Thank you for taking care of the cabin, and especially for these." Her hand lightly touched the three figures, stopping before the last one.

Devon saw the gesture and he had a hurt look in his eyes. He came to stand beside her and lifted the fourth sculpture, holding it lightly. "You don't like this one?" he asked quietly.

"I . . . Well, yes, it is very nice," she said hesitantly.

"Jessie wasn't so easy, his face changes all the time, but you were real easy."

She stopped in the middle of setting the table. "Me?" she asked incredulously.

Devon looked at her in surprise. "Maybe I didn't get you so good. You didn't know it was you?"

She put the plate down and took the statue from him, studying the girl. She had no idea she looked like that, so young, so naive. "No, I didn't know it was me," she said quietly as she looked up at Devon.

He grinned and noticed the way her fingers curled around the dark wood. He swung a long leg over the bench. "I'm ready to eat. Gaylon tried to kill me with his cookin' while you was gone."

As she served him enormous helpings of everything, she realized he was going to ignore the whole incident with Cord. She didn't know whether to be relieved or angry.

"Who'd you think it was?" he asked through mouthfuls. "Ain't nobody else here looks like that."

"I . . . I didn't know. I thought she was someone you had . . . known another time."

He frowned. "You're not a very good liar."

There was silence between them. "Devon, I want to tell you . . ."

His head came up sharply. "You don't have to

99

tell me nothin' about anythin'. You're my teacher and that's all, and whatever you do is your own business, not mine. I got no claim on you. Now, let's just keep our conversation to matters of interest to us both, like givin' me another piece of that pie." He smiled at her but the smile did not spread to his eyes.

"All right," she said after a while. "I understand your feelings." She cut him another generous slice of the pie.

"Gaylon said you probably went to see your great-grandfather," she said.

Devon ignored her.

She angrily snatched his empty plate away. "Perhaps you are uninterested in my life, but as your teacher I am concerned about yours. Is your grandfather as blindly stubborn as you are?"

Devon leaned back in his chair, looking at her in surprise. "I went to get them children you wanted so much. Turned 'em over to some missionaries to take back east."

She was so astonished she could barely speak. "All of them?" she whispered.

"Your six and a couple of others Crazy Bear took on another raid."

Chapter Eight

By silent mutual agreement, Devon didn't return to Linnet's cabin for the next few weeks, and her life began to fall into a pattern. She felt she owed him more than ever for rescuing the children; so three times a day she left hot food with Gaylon. And Devon always seemed to be out of the store when she arrived.

When the Christmas season arrived, she and everyone else looked forward to the planned festivities. Agnes came to the store and gave orders to everyone. Gaylon was sent into the woods to bring in fresh game, while Doll was told to practice his fiddlin' and Linnet was ordered to decorate Devon's store, where the dance would be held. Agnes fixed Devon with a glare. "And you stay beside Linnet and help her."

Linnet could have sworn she heard deep chuckles from Gaylon and Doll.

"All right, what do you want to do?" Devon said nastily.

Linnet tightened her mouth. "I need nothing from you. I am quite sure I can manage alone." She quickly went across the room and nearly slammed the door behind her.

"Linnet?"

She whirled to face him. "Don't come out here to say any more hateful things to me. I am quite sure I can manage alone."

"You said that already. I just brought this." He held up her shawl. "I thought you might need it."

She realized she had been so angry that she hadn't noticed the cold. She slung it about her shoulders. "Now, if you'll excuse me." She swept away from him and went into the woods, but to her further anger, Devon followed her. "You do not have to stay near me."

"I know—you are quite capable," he mimicked her crisp accent. "But, last I heard, it was a free country."

She tried to ignore him as she considered some greenery for the mantel. To her disgust she found she had forgotten to bring a knife. Rather than return to her cabin, she tried to twist one of the lower branches from an evergreen.

Devon watched her struggle for a while, then stepped forward. "Can I help?" He held a razor-sharp knife and quickly cut the branch away. "Or maybe you'd rather Cord helped you."

"Yes," she whispered. "I'd much rather have Cord, or anyone else for that matter." She didn't watch as he turned and left. With shaking hands she carried the evergreen back to the settlement.

The store was full of people when she returned, the children running around, excited about the dance that was to be held the next day.

"A hoedown," Doll said to Linnet. "Put your hoe down and come to town."

Caroline Tucker spent the day with Linnet, and they cooked, using ingredients the women had stored all winter. Jessie constantly stayed underfoot, and soon Lonnie Emerson joined him. Lonnie felt that he had saved Linnet's life and therefore she was his personal property. Jessie didn't take to the idea at all and, that being as good an excuse as any, they had to be pulled apart from several fights.

Once Devon kicked open Linnet's door, a squirming boy in each hand, and demanded she do something with them. He also had a few remarks to say about how she had all the males in Sweetbriar fightin' over her and he'd be damned if he was gonna join them. He stomped away before she could answer him.

The night of the festivities dawned clear and cold, and Linnet donned the new dress she had made for the party, a lightweight blue cotton,

103

gathered at the low neck and the waist. It had big, puffed sleeves that stopped at her elbow. She knew it was more for summer, but guessed the room would be very warm with so many people. She combed her long freshly washed hair about her back and shoulders, and it curled softly about the edges.

She stood by the fire a moment, nervous, chiding herself for the giddiness. As she turned around, the full skirt swirled softly about her. If only Devon would think she was pretty, if only Devon— She laughed aloud. She wondered what he'd say if he knew how much time she spent thinking of him, how she had spent so many hours on this dress, just for him. Would he ask her to step outside for some fresh air tonight? She'd go. She'd go wherever he asked.

She opened the cabin door and breathed deeply of the night air, not aware of the cold as she walked the few yards to the store. Timidly, she opened the door, and many eyes turned to her, but none of them were Devon's. He sat in a secluded corner with Corinne and hadn't even noticed her.

Agnes Emerson came to Linnet. "Lynna, why don't you come walk with me a bit? You ain't thinkin' of marryin' him, are you?"

Linnet was confused for a moment, then smiled absently at the boy Worth Jamieson who'd come to stand near her.

"How did you know he'd asked me?"

"Ever'body in Sweetbriar knows ever'thin' about ever'body else. Like I know you and Mac been quarrelin', hardly spoke a civil word to one another."

Linnet bent her head to stare at her hands. "Devon has some misconceptions about me and, besides, I think he'd rather have someone else."

"He don't want Corinne, 'cept the way any man wants her." Agnes went to the heart of the matter. "If Worth or any other man asked her to marry him, she'd probably drag him to the preacher's. It's just that she thinks she's gonna get Mac and she thinks he's rich."

"Agnes, do you think I'm so obvious to everyone?"

"You shore are. You look at Mac and you nearly melt at the sight of him."

"No! Please don't say that."

"Can't help but say it, it's the truth. Now let's go see him and see if we can get him away from Corinne. One look at you, and I don't think he's gonna see anybody else. Mac," she called, "get out of that corner and come here and look at our Linnet."

Devon looked up and his eyes registered surprise.

"I think you got 'im now, just don't let him go," Agnes whispered to Linnet as she walked ahead to intercept Corinne.

"You're pretty, Linnet," Devon said quietly.

"Better than a tar baby?"

"Much better." He grinned.

Doll started his fiddle going and Devon grabbed her arm. "You ready to dance?"

"I think you'll have to show me the steps."

"Ain't no steps, just stompin'." He caught her hands and whirled her around. The dancing was more than strenuous, and she became very thirsty.

Devon held her hand and pulled her to the barrel of cider and filled a mug for her. They looked at one another over the rims when, suddenly, he set his cup down, put his arm around her waist and drew her close to him. "I think your eyes are honey-colored with little flecks of silver, but I swear once they were almost red."

"No more of that," Floyd Tucker called to them. "You can see where that leads to, Mac." He pointed to several young children sitting in a row beside the heavily pregnant Esther Stark.

Linnet's face flooded pink, but Devon squeezed her to him and grinned. "Best idea I've heard all night, Floyd." He laughed.

"Devon!" She pushed away from him, but he grinned roguishly at her until she had to smile back.

"Agnes," Lyttle called to his wife, "I think it's time we got on with the shuckin' 'fore these young'uns lose control."

"Can't say Lyttle's idea's as good as Floyd's, but it'll do," Devon answered.

The way everyone laughed made Linnet know

that what Devon had said was not of an innocent nature.

Agnes came to stand beside her. "We always save a few bushels of corn each year and then shuck 'em here. Whoever gets a red ear, man or woman, gets to kiss whoever he wants."

"Oh," Linnet said as she began to understand Devon's jest.

"Come on, you better get started or ever'thing'll be gone."

"Me?" Linnet asked.

"Sure," Agnes laughed. "You get a red ear and you can kiss anybody you choose."

Linnet looked up at Devon as he watched her. She didn't hesitate. "Let's go," she said as she hurried to the big pile of corn.

Doll Stark found the first red ear and unerringly went straight to his wife. He was deft in getting his arms around her big stomach. Someone called that he knew how 'cause he'd never seen her any other way. Doll kissed her passionately, lifting her off the floor while everyone laughed and hooted.

Agnes poked Linnet. "From what I gather, there's the reason Esther puts up with Doll's laziness. A woman couldn't ask for more."

Doll abruptly dropped his wife on the bench and returned to his fiddle. Everyone laughed at the adoring look on Esther's face.

The door to the store flew open, and Cord Macalister filled the narrow portal. Linnet hadn't seen him since she fled him from the cave. He seemed to have no regrets about the incident, for he searched for Linnet's eyes and grinned at her. "Cord!" some of the children screamed and ran to him, their hands catching the long, swaying fringe.

"Well, just in time." He eyed the pile of corn. "This here is my favorite game. Look out, young'uns, Cord is gonna find a red ear of corn."

The children laughed as the big trapper tore into the pile. "Got it!" Cord shouted triumphantly minutes later. He bounded across the pile, fringe hitting Wilma in the face, and pulled Linnet to her feet.

She pushed against him. "No, Cord, leave me alone."

"No sir, I won you fair and square, and you're my prize." He pulled her to him roughly and hurtfully bent her head back as he thrust his tongue in her mouth. She thought she was going to gag.

He released her abruptly, her feet hitting the floor very hard. He glared at her, his eyes hard in hatred, then turned and left the store, the door slamming behind him.

The room was silent. "I guess I forgot to sweep all the varmints out of the corners," Gaylon muttered, and everyone laughed nervously, but their spirits were dimmed.

Doll struck a chord on his fiddle. "He ain't gonna ruin my party spirit," he called. "You folks get that corn shucked so my wife and kids don't have to do it."

They all laughed in earnest at Doll's gibe at his own laziness. Several more red ears were found, and the laughter increased. Toward the end of the pile Devon found a red ear and they all waited nervously, giving Linnet several little secret smiles.

Devon looked at her a long while, his face serious.

"Come on, boy," Gaylon called. "You got so many women you can't decide?"

"No, I don't," he said flatly. "Corinne, come over here." He turned to the voluptuous girl. There was a hush as Devon pulled Corinne into his arms, and Linnet couldn't take her eyes from them, couldn't help but see Devon's smooth, dark skin touch another woman's. She saw how his mouth opened before closing on Corinne's and how the girl eagerly pressed her body against his.

She looked back to her lap and saw the first kernels of a red ear. Quickly, she thrust the corn into Agnes' hand and murmured something about not feeling well. She quietly left the store, but there wasn't one person who wasn't aware of her going, including the man who kissed another.

109

Chapter Nine

LINNET RAN TO HER CABIN AND THREW HERSELF down in a burst of tears, feeling the empty desolation of one who is lost.

"Well, now, you're gonna ruin that pretty party dress o' yourn."

She turned over and through tear-filled eyes saw Cord standing over her. "Go away and leave me alone." She could see his eyes harden.

"I think I've had about enough of you and your high and mighty ways. You ain't so pure as you make out. I've heard about the way you pant after my little cousin, and I'm sure he's had whatever you can give him. So it seems to me that I'm due a little of what you been givin' out so freely."

"You're wrong! Now get out of here or I'll scream."

"Go right ahead." She opened her mouth, but

before a sound escaped, she felt his hand covering her face, blocking all air. After several seconds, he released her. "Now, you see what I mean? Just go ahead and scream. But, come to think of it, it could be unpleasant to have to tie your mouth while I taste that sweet little body of yours."

"Cord, no—" She backed away from him, scared now.

"You think you gonna talk me outta this? There ain't enough words to make me leave without havin' you." Someone's voice came from outside the cabin and Cord immediately leaped atop Linnet and covered her mouth. "Damned busybodies! They'll be comin' to see why their little Lynna-girl ain't at their party no more. Looks like I'm just gonna have to take you away from here."

"No—," she began.

"Don't tell me 'no' no more," he snarled. "I don't like it. Now I got to think on this a minute. I don't want them people followin' me. That cousin of mine could track a snake upstream." His face lightened. "You been teachin' him to read, ain't you? Well, you can just write him a letter sayin' you run off with me. He'll believe that." He grinned. "Mac ever tell you about that Trulock girl? He was so hot after her his tongue near touched the ground, but I come along and she never even seen Mac no more."

Linnet was frightened, very frightened. Cord was a madman. She could hear the jealousy and hatred of his cousin in his voice and wondered again at its cause.

"Here now, you write what I tell you."

She had no pen or paper and only the slate that Devon used in his lessons.

"You say you've run away with me and won't be back. And be careful 'cause I can read it." When he saw she hesitated, his lip curled. "I'd hate to have to break one of them little bones of yours, but I shore will and then I'll still take you with me. As you said at the cave, you ain't got no choice."

She wrote exactly what he said, and when he picked it up to stare at it, she realized he had tricked her, for he obviously could not read.

He grinned as he read her thoughts. "I hate to do this, but I don't reckon you're gonna come willin' like." He tied a scarf across her mouth and then her hands behind her back. He thrust her behind him as he put his head outside the door and looked around. When he was sure no one was about, he put Linnet on his horse, and they rode away into the dark forest.

When Devon released Corinne, he met the hostile stares of nearly everyone in Sweetbriar. He knew Linnet was gone and for a brief moment he had felt good that she had had a taste of her own medicine. She could not have felt half as horrible as he felt when he saw her in Cord's arms or before, when he knew she had spent the night with Cord. Now as he pushed Corinne from him and he sat alone on a bench by the wall, he didn't feel so jubilant. He swore he'd never let another woman hurt him, but Linnet had. She hadn't been out of his mind since she looked at him with those big eyes in Crazy Bear's camp.

He went behind the counter and poured himself a stiff drink of whiskey. Why didn't he just marry Corinne and raise a bunch of kids like a man ought to? Why'd he have to go pining for some little girl who took up with every man in Sweetbriar? The bottle was half empty before Gaylon took it away from him.

"You done made a fool of yourself once tonight. I ain't aimin' to let you do it again. Go outside and walk around. Get some air." He pushed Devon out the door.

The first thing Devon saw was Linnet's cabin, the door open, the light from the dying fire shining on the front step. He walked toward it slowly, his mind fuzzy with the whiskey.

"Linnet?" he whispered thickly as he stepped inside, closing the door behind him. She wasn't there. He tossed another log on the fire, his actions slow and clumsy. It was then he saw the slate. He read it carefully, repeatedly. She had left Sweetbriar with Cord. There was a finality in the words that could not be relieved.

He held the slate and walked to the bed, Linnet's bed, and fell on it. He went to sleep, the slate in one hand, the other outstretched in a helpless, palm-up gesture.

In the morning, Devon's head hurt, his tongue was thick and dry. When he looked about for water he realized where he was and he began to come alive again. As he swung long legs over the side of the bed, the slate clattered to the floor. Memory came back to him as he read the words and, with it, an overpowering anger.

So, she'd run off with Cord, he thought, and he remembered how she'd looked in the big man's arms the night before. He also remembered how Linnet had tried to push Cord away. Of course that had been an act. He read the slate again and frowned. Linnet would never pretend. She would put out her little hand and say, "I'm Linnet Blanche Tyler and I'm going to be married. Will you come to my wedding?"

The more he looked at the slate, the more he was puzzled. It just wasn't like Linnet to run away. He looked about the cabin and saw her shawl on the peg by the door. Nothing in the cabin had been moved or rearranged. Her two dresses also hung on pegs. The four carvings he had given her were in their places on the mantel. She wouldn't have gone away without her clothes. Maybe Cord promised her new things when they got where they were going.

Devon stood and his head throbbed. Cord! He couldn't believe it of Cord, that he would take Linnet away against her will, at least not when she already gave him what he wanted. Or did she? What was she doin' out in the snow that day unless she'd run away from Cord? Devon could imagine that if she had run away, Cord would be mad enough to do anything.

He drank several gourds full of water and went outside into the early morning. Gaylon was snoring on some bags of flour. He'd obviously finished the bottle of whiskey that Devon had left.

"Gaylon!" Devon shouted, and the old man opened one eye. "I'm goin' after Linnet. It looks like Cord's taken her off."

"You sure she didn't wanta go? It ain't like there's another man around here pays her any mind."

"I ain't got time to argue with you. Get me some jerky while I saddle my horse."

Linnet sat in front of Cord rigidly. He had run his hand over her body freely at first, but had grown angry at her stiffness and had soon ceased. Now they rode in silence. She would not allow herself to relax for fear she'd fall asleep, and she wanted to stay very aware of the direction they traveled. She would wait for a chance and then escape and make her way back to Sweetbriar.

He did not stop until well into the next day, and Linnet was so tired she could barely walk, but Cord looked as fresh as if he had just rested. "Here, sit down." He pushed her to the ground. "Ain't nobody followin' us." He laughed. "It ain't gonna be easy keepin' this from my little cousin. After I get tired of you, I'll sell you to one of the other trappers, then I'll just breeze into Mac's town sweet as you please, and he won't know the difference."

She listened to his words, but to his voice more. "Why are you afraid of him?" she asked quietly.

Cord's face nearly turned purple as his rage mounted. "Afraid! Cord Macalister afraid of a little thing like Mac?"

"You say you're not afraid, but I hear something else in your voice."

He drew back his arm to strike her but she sat still, her eyes steady and unafraid. She knew there were worse things than being beaten.

Cord recovered his smiling facade. "I guess you're a right smart girl. It ain't that I'm afraid of Mac but it goes a little deeper than what most people see. Somethin' I know and he don't is that he's not my cousin, he's my brother."

Linnet's eyes widened.

"Slade Macalister was my pa, too. He warn't much more than a boy hisself when I was born, but even so he should of claimed me, 'stead of leavin' me with them people. Never could abide those preachin' people. I was Mac's age 'fore I found Slade, and it always galled me that he never told nobody I was his son."

"But I don't understand," Linnet said. "Agnes knew Slade, and all the people knew him long before he came to Kentucky. They would have known he had another wife."

116

"Not wife, little missy. I was the result of one night's tumble in a field when Slade Macalister was just a pup."

She considered for a moment and then said quietly, "Did Slade ever know about you?"

"He should a' knowed!" Cord said with venom.

Linnet began to understand. When Cord was an adult, he came west searching for his father, expecting his father to recognize him, the hate in him building when he was not recognized. "You must resemble your mother."

He eyed her carefully. "My ma died cursin' Slade Macalister. He made her life hell. I grew up with her livin' with her parents, ol' man always preachin' at me, tellin' me I was a child of lust and sin." He gave an ugly grin. "I broke his jaw 'fore I left, the same day my ma died."

"So now you're repaying Slade by hurting his son."

"That's right. Last year I took some little girl away from him and now I'm takin' you."

"But there I'm afraid you're wrong. Devon doesn't care for me. Didn't you know that when he had a chance to kiss someone, it was Corinne, not me? I only teach him to read."

"You tryin' to get me to go after Corinne?"

"No!" She hadn't realized that it sounded that way. "No," she said more quietly. "It's just that Devon doesn't love any woman since what happened with Amy Trulock."

"Know her name, don't you? Look, I ain't

crazy, and you can't talk to me like I was. I wouldn't of carried you off 'cept you made a fool of me 'fore ever'body in Sweetbriar."

"I didn't! Cord, at least I didn't mean to."

"No use tryin' to talk your way out of this. Fact is, I'm beginnin' to feel like a little lovin' right now. Come here." He grabbed at her, and she jerked back, his hand tearing away the shoulder of her dress. "Ain't gonna do no good to fight me. Why don't you just be real still and enjoy what I'm gonna do?"

She walked backward, away from him, and tripped over the trunk of a fallen tree. She fell heavily, her back on the ground, her legs over the tree.

Cord stood over her, hands on hips. "Just the way I like 'em—legs up in the air." He knelt and ran his big hand along the inside of her thigh. "You're rounder than I'd thought. I like nice round legs." His other hand ran inside her other leg.

She pushed up on her elbows, trying to get enough leverage to be able to move away from him. Her long skirts tangled about her, one calf pressed between the log and Cord's heavy body. His hands moved farther up her body. She felt a rock against her fingertips and stretched to reach it. With all her force she brought the rock down on his head, surprised when so much blood began to flow all over her and the masses of white fringe entangled about her.

Her heart pounded, raced, as her first thought was to see to his wound. No, she cried to herself. She could feel his heart against her thigh and knew he was alive. She would have little enough time to escape before he woke. She pushed hard to get him off her body and tore her skirt from waist to hem on the tree.

She stood, dazed for a moment, unable to think what to do or where to go. Think, Linnet, think! she commanded herself. Get away, south toward Sweetbriar. Go quickly and steadily. Do not run, but keep an even pace. She walked as fast as she could, taking long, steady breaths, listening always for any sounds of pursuit, trying hard to be as quiet as possible.

She was so incredibly thirsty, yet she did not dare stop for water. By the sun it was late afternoon when she fell. She landed on her back but her fall triggered a rotten tree and it crashed across her leg. She bit her hand to keep from screaming when she saw it strike her leg, but then she recovered enough to wonder at the lack of pain. She sat up to examine what had happened, unable to move her foot. Her foot was in a hole and that was what had made her fall, yet the heavy log now pinned her to the place. She pushed but didn't have the strength to move the log.

Somehow, she was just too tired to care at the moment, too tired to expend any more energy, and she lay back and looked up at the sun filtering through the elm leaves and went to sleep.

"Where is she?"

Cord looked up from the stream, a wet cloth on his bleeding head, to see Devon standing over him. He turned back to the water. "I don't know what you mean."

"Cord, I want to know *now!*" Devon's voice was deadly.

When Cord turned again, he held a pearl-handled skinning knife. "You been askin' for this a long time, and I'm gonna give it to you."

Devon also withdrew the knife at his side and they circled one another, bent, eyes locked together. Cord had never believed in the strength of Mac, had always thought him skinny, but Devon's body was trim, steel, and now he was drawn taut and ready, his long years with his Indian relatives showing in every move.

"You look more like one of them Injuns ever' day," Cord sneered. "Tell me, how come you want this girl? She don't look like no squaw."

Devon did not speak, his face a solemn mask, unreadable, his mind cleared of all thoughts but survival. Cord frowned when he saw he did not ruffle Mac's concentration. He lunged with his knife, but Devon easily sidestepped, his maneuver almost graceful.

Cord had killed many men in knife fights, but he'd never fought one of Devon's ease and whiplash movements. "Think you're real fancy, don't you, boy, dancin' around like that? But how'll you do with a real man?"

Cord's powerful arm swept out and encircled Devon's waist, an unexpected move, and Mac's knife flew out of his hand. Devon brought his elbow down into Cord's ribs, feeling them crack beneath the blow. Cord released him, but only briefly as his foot went out and both men rolled together on the ground, Cord on top. He lifted his arm to plunge the knife into his brother's throat, but Devon caught his wrist and there was a battle of strength, of testing arm against arm, man against man, as sheer brute strength would show who would be the winner, the man left alive.

Cord's face showed not only the strain but his puzzlement at the incredible strength of the smaller man. Minutes passed, immobile, as they each tried to move the hovering knife, but Devon's training, the perseverance he had learned from his Shawnee brothers, won out. The knife slowly began to turn toward Cord's stomach and the sweat rolled off the man as his fear began when he saw where the path of the knife led. He grunted when it sank into the hard muscles.

Devon pushed the man from him, saw that he was still alive, then went to the stream to clean some of the blood and sweat from his body. The cold water helped revive him and he hid his face in his hands for a moment. He was not a good Shawnee, for he did not enjoy the sight of his enemy's blood.

He went back to Cord and pulled the knife out of his stomach, wiping it on some moss before returning it to the sheath at Cord's side.

"Where is she?" he asked the staring man. "Cord, I don't want to kill you, but I will. Tell me where she is and I'll put you on your horse. There's another settlement just north of here. You can get help there. You'll live if you tell me where she is."

"I don't know," Cord finally managed to rasp. "She run off seven, eight hours ago. I been followin' her, but can't find her."

Devon nodded, then put his arm under Cord's wide shoulders and helped him stand. Cord didn't protest when Devon half-lifted him into the saddle. He'd already underestimated Mac's strength once and he wouldn't do it again.

When Cord was on his horse, bent, one hand on the oozing knife wound, he looked into his brother's eyes and for the first time there was no hatred between them, only a bond bought with shared blood, both spilled and what came from a mutual father.

Chapter Ten

LINNET HEARD THE HORSE'S QUIET HOOFS LONG before she saw anyone. She tried frantically to move the log that pinned her but could not. A twig snapped, and she knew someone was near.

"Lynna." It was no more than a whisper, but she twisted toward the sound, tears already beginning to flow. She saw him outlined by the early morning light, and her eyes filled. She opened her arms to him. "Devon," she whispered.

He came to her quickly and clasped her to him, soothing her. "Are you hurt?"

"No," she managed to choke out. "My leg—"

He left her to examine her leg and quickly moved the log away. She moved toward him, pulling him once again close to her. "Oh, Devon," she said in his ear. "You came. You knew. I don't know how, but you knew."

He buried his face in her hair, smelling the rich forest smell of it. "You wouldn't run away. You'd never run away."

She laughed, joyous, knowing what he meant. It was so wonderful to have him near, to think everything was going to be all right. "You are always there when I need you, always near. You are the brother I never knew."

He drew back from her, his face contorted with rage. "I watch you with other men," he said through clenched teeth, "and you call me brother. It's time you learned I was a man."

She opened her mouth to speak but could not as he ran his hand down the front of his shirt and half tore it open, then jerked it from his body and threw it aside. His skin gleamed, so alive, so smooth, the Devon she had first seen, muscle and quiet strength.

He pulled her roughly to him and for the first time his mouth touched hers. How unlike the kisses of Cord! Where his had been pleasant, Devon's kiss was fire, a startling sensation that started at her mouth and seared its way down her body to her toes and back again. He did not need to force her mouth open because Linnet just as eagerly wanted to taste his sweetness as he hers. Her arms went around his neck to draw him closer, his skin touching hers at the torn shoulder of her dress, and it sent little shivers, tremors to the depths of her.

She pressed her body against him, and he lowered her to the ground and she felt his weight on top of her. She was burning. His mouth left hers and she moaned in protest, but he ran his lips along her neck and she arched to give him access to any part of her he desired. Her hands touched his hair, luxuriating in the soft thickness of it.

His hands tore away part of her dress and he touched the beginning curve of her breast. "Oh, Devon," she whispered, the sound blending with the lush richness of the forest around them.

"Yes, Devon," she murmured, "Devon!" His hand encircled her breast, the thumb arousing the pink crest. She pulled his mouth back to hers, the aggressor as she explored the moist cavity, honey, nectar so sweet yet so demanding. His hand ran along her leg, the skin exposed from hip to ankle. Her heart thundered in her ears.

He pulled away from her and her body felt lost, needing more of him. She held her arms up but touched only the now-cold air. She opened her eyes. Devon knelt over her, legs apart, straddling her hips, and he was smirking at her, one lip almost curled.

"Remember this the next time you're with one of your other men and the next time you think I'm your brother."

She realized he was laughing at her, that what to her had been a new and beautiful experience had been nothing to him but an act to prove his maleness. Her hand came from the ground and she hit him across the face with all her might.

He did not try to stop her, and the sound echoed in the forest. She lay still as she saw the red print of her fingers on his cheek.

He stood then and walked away. She was too angry to cry, and her fingers shook as she tried to put the pieces of her dress back together. She didn't hear him walk back, but Devon slipped his shirt about her shoulders. She threw it from her as if it were a vile, filthy thing, the way she felt after his humiliation of her.

"You are less than a mile due north of Sweetbriar," he said, his voice heavy. "Take the horse and return there."

She did not look up but knew he was gone.

She sat in silence for just a moment before hot anger raged through her. She was innocent of the things he accused her of! She grabbed his shirt, ran, leaped on the waiting horse and began a frantic search for him. He must have heard her approach because he stood still, looking up at her expectantly.

She had nothing as a weapon but his shirt, which she used as a whip to strike him. "Cord Macalister is a better man than you are!" she screamed at him. "At least he's honest! No wonder Amy Trulock chose him."

With that, she dropped her end of the shirt, kicked the horse forward to ride away from him.

But Devon was faster than she as he made a leap, and in a moment both of them were tumbling to the ground, his mouth taking hers with a breathtaking force. Linnet buried her hands in his hair and returned his kiss with matching fire.

"Damn you, Linnet! Damn you!" he murmured, his mouth moving down her neck.

She tried to bring his mouth back to hers, but he stopped her.

"I've waited too long for this and you'll not rush me." He began to kiss her slowly, softly, his hand against her cheek. Forgotten were any grievances, any hostilities, there only existed before them the culmination of long months of stored and buried desires.

Devon unbuttoned Linnet's gown, the pale skin exposed to him. "I want to look at you," he said very quietly, only a whisper really, but with none of a whisper's harshness.

She looked at him, his eyes so gentle, and she had no thoughts but that Devon was near her, that he touched her, that he was finally hers. Her look answered him, and carefully he slipped the torn dress from one slim shoulder, his lips following his hands. Linnet was not aware of the rest of the gown going, but she lay nude before him and she was glad she pleased him.

"You're beautiful, Lynna, beautiful."

His hand on her sent little shivers of delight through her, the contrast between her smooth skin and his work-hardened palm making her more aware of the maleness of him, the vitality of him. He did not kiss her mouth again but her neck, the line below her cheek, the soft spot below her ear. He ran his face along her perfect, jewel-like collar bone and she felt the soft beginning whiskers on his jaw.

When his mouth first touched her breast, she gasped aloud, in wonder as well as pleasure. She arched against him, felt him draw her closer, the rough, heavy, coarse bottom of his pants against her thigh, and the contrast of him was wonderful.

"Devon," she said.

He came back to her mouth, smiled at her, his lips curving, so close, so warm. He sought her mouth and she opened it to him and he drank of her, needing her. The passion in her began to rise, replacing the wonder and the awe. She met his kiss, pressing her body closer, pulling him to her, hands in his hair, entwined about her fingers. She greedily tasted his mouth, roughly, hungrily.

"Wait, sweet, you go too fast."

He pulled away from her and smiled, touched her temple with one finger. She felt angry, cheated. She did not want him to leave, but wanted more kissing, more touching, more and more, until she would die from the want.

Devon moved farther from her side, lightly touching her body, her stomach, thighs. Suddenly, he did not want to wait any longer. He knelt beside her on the forest floor, watching her. Linnet's fingers ached to touch the golden skin and she put her arms up to him again and he grinned at her as he removed his pants.

Linnet gasped at the sight of him, his maleness alarming to her and she drew back from him, but he did not seem to notice as he quickly lay beside her again. In spite of her fear of the unknown, she responded quickly to his touch, to his breath in her ear, his teeth on her earlobe. He pulled her to him, his arms strong, his skin touching hers, so hot, so cool, so alive, vibrating almost. His kisses changed as his passion increased and she met that desire, tasting the skin of his neck with her teeth, so firm, so smooth.

He pulled her beneath him and the weight of him startled her, his strong, hard thighs touching her smooth, soft round ones, the dark skin of his chest touching her breasts, catching them between their bodies, and the feelings that flooded her!

At his first probing touch, her eyes opened and she tried to move away from him.

"Linnet?" he questioned in bewilderment.

"No," she whispered desperately.

He pulled her back to him and brought his mouth down on hers forcefully. All thought of protest was gone until the first sharp pain, the hurt that caused the idea of love to flee her mind. He held her face in his hands.

"Linnet, I didn't know. I didn't know. Please, look at me."

The pain had subsided some as he lay still and

she opened her eyes to him. It was Devon, her Devon, and she wanted to please him. She managed a small smile and he kissed her again as he seemed to fight some inner agony.

"I . . . cannot . . . ," he whispered, and began to move. He still hurt her, but she saw the pleasure in his face, the almost ethereal look as his eyes closed and his lips parted. He collapsed on her quickly, roughly drew her to him and slept almost immediately.

Linnet lay still under his heavy arm, thinking how she wished the kissing had not stopped, for her hunger for him was not in the least assuaged. She lifted a bit and looked at the long, smooth muscles of his back and her lips wanted to touch him. How many times had she seen that skin and wanted to touch it?

He slept heavily and did not waken when she slipped from under his arm. She did not hesitate as she pressed her lips against the back of his neck, hidden and secret under black curls. His hair smelled of smoke and the strong, rich Kentucky earth. She ran her teeth along the back neck muscle, marveling at the power there, the power she held over him—the power to give him pleasure.

She felt him stir beneath her as if he came out of a stupor, but he did not turn. She began to forget who she was, no longer remembered the strict upbringing of an English nanny, the many words of "a lady doesn't do that!" She was a woman, alone in a quiet place, and the man she loved lay beneath her, dark and warm and untouched, and months of looking had made her insatiable in her desire to touch him.

She put her hands on the round, hard muscles of his shoulders and slid her sensitive fingers along his arms until she lay on top of him, then lifted again, the sensitive tips of her breasts against his skin. She kissed him then, over the entire back of him, her hungry fingers and mouth caressing and exploring, curious, interested, excited.

"Lord, Linnet! I can't stand any more. Come here." He grabbed her arms and pulled her beside him and he felt her stiffen again. "I won't hurt you again. Trust me."

She did trust him, the trust he had asked for and received so long ago in the crude Indian hut, the trust she had since withdrawn, but now she returned it to him, with forgiveness and overflowing love. He did not hurt her again, and this time she understood the culmination of her desire. He moved slowly, carefully, until he saw that she too wanted him. She pulled at him, her fingers biting into his arms, and she moved with him, together, towering, soaring, building, and exploding as one. They lay together, entangled, wet, sated, and slept.

Devon woke first and silently, trying not to look at Linnet, sunlight drenching her lovely body, as he dressed and walked away from her.

He'd had what he wanted, she'd at last repaid him for saving her and now she could have Cord, or any other man she wanted.

Without thinking about where he was going, he turned north toward his Shawnee grandfather's. He needed time to think.

The young man who walked into the Shawnee village with a freshly killed deer across his shoulder was greeted with great affection and no little noise. The women took the deer from him and he made his way directly to the large, round wigwam of his great-grandfather. The old man's face was a spider's web of wrinkles, and they rearranged as he smiled up at his tall, lean grandson.

"The white man's ways have made you soft," he greeted the boy.

The young man self-consciously ran his hand over his hard, flat stomach and then grinned as he sat before his grandfather. "I ask permission to stay with my Shawnee brothers for a while."

The old man nodded and took a long clay pipe from the wall of the dwelling. "You are welcome. You know that. There is something which troubles you?" He looked across the pipe bowl.

"It's nothing that time won't heal."

The old man paused a moment and stared, his black eyes like tiny glass beads. "It is a woman who does this to you," he said calmly.

The man's head came up sharply, and the old man chuckled, a dry sound.

"I have not always been as I am now. I was young once also. You may stay and try to forget or remember this woman."

"My grandfather is very wise." He took the pipe from the long, thin, dry fingers and they smoked together, needing no more words.

When Linnet woke and found herself alone, it was almost as if she'd expected to find him gone. Obviously his hatred and jealousy of Cord were more than any feelings he had for her.

Quietly, she rode back to Sweetbriar.

Six weeks later, Devon had not returned, and Linnet was sure she was pregnant. She wasn't sure what she was going to do and wondered if the people of Sweetbriar would still care about her if she bore an illegitimate child.

Corinne made her decision for her. The girl, in tears, came to Linnet and begged her to tell where Mac was. She cried harder, sneaking looks at Linnet through her wet fingers when Linnet said she had no idea where Devon was.

Corinne dramatically confessed she carried Mac's child and he *had* to marry her.

Linnet began to laugh so hysterically that Corinne fled the little cabin.

In the morning, Linnet began to pack her few belongings and she asked some traders at Mac's store if they could help her travel east. They told her of some settlers who would be traveling through day after tomorrow.

Chapter Eleven

"I hear you're leavin' tomorrow," Agnes said, her face rigid.

"Yes, I am." Linnet answered her in the same tone.

The two women stared at one another, neither flinching. Agnes spoke first. "You're a fool, you know."

"I know nothing of the sort." Linnet brought a long-handled axe down on a piece of wood.

Agnes took the axe from her. "You can maybe fool the others but you ain't foolin' me."

"Agnes, please excuse me. I've told you before that I have no idea what you're talking about."

"About you and Mac."

"Mac? Oh yes, I believe I have met the man, but I don't recall much else, certainly not enough to make us a pair."

134

Agnes grabbed Linnet's upper arms. "What's he done to you to make you this way?"

"No one has done anything to me that I did not ask for. I am returning to the East where I belong. I refuse to remain here and wait for a selfish, pigheaded man to return and laugh at me."

"There's more to a man than bein' just what you have all picked out."

"And what possibly could be more?" Linnet asked sarcastically.

"There's a feelin' that's left when you're tired after all day washin' diapers for a man's kids, when you're sick and he holds the pan to catch your heavin's. And there's a feelin' for a man that makes you forgive him when he does ever'thin' wrong, when he says and does mean things he don't intend. And that feelin' is love, somethin' I think you know a right smart about."

"But you're wrong, Agnes," Linnet said quietly. "I know nothing about love. All I know about is a childish hero worship for a man who isn't capable of any feelings but anger and hostility. Do you expect me to go on chasing after a man like that? I might have once, but no more. There are things, unforgivable things, between us."

"You can't tell me about no high-falutin' hero worship. I know what I seen, and I'll tell you again that you're a fool. Go to him now, go tell him that you love him."

Linnet's eyes lit into an amused twinkle, but it was not a pretty expression. "But you don't understand, Agnes. I did tell him. I told him that I loved him in the best way I could, but he just frankly doesn't care. So now, if you'll excuse me, I must start preparing supper." She walked past Agnes, and for once the big woman was speechless.

The morning came all too soon and Linnet could hear the sounds of people outside her cabin, the wagons rolling into place. She gave one last look about the little room. Whatever happened in her life from now on would be without Devon Macalister. The four carvings still stood in their places on the mantel. No, she wouldn't take them with her. That part of her life was over. She walked toward them, touching the dark wood one last time, and then she sighed and scooped the four of them into her small bundle of clothing. No matter what, she justified herself, she could always sell them.

She opened the door to Lyttle Emerson's knock.

"It's time to go, Lynna. The people of Sweetbriar have come to say good-bye," he said sadly.

Linnet stepped outside and saw they waited for her. She went first to Wilma and Floyd Tucker, their four children standing quietly beside them.

"We're gonna miss you," Wilma began, throwing her arms around Linnet. "Thanks so much for goin' after Jessie that time."

Linnet turned away to hide her tears.

Floyd shook her hand, his face solemn. Jonathan, Caroline, and Mary Lynn smiled at her and said they were sorry she was leaving. Linnet knelt in front of Jessie and he held out his hand to her.

"I thought you might like it. Ain't much, just a rock, but it's got a hole in it."

"Thank you, Jessie," she said, her eyes too blurred to see. Jessie shrugged and walked away.

Esther Stark hugged her and thanked her for helping deliver the baby, Lincoln, and the four twins cried and begged her to stay. The Emerson family was the hardest. Lonnie was indignant, saying he had saved her life and she had no right to leave without his say-so.

Agnes nearly crushed her in a vigorous hug. "You 'member what I told you. You'll always be welcome in Sweetbriar."

Linnet shook Lyttle's hand. The tears were running down her cheeks. She had never before realized how happy she had been in Sweetbriar until now.

At a distance stood Doll and Gaylon, no laughter in their eyes. More tears came as she thought of never seeing these two men again, hearing their teasing, their baiting of Devon. She stopped by the wagon, a few feet from the men, and dropped them the lowest, most elaborate curtsy she could manage—a curtsy for kings.

Lyttle stood ready and helped her onto the wagon seat and she never looked back.

Chapter Twelve

Sweetbriar, Kentucky—April, 1787

THE TRAPPER SLUNG THE BUNDLES OF FURS ONto the counter and went to the fireplace to warm
his hands. This was the first time he'd been to
Sweetbriar in nearly two years and it had
changed a lot. The settlement had nearly doubled in size, and he didn't know very many of the
people anymore. He wondered where Mac and
Gaylon were and that old man who usually sat in
front of the fire, Doll was his name. The trapper
looked around the store and realized it had
changed, too. Mac usually kept it pretty clean or
made sure Gaylon did, but now it looked as if a
couple of bears had spent the winter in the
place.

Zeke sat down and stretched his long legs
toward the fire. Maybe it had somethin' to do
with that little gal he'd seen in the Squire's
town. He was surprised when he'd seen her

there, playin' with a bunch of kids, some no taller'n her. He'd been surprised because the other time he'd seen her she'd been livin' in Sweetbriar and was causin' a whole lot of problems amongst the men.

Zeke had to smile as he remembered Mac sulkin' after the girl, watchin' her all the time and then pretendin' not to look at her. He, Zeke, had been the same way when he was Mac's age, but, thank the Lord, Molly had had enough sense to see through him. She'd had to use her big belly to drag him to the altar, and he'd been pretty mean to her for a while afterward, but she straightened him out, and he'd been the happiest man alive for ten years. He didn't like to remember Molly's death and his drinkin' and finally how he'd sent the kids east and set out for the woods.

Zeke shook his head as he cleared away the ugly thoughts and went back to the early years with Molly. Mac was just like him—scared to death of what he felt for the girl. It does somethin' to a man to love somebody so much, because then he gives up too much of himself.

The door opened and Gaylon entered, his shoulders drooping, looking much older than the last time Zeke had seen him. "Mornin', Gaylon," the trapper called.

Gaylon stared. "Who are you?"

"You 'member me, Zeke Hawkins. I brung you some furs."

"Hmph!" The old man hardly looked at the furs.

"What's the matter around here?" Zeke asked. "Where's Mac and where's that old man used to sit by the fire all the time?"

Gaylon looked up in surprise. "You ain't been here in a while. Things is different now. Now we got a devil runnin' the Macalister store. Don't allow nothin' but work." He spat a healthy black wad of tobacco juice on the floor.

The door burst open, and Mac entered the store in a rush. Zeke gasped at the sight of him. He'd lost a lot of weight, his eyes were sunken as if he hadn't slept in days, and his hair and clothes were dirty. "Mac." Zeke stepped forward, his hand extended. "It's been a long time."

The tall, dark young man ignored him and went to the counter. "You bring these furs?"

"Yes," Zeke answered hesitantly.

Mac turned to Gaylon. "How come you ain't got 'em counted yet?"

Gaylon spat again, the juice barely missing Mac's foot. "Ain't had time. You so all-fired in a hurry, you do it. I got other things to do."

"I'm sure they're real important," Mac snarled as Gaylon slammed the door.

Zeke moved away from the counter. Whatever had happened to Mac in the last two years, he certainly didn't like. "Mind if I stay around here for a few days?"

"Do what you like," the dark man answered. "I got no claim on you."

"I know." Zeke tried to sound pleasant.

The door opened, and a tall, big-boned woman entered.

"What do you want, Agnes?" Mac snapped.

"None of your bad temper, I can tell you," the woman returned. "I come over to look at the cloth that just come in."

"You know where it is," he said disinterestedly.

Agnes ignored him and then saw the trapper. "Why, Mr. Hawkins! We haven't seen you in Sweetbriar in a long time."

He removed his fur cap and smiled. "I'm pleased you remember me. I been farther north, around Spring Lick for a while now, near two years."

"Spring Lick? Ain't that where they're doin' all that talk about Kentucky bein' made a state?"

"Some of it's goin' on there. They got a man there name of Squire Talbot what thinks he's gonna be the first governor."

"Governor! You hear that, Mac? Kentucky's gonna have its own governor."

Mac ignored her.

"Well, Mr. Hawkins—"

"Zeke."

She smiled. "Zeke, I sure would like to hear all your news. Why don't you come to my house for supper?"

Zeke grinned. "That's the best offer I've had in months. I sure miss a woman's cookin'. In fact, that's somethin' like what I was just gonna ask Mac 'fore you come in."

Mac lifted his head. "I don't run no free kitchen for ever' trapper comes through here."

"No, it's not that, it's my rheumatism. These spring rains bring it on worse and worse, and sleepin' on the ground don't help it none."

Mac slammed the ledger shut. "You're welcome to sleep on the floor here anytime."

"I wouldn't want to put you out none, but when I was ridin' in, I saw an empty cabin in the clearin' and I wondered if'n I might stay there."

"No!" Mac fairly shouted.

Zeke looked in puzzlement to Agnes, and she glared at Mac. "I'm afraid we're keepin' that cabin like it is so we can all remember some people's ignorance," she said.

Mac returned her stare. "You find what you need, Agnes? I got other things to do than stand around here all day."

Zeke stepped between the two people. "Look, I didn't mean to start nothin'. I know ever'body was right fond of that little lady who used to live there, but since she ain't comin' back, I thought—"

Agnes whirled on him. "What makes you so sure she ain't comin' back?"

"Well, 'cause I seen her." Zeke felt like a bolt of lightning couldn't have affected the two people more.

Agnes recovered first. "Where'd you see her?" she asked quietly.

Zeke looked away from the staring Mac. "She's been livin' in Spring Lick for over a year now. Come out on a wagon with some missionaries last spring, about this time, I guess. She's the schoolteacher at Spring Lick." Zeke chuckled. "She may be little but she's sure got them kids under her thumb. I seen her out playin' with 'em many a time but as soon as she tells 'em to get back inside the schoolhouse, they go and, funny thing is, about half of them kids is bigger'n her."

Agnes laughed. "That's Linnet all right. She's sure got a way about her. But why's she in Spring Lick? She left here to go to Boston or some such place."

"Ain't you two got no place else to go so you can talk over old times without botherin' me?"

Agnes didn't even turn to acknowledge Mac's outburst. "Zeke, I don't think I'm gonna be able to wait 'til supper to hear the news. Why don't you come with me now?"

Zeke was glad to get away from whatever was eatin' at Mac. "I'd be pleased to, ma'am."

Mac stared for a moment at the closed door. So, Linnet was in a place called Spring Lick. He grabbed a half-full bottle of whiskey from the shelf and went to the old oak tree by the spring. He placed the bottle to his lips and hardly noticed the burn of the raw whiskey; he was used to the sensation by now.

The girl ate at him, he thought. Night and day she ate at him. How many times had he gone to her empty cabin and looked around, remembering the hours they had spent there? It wasn't that he missed her, it was just that she was like a sore that grew in him, a sore that hurt all the time.

Mac drained the last of the whiskey and found there hadn't been enough to stop his thoughts of Linnet. What was so different about her? He'd been in love with Amy Trulock but he'd gotten over her leaving him. Why did he still think of Linnet constantly? There was only one way to rid himself of her ghost, and that was to go to Spring Lick and see her. She'd probably be married now with two dirty, ugly kids and she'd be fat and tired like the other women. When he saw her like that then he'd be able to laugh at himself and he'd be content never to see her again.

He smiled for the first time in a long while. It would be good to get her voice out of his mind, those precise little words, good to never again see those strange eyes that changed from gray to green to blue to angry flashes of red. He tried to suck more whiskey from the empty bottle but couldn't and in anger threw it and watched it shatter against a distant tree.

Linnet sat bent over a quilting frame, her needle flying in and out, while around her the women gossiped nastily, ripping Linnet's friend

Nettie Waters apart. Linnet didn't dare say a word or she knew she'd cause the wrath of the people to come down on her own head.

She'd been in Spring Lick almost a year now and she was counting the hours until she could leave. She'd left Sweetbriar in anger and haste, not considering the fact that she had no money, no one to help her. For months she'd worked at any job she could find, usually being some lazy woman's maid. By the time she had reached Boston, her advancing pregnancy had made even those jobs difficult to find.

Her daughter Miranda was born in a Catholic hospital for unwed mothers, and Linnet was urged to put the baby up for adoption. But Linnet looked into those blue eyes so like Devon's and she knew she'd die before she parted with the child.

In the hospital, her luck seemed to change, for she read an ad in a newspaper that a man in Boston was looking for a schoolteacher in Kentucky. Linnet wanted to return to the wilderness, wanted to raise her daughter away from the city, away from people who might call her child ugly names.

Linnet applied to a man named Squire Talbot, and after six long days of waiting, she was given the job.

It didn't take her long to realize what a mistake she'd made. "The Squire," as he wanted to be called, had found out that her story of being a widow was a lie and he assumed she was an easy woman. Once, on the trail into Kentucky, Linnet applied a heavy skillet to the Squire's head, and the man began to get the message.

But Linnet had made an enemy.

The Squire stayed away from her, but his pride was hurt and he wanted revenge. He introduced her to the people of Spring Lick as Mrs. Tyler, widow, but within days they knew Miranda was an illegitimate child, and Linnet knew the Squire had told them the truth.

The people of Spring Lick were narrow-minded gossips who used religion to back up whatever they wanted. At first the men of the town had seemed to expect favors from Linnet, but she'd been able to repulse them—and made more enemies. The women hated her because she tempted their husbands, and the men thought she should give them what they wanted because she'd obviously given it to some other man.

Now Linnet tried to save every penny she made at teaching so she and Miranda could soon leave the town, where she had only one friend— Nettie Waters.

"Miranda's growing quickly, isn't she, Linnet?" Jule Yarnall asked from across the quilting frame. "Tell us, does she look like your family or your . . . husband's?"

Linnet didn't look at the woman. "She looks like my husband. At least she has his eyes. His hair was much darker, though."

The door burst open before the women could really get started, and a pretty woman entered, her clothes faded but clean and showing her good figure. "Linnet, I just got some wax goin' for some candles and I wondered if you'd help me with the molds."

Jule protested. "Can't Vaida or Rebekah help you, Nettie? They seem perfectly capable girls, or maybe they're busy at other things?"

Nettie gave her a deadly smile but no answer and then turned back in question to Linnet.

Linnet smiled gratefully. "I'll be glad to help." She hastily put her sewing scissors, needle and thread in the little reed basket, before bending and scooping up Miranda. "I can't thank you enough," she said when they were outside.

"I figured now'd be a good time to rescue you since they've had enough time to finish with me and my family and it's about time to start on you and Miranda."

Linnet had to laugh at Nettie's correctness. Miranda pushed away from her mother and wanted to get down. Linnet held the little hand, and the two women slowed their pace for the child.

"This sure is a beautiful spring," Nettie said. "Nice time for a weddin'." She looked shrewdly at Linnet. "When's the Squire gettin' back?"

"I'm not sure." Linnet avoided her friend's eyes.

"I guess you know he's spreadin' around hints that Miranda's his, don't you?" Nettie said quietly.

"No!" Linnet gasped. "Even he—"

148

"I wouldn't put anythin' past him. You've hurt his pride. Speak of the devil, look who's comin'."

Approaching them was a tall, gray-haired man on a horse. He carried himself well and looked younger than his fifty years, his shoulders back, his stomach sucked in. He was a man used to getting what he wanted out of life, and Linnet suspected that her major appeal to him was her refusal of him.

The Squire stopped his horse before the two women, his brown eyes smiling down at Linnet for a moment before he even saw Nettie and the baby. He tipped his hat. "Hello, Nettie. Everything all right at your house?"

"Just fine, Squire," she answered. "Ottis wants you to come by and look at some new corn seed he bought from some trapper. I don't think it's worth much, but Ottis seems to think each seed's gonna grow a stalk of corn that'll take four men to carry."

The Squire chuckled. "I'll have to go by today and see the seeds. I wouldn't want to miss anything like that. Is there no school today, Linnet?" He smiled down at her.

"There will be this afternoon. Everyone begged so to have this morning off that I couldn't resist the chance to play hooky myself."

"You're too easy on the children, Linnet," he said seriously.

Nettie made a little noise in her throat. "How she handles them kids of the Gathers is beyond me. You know, Squire, you ought to speak to

Butch. If he'd stay away from that store a little more and have a little say in them kids of his, they'd be a lot better off."

The Squire dismounted his horse, standing close to Linnet. "Nettie, you're sounding more and more like Jule. She says I ought to do something with your oldest daughter."

"Ain't nothin' wrong with Vaida and you know it. They're just jealous 'cause she's prettier'n any of their kids."

"Be that as it may, I still have to listen to all complaints. If Linnet has any complaints about the discipline of the schoolchildren, I'll have to step in, but until then—" He broke off and they both stared at Linnet, expecting an answer.

"No," she said quietly. "I have no complaints. I must go back to the school now. I have some lessons to get ready before the children arrive." She knelt and hugged her daughter, who grinned happily at Linnet. "I have to go to school now, Miranda, so you go to Aunt Nettie and be good, will you?"

Miranda gurgled an incoherent answer to her mother and readily went to Nettie.

"I'll walk with you," the Squire said as he took her arm.

"Did you have a pleasant trip?" Linnet asked when they were alone.

"Yes." He looked into her eyes, a deep, rich gray. "But I was anxious to return home. Did you have any more unpleasantness from Jule or Ova?"

"Very little." She smiled. "I must go now," she said at the door of the little schoolhouse.

"I'll just come in with you and—"

"No!" she interrupted.

He stepped away. "I guess you're right. Wise, sensible Linnet. Of course, you owe me nothing for taking you and your child out of Boston. Oh well," he said when he got no response from her. "That's past history. I do have a lot of work to do today. May I see you tonight?"

Linnet turned and fled inside the school without answering. Her first action was to slam the big dictionary on the desk with her fist. The Squire! Everyone adored and worshipped him, went to him to ask his permission for anything they planned to do. Spring Lick was even called the Squire's town, the way Sweetbriar was Devon's town. But what a difference! Devon loved the people of Sweetbriar but the Squire collected people. He always did things for people, lots of things, and he always refused to be paid for his deeds, refused to ever ask any help from anyone.

For a while Linnet had tried to get along with him and he'd come to supper with her and Miranda a few times, but soon Jule and Ova had come to talk to her "for her own good." They said it didn't look good for her to have a man in her house each night like that, that people were bound to talk, not that they, of course, ever would, but there were some people a lot less Christian and charitable than they were.

At first Linnet had been stunned by the people of Spring Lick's attitudes, but she had grown to understand them, even to anticipate their reactions. The women very much liked having a handsome bachelor in their community and they didn't like a single woman around. So Linnet had to bear many snide comments. Spring Lick was four times as big as Sweetbriar, yet she'd had more real friends in the smaller town than she could find in all the population of the larger settlement. Nettie was the only one who didn't ask questions, who didn't sometimes stare at Miranda as if she were a little odd or maybe a little dirty.

The thought of the children brought her mind back to the schoolroom. Her first experience with children had been on the trip to Kentucky with her parents. They were happy, honest children and she had loved them, like those in Sweetbriar. She thought of the carving of herself and Jessie Tucker on the mantel in her house, and wondered how much Jessie had changed in the past years, how much everyone had changed. Did any of them even remember her now?

She forced her mind away from her thoughts of Sweetbriar and back to Spring Lick. When the Squire had first given her the teaching job, she had been happy, but things were different now. As two towns could be so different, so could two groups of children. Whatever love she had given the children of Sweetbriar, they had returned

several times, but that was far from the case of
the children of Spring Lick. She felt sometimes
that she could fall dead in the middle of the room
and maybe, only maybe, the children would
remember to step over the body.

They looked at her with vacant eyes. Nettie
had said the Gather children were a problem but
they were far from it. How she wished for a boy
like Jessie who defied her or pulled the girls'
braids. Anything but those cold children who
stared at her and didn't seem to realize she was
a human being. Once, at recess, she had heard
Pearl Gather say, "She said to do it." Linnet was
stunned when she realized the girl had meant
her, not Mrs. Tyler or even Teach or the old lady,
nothing so personal. Even now, remembering,
Linnet was stunned. It wasn't the words but the
girl's tone.

She heard the children outside and when she
opened the door, none of them looked at her.

Chapter Thirteen

"MIRANDA, WOULD YOU LIKE TO GO FOR A WALK?"
Linnet asked her little daughter. The child awkwardly pushed herself up on her hands and knees, then stood, precariously, and walked to her mother's arms. Linnet's smile faded when she heard the knock on the door. She had hoped to be gone by the time the Squire arrived. "Hello," she managed to say pleasantly. "Miranda and I are ready."

The Squire ignored the child, as always. The little girl looked at him too seriously, her gaze too piercing for him to be really affectionate with her. Besides, it wouldn't do for someone of the Squire's class to touch a "tainted" child.

"The evening's beautiful, isn't it?" Linnet asked as she smelled the spring flowers, the new growth.

"Yes," he said, his eyes on her.

"What happened in Danville?"

The Squire puffed his chest out visibly. "I think my speech really impressed them." He gave her a sidelong look. "Thank you for helping me with it."

"You're welcome; I enjoyed doing it. So you think it's fairly certain that you'll get your wish to be governor?"

"Yes, I do, Linnet, and—" He broke off as Linnet went to retrieve Miranda from falling into a mud puddle. "Linnet, I—," he began as he took her arm.

She pulled away from him as politely as possible. Too often his touches led to more than she wanted to endure.

He noticed her movement. "Let's go back, shall we? It's getting dark."

The tall man walked into the store, eyeing it professionally.

"Can I help you?" The voice came from a hideously obese man, his little head set on top of several rolling chins, his shoulders and the rest of his body form lost in massive amounts of flesh. "You from around here?"

"No," the man said. "I'm from Sweetbriar. I been thinkin' of openin' a new store up this way but I can see you already got me beat."

The fat man showed pleasure at the compliment. "Name's Butch Gather." He held out a hand, the back and palm ballooned with short little digits protruding.

"Macalister, called Mac." He shook the offered hand.

"You gonna stay 'round here?"

"Thought I might for a while, if I can find a room or someplace to stay."

"I got a room out back if you can pay for it."

Devon tossed a silver coin onto the counter.

Butch studied it, close to his little eye. "For silver, mister, I'd give you my room."

Laughter came from behind Devon and he turned.

"Ova gets a taste of a real man, and you'd never get your bed back," one of the three men said.

Butch gave a little smirk. "I ain't heard her complainin' when I done give her six kids."

"Come over here, Mac, is it? Set a spell and tell us your news."

Devon listened and talked with the four men for a long while before he heard a word about the new schoolteacher.

"Real purty little thing, and the Squire better lay claim to her real soon."

"The Squire?" Devon asked. "I heard he was gonna try for governor when Kentucky gets to be a state."

"You heard right."

"And this schoolteacher is his wife?"

The man winked at Devon. "Not in front of a preacher she ain't, if you know what I mean."

Devon forced a smile. "I sure do."

* * *

Linnet left the schoolhouse as soon as she could. She should go to Nettie's house and get Miranda, she thought, but she really wanted some time alone. She walked into the woods, the shade cool and fragrant. She smiled and stretched, loving the solitude, the peacefulness.

"Hello, Linnet."

She froze at the voice she knew so well, then began trembling. Very slowly she turned and looked into the brilliant blue of Devon Macalister's eyes.

She could only gape at him, incredulous that her heart pounded so hard, that she could not be so at ease as he seemed to be.

"You do remember me?" he asked, his eyes laughing.

"Yes," she managed to whisper, working hard at controlling her breathing and calming her pulse.

"I was just travelin' through," he lied, "and I heard you was here so I thought I'd say hello. You look like Spring Lick agrees with you." His eyes swept her body, remembering every detail.

Linnet put her chin into the air. "I have managed."

"From what I've heard, you've done more than manage." He leaned on a tree negligently, but Linnet saw a brief flash of anger cross his eyes.

How could he just stand there so easily? Why was her body still trembling? He sat down on the ground, cross-legged, and plucked a long blade of grass. She had forgotten how graceful he was, how he moved so fluidly, as if he were made of water under his skin rather than hard bones like other people. His hair was blacker than she remembered, but it curled exactly as it always had. She knew how it felt under her fingers.

"So tell me what you've been doin' the last couple of years."

She brought her eyes back to his. She must act as if she felt as little as he obviously did. "Oh, simple, really. I lived in Boston for a year and then here in Spring Lick for the other year. I'd much rather hear about Sweetbriar. How is Agnes?"

Devon smiled and she saw his strong, white teeth, looking even whiter against the dark skin that she could almost taste—Stop! she told herself.

"Agnes had another young'un, a little girl, not long after you left." He watched her. "Named the baby Blanche."

Linnet was startled "Blanche?"

"Yeah. Like in Linnet Blanche Tyler, I reckon. Only she didn't ever say so in so many words."

Linnet couldn't help feeling pleased.

"And Esther's expectin' again," he continued. "And Lester's—oh, you don't know Lester. Sweetbriar's grown considerable since you left."

"And Jessie Tucker?" she asked. "And Lonnie?"

"Jessie and Lonnie are growin' faster'n their mas can keep 'em in clothes. You wouldn't hardly know 'em now. And Esther's baby, Lincoln, the one you helped birth, is walkin' and startin' to talk and he runs the whole household of all them women. The twins still look just alike, all four of 'em."

"You never thought so. You could always tell them apart."

He smiled at her, silent a moment and she looked away. It was as if the air between them was charged with thin, brilliant bolts of lightning. At least it felt that way to Linnet.

"And how is your wife?" she asked quietly, hoping to douse the lightning.

"Wife?" he asked incredulously. "What would I be doin' with a wife? I made it this far without gettin' a ball and chain, so I figure I can make it the rest of the way."

She was stunned. "But your child . . . What of the baby?"

"I don't know what you're talkin' about." He leaned back against a tree trunk and pulled his knife from its sheath and began to carve on a pine knot.

Linnet sat down heavily on a rotten tree that had fallen across the forest floor. "But what about Corinne?" she continued.

He looked up at her briefly. "Last woman I'd marry would be Corinne. I don't take Cord's leavin's." He gave her a swift, angry look before

159

returning to the pine knot. "Corinne got married all right and had herself a young'un right after the weddin', but that was all Jonathan Tucker's doin'. What made you think I was gonna marry Corinne?"

She braced herself and answered truthfully. "She told me she was going to have your child."

After a quick, hard look, Devon laughed, the cords in his powerful neck standing out. "Corinne always was a liar. Ever'body knew that. It wasn't me she wanted but my store. She tried ever'thin' to get me to—" He stopped and looked at Linnet until her face warmed with embarrassment. "Well, let's just say it wasn't possible that she could be carryin' my baby."

Linnet only blinked at him and wondered if he wasn't the liar.

He seemed to read her thoughts and looked away. "I ain't sayin' I didn't fool around with her some, but then a lot of men did. I wouldn't wanta be in Jonathan's shoes. But who knows, maybe he'll straighten her out."

"Yes, maybe," Linnet said. She was digesting this information. If only it weren't too late! But even if Corinne lied, it was Devon who left her alone after he'd made love to her in the forest.

"Now tell me about you. We been talkin' too much about me."

"No, we haven't. You haven't said a word about you." She took a deep breath. "You look tired and you've lost weight."

He gazed at her steadily. "I been eatin' Gaylon's cookin'—or my own, which is worse. It's a wonder I have any skin left."

She suddenly wanted him to go away, to kick him, bite him, kiss him, touch him—No! she must not think that way. She must be as calm as he. "I baked bread yesterday. Would you like to eat some of it?"

He grinned and she felt her heart pound again. "I would love to eat some of your cookin'." He rose and stood before her but she wouldn't look at him, couldn't, not when he was so close.

She moved away from him, and they walked together to the edge of the woods. The first thing Linnet saw was Nettie holding Miranda by the hand. Linnet was astonished and then appalled at herself. She had completely forgotten her daughter. She had no time for explanations, but threw an, "Excuse me," over her shoulder, lifted her skirts and ran to Nettie.

She was out of breath and gasping when she grabbed Nettie's arm. "If you're my friend, if I've ever done anything for you, please do this for me now. Do not tell him Miranda is my daughter."

Nettie looked over Linnet's shoulder to see exactly who "him" was. She saw a tall, slim, handsome man, with dark hair and . . . Miranda's eyes. It didn't take much intelligence to know who he was.

161

Devon came to stand beside the two women.

"Nettie, this is Devon Macalister. Everyone calls him Mac."

Devon lifted one eyebrow at Linnet. So, she didn't want other people to call him Devon. It was still her personal name for him.

"And this is Nettie Waters."

Devon inclined his head slightly to the woman.

Nettie bent and lifted Miranda high. "And this is Miranda." Nettie was very aware of Linnet's sharp intake of breath, but ignored her as she thrust the baby into Devon's arms. "Would you like to hold her?"

Devon was surprised. He liked children, but always managed to stay away from the little ones. They seemed to instantly become wet or very noisy. He looked with detached interest at the child in his arms. "Pretty little girl," he said as he handed her back to Nettie. "Nice eyes." He didn't know why she seemed to think that was such a funny remark.

Linnet began talking rapidly, after giving Nettie a fierce look. "I used to know Devon when I lived in Sweetbriar."

"I didn't know you lived in Sweetbriar. I thought you came here from Boston."

"I did, I . . ." Linnet felt confused. Seeing Devon holding Miranda made her lose what little composure she had. "I'm going to cook some supper for Devon now. I'll see you later."

Devon sat at the pine table in the little cabin. It was bigger than the one she had in Sweetbriar but basically the same, except for a high porch in front. "You still haven't told me about your life here. You're the schoolteacher?" he asked with his mouth full.

How could he sit there so calmly? How could he hold his daughter and not know who she was? Nice eyes indeed! They were identical to his, the vain, infuriating man! "It's all right here. The people are different from those in Sweetbriar."

"I met a man, Butch Gather, down at the store—" He stopped and went to the fireplace to look at the carvings.

"You kept them?" he asked quietly.

"Yes, I kept them." She could feel her anger rising. What right did he have to come back into her life? She had adjusted to a world without him. There were whole hours when she didn't even think of him, so what right did he have to come back? "Why are you here?" she demanded.

He sat down again at the table and resumed eating.

"I asked you why you are here and I want an answer!"

He put the chunk of bread down calmly. "I was passin' through and when I heard an old friend was here I thought I'd stop and say hello."

"Old friend," she said, quietly, deadly. "You

can sit there just like it was the same, just as if we were in Sweetbriar and I was giving you a reading lesson?" Her voice began to rise, becoming shriller. "You can talk to me calmly after all that has gone on between us? After that night we—?" She felt tears forming. "Well, I can't!" she shouted. "I left Sweetbriar because I never wanted to see you again, and I still don't. I want you to leave, to go away from here and never come back. Do you understand me?" She was shouting as loudly as she possibly could, and tears blocked her vision. She ran out the open cabin door and into the woods.

Devon sat quietly at the table, watching her run. She still runs just as slow and clumsy as ever, he thought, then turned back to the food and grinned. It seemed to him that it was the first time in two years he really felt like eating. Too often he had pushed his food away and reached for a jug of whiskey. Right now he had no desire for drink.

So, she did remember him! Spreading the bread with an inch-thick layer of fresh butter, he bit it, then studied the marks his teeth had made in the creamy substance. She thought he'd forgotten that night they spent together. That one night with her had ruined all women for him for the last two years. He'd been to bed with other women but not one of them had made love to him in return, not one of them had—

He smiled and ate another bite of the bread. If

she still remembered him so clearly, maybe they could have a little fun before he went back to Sweetbriar and returned her to the Squire. Lord! What kind of man would allow people to call him "the" Squire? Oh well, it didn't matter to him as long as he got what he wanted.

Chapter Fourteen

"I THINK IT'S DISGRACEFUL THE WAY SHE BRINGS him here in front of us good Christian folk. Anybody with half an eye can see who he is. Why, that child is the spittin' image of him," Jule said.

"An' her takin' up with him again, just where she left off before. Butch says he didn't come back to his room till the wee hours of the mornin'." Ova stabbed at the quilt, taking stitches much too large.

"What I want to know," Jule said, "is what we're gonna do about all this. Spring Lick is a good God-fearin' community, and I don't like what's goin' on under our very noses. And her the schoolteacher, too. What's she gonna be teachin' our children?"

"That's right," Ova answered. "A teacher should set an example, and if that's an example of what she believes is right—well, you know what I mean."

"I certainly do!" Jule began to sew faster, her voice rising. "I always knew she warn't no good, always moonin' up at the Squire."

"The Squire!" Ova stilled her needle. "We've forgotten about the Squire."

"Now there's an innocent lamb that needs protectin'."

"He shore does, and I think someone ought to tell him just what is goin' on under his very nose."

Jule and Ova looked at one another.

"It's our duty," Jule said.

"As Christian women," Ova said, and the two women put their sewing things away and went outside, walking briskly toward the Squire's large log house.

"Mornin', ladies. It sure is a fine day to be out, isn't it?"

Ova looked at her feet, suddenly embarrassed, but Jule had no such emotion.

"Squire, I'm afraid we've come on some unpleasant business."

The Squire's face became serious. "No one is hurt, are they?"

Ova sighed. "That's just like you to think of someone else's hurt first. No, I'm afraid the only one to be hurt is you, and we felt it was our duty—"

"Our Christian duty," Jule interspersed.

"Yes," Ova continued, "our bounden duty to

tell you what's goin' on in your own town, own household, so's to speak, somethin' you'd be much too kind to ever see."

"Won't you sit down, ladies, and let me hear what you have to say?" He indicated the chairs on the porch, and when they were seated, he said, "Now what can I do for you?"

"It's about that schoolteacher."

"Linnet?" he asked.

"Yes, Linnet Tyler. At least that's what she calls herself."

Jule continued talking. "We were willin' to overlook a lot of things, such as that baby havin' no father, at least not in the eyes of the Lord, but when she brings the child's father to our town and expects us to—"

"What!" The Squire stood, astonished.

"That's what we said," Ova added. "She brung the baby's father here. He's stayin' at my Butch's store now."

The Squire leaned against a porch post for support. "Ladies, I want you to start from the beginning and tell me about this, every detail."

Linnet swept the floor of the little schoolhouse. She regretted her actions of the night before, but there was nothing she could do to repair the damage. If she'd only been calm in his presence, then maybe he would have gone away. At least he had been gone when she returned to her cabin, but all night she had felt him near her, as if he still sat at the table and watched her.

"Mornin', Teach." Devon stood in the open doorway, reclining against the jamb.

"Good day," she said as calmly as possible. "What can I do for you this morning?"

He smiled lazily. "Just thought I'd come by and see where you spend so much time." He roughly thumbed through the big book on her desk. "What's this?"

"It's a dictionary. If you don't know the meaning of a word, you can look in there and find it."

"That don't make sense. Why would anybody use a word they don't know the meanin' of?"

She gave him a look of disgust. "What if someone said something to you in Shawnee, and you knew what every word meant except one? Wouldn't you like to have a book where you could look and find the meaning?"

"No," he answered seriously. "Then I'd have to carry a book like this around. I'd rather ask a Shawnee."

"But sometimes—," She stopped when she saw the Squire enter the school.

"Linnet, I've just been told we have a visitor to Spring Lick, a friend of yours."

Linnet stood, a man on each side of her. "Yes. This is Devon Macalister from Sweetbriar, Kentucky."

"Well, Devon." The Squire held out his hand.

"Mac!" both Linnet and Devon said in unison.

Devon's eyes twinkled and Linnet hurried to explain. "He's called Mac by everyone."

"Oh," the Squire said, seeing more than he wanted to see. "Linnet, may I see you outside for a moment?"

"Of course." She didn't look at Devon because she knew what he was thinking. His jealousy had torn them apart once, and she had no reason to believe he'd changed.

"Is he the father of your child?" the Squire demanded when they were barely outside the door.

Linnet blinked once in astonishment. "It didn't take them long."

"Did you spend last night with him?"

"You mean did I accept him when I've turned down the generous offers of every other man in this town? Excuse me, I have work to do."

The Squire caught her arm. "I brought you here. I paid for you to come here and you owe me—"

"I owe you nothing! I've paid your price since what little reputation I had you've ruined by letting everyone believe you do spend your evenings with me." She pointedly looked down at his hand on her arm. "It would hurt you in the eyes of the men if I let it be known I chose a shopkeeper over our next governor, wouldn't it?" She jerked away from him and briskly walked back to the schoolhouse.

"A lovers' quarrel?" Devon asked from his place by the door.

"Yes!" she hissed at him. "The Squire is just one of a long string of men I have here. Now would you please get out of my life?"

"You plannin' to marry the Squire?"

She didn't bother to answer him but went to her desk.

"I hear he's pretty rich. He can buy you lots of pretty things."

She glared at him steadily. "How wonderful since my whole life revolves around silk dresses and maids. Did you know that the house I grew up in was so large you could put every house in Sweetbriar in the dining room? Include the kitchens and you could add most of the gardens of Sweetbriar. As a child I never had to lift a finger to do any work. My father had twelve people hired just to care for me. I had two personal maids, a governess, a cook, two footmen, a driver, a—"

"You had your say. So now you're gonna marry the Squire and get some of it back."

"Certainly," she said, eyes wide.

He studied her silently.

"You must excuse me. I have work to do. I must work for a while longer until someone provides me with the life I've always been accustomed to."

Silently, Devon left the schoolhouse, walked through the town and into the forest.

He sat down heavily on a stump, his head in his hands. Why'd she say all those things when they weren't true? Lord, but the woman was driving him mad. He'd worked it all out, how he'd rid himself of her when he saw her again, but it was worse now, much worse.

"Mac?"

He looked up to see a woman standing near him. It took him a moment to realize she was Linnet's friend Nettie.

"Could I talk to you a moment? Miranda, don't go too far."

Devon watched the toddler, his mind bleak.

"I know it's none of my business, and I've been told so several times, but I think you ought to know what's goin' on in Spring Lick."

"I didn't know anythin' was goin' on," he said.

"I know. But you see, you're causing a great deal of commotion here."

"Me? But I don't even know anybody."

Nettie smiled at him. She could see why Linnet had fallen for him. "It's pretty obvious that you and Linnet have known one another rather well."

He lifted an eyebrow and she laughed. "Miranda, come here to Aunt Nettie. I'd like to show you somethin'."

The baby walked clumsily to Nettie's open arms. "You said she was a pretty little girl. Does she remind you of anyone?"

Devon looked from the child to the woman as if she were insane.

"How about her eyes? Ever seen them before? Jule and Ova recognized them right off."

"I have no idea what you're talkin' about."

Devon was deciding he didn't like the woman. "And who are Jule and Ova?"

"They're the town gossips. Gossip and, unfortunately, rather hurtful gossip is their life's work. If it hadn't been for them, no one would have cared who was the father of Linnet's daughter, and she wouldn't have been such an outcast here with all the men after her."

"Father! Linnet's daughter!" he exploded. "She didn't tell me—"

"No, she didn't." Nettie cut him off. "In fact, she's taken a great deal of trouble to hide her daughter from you. I would suggest you take a real close look at Miranda and then see if you remember seein' those blue eyes before, maybe in a mirror."

Devon stared at the child, seeing Linnet's chin, so often stuck in the air, and his own eyes. "Lots of people have blue eyes, maybe—"

Nettie stood and dumped Miranda into her father's lap. "You are a stupid man, Devon Macalister. Stay here and get to know your daughter." Nettie left them alone.

Devon was too stunned to even think. Miranda pulled on the buttons on his shirt, then lost interest, turned and scrambled from his lap. Devon watched her. His daughter! Could it be true that Miranda was his daughter?

"Miranda?" he said softly and the baby turned and smiled at him, her eyes brilliant. He reached into his pocket and withdrew a necklace of glass beads and handed it to her. She immediately put the necklace in her mouth and her father laughed with her.

"Well, little daughter, you now have a father. I'll bet your name is Miranda Tyler. How about if we change it to Miranda Macalister?" He swept her into his arms and she laughed at the motion.

"Miranda. Silly name, but I guess if your father can give you the Macalister, your mother can choose whatever name she wants." The baby hit him with the bead necklace, and he hugged her to him. "I think I like being a father."

Linnet saw them walking slowly from the forest, hand in hand. Devon stopped in front of her and Miranda went to look at the kittens under the porch.

"Is it true? Is she my daughter?"

"Yes, Miranda is your daughter."

He sighed and then took a deep breath. "All right," he said with resignation. "I'll marry you."

Chapter Fifteen

"MARRY ME?" LINNET SAID INCREDULOUSLY. SHE felt such anger in her head that she thought something might burst. "So, you will marry me. After two years and one daughter, you vile, insufferable creature, you now say you'll marry me!"

"Now hold on a minute—"

"No! You just hold on a minute. I have listened to you for a long time, but now you're going to listen to me. When you first walked into that little hut where Crazy Bear's people held me, when you risked your life for me, I fell in love with you. Yes, you should look astonished. I fell in love with you so hard that it has taken sheer hell to make me realize what a fool I was. What do you think it's like loving someone who's always angry with you, always accusing you falsely?"

"Falsely hell! I watched you with man after man."

"Man after man!" she gasped. "There was only Cord and he was as eaten with jealousy as you are. The two of you used me to repeat a game you'd already played. You lost one woman to him so you weren't going to let your pride be hurt by losing a second woman."

"How was I to know which man you wanted?" he said softly.

She threw up her hands. "There were times when you barely spoke to me. Cord dragged me away from the town and rather than stay with him I went into a snowstorm and nearly died. But did you care? No! All you thought of was that perhaps your rival had touched me."

"Why did you call me your brother?" he whispered.

She laughed, an ugly, mocking laugh. "You were everything to me—brother, father, mother, sister—all. I loved you so much. You in your selfish ways could never know how much. Why do you think I let you make love to me? I was such a fool about you that I would have lived openly with you at any time. All you had to do was snap your fingers and I would have come. It's not possible for you to know what I felt when you left me that day. Well, it's all over now. I've finally come to my senses. What I felt for you is gone, killed, bit by bit, by your suspicions, your accusations, your constant anger. Now I want you to get out of my life. I never want to see you again. And I assure you it will take me no more than ten minutes to rid myself of your unpleasant memory."

She stepped past him, but he grabbed her arm and pulled her to face him.

"I've been a fool, haven't I?" he said simply, a new knowledge in his eyes.

"Yes, you have," she said, her voice heavy, still angry.

"That's what's been wrong with me since I met you, ain't it? I've been in love with you and didn't even know it. I was afraid to love anybody again. After what happened with Amy, I was afraid. You knew it, probably ever'body in Sweetbriar knew it, 'cept me. I've been in love with you for a long time and I was too big a fool to see it."

She jerked away from him. "And now am I supposed to fall into your arms and forgive you, and we live happily ever after? It just doesn't happen that way. Do you realize what you've done to me? Not an hour ago you accused me of marrying someone for money. Has it ever occurred to you that I might want some kindness in my life, that I might want someone who can even say, "Good morning," to me without sneering, without some hidden meaning that was supposed to insinuate that I'm a woman of the streets? You've accused me of going to bed with every man who ever looked at me, but I'll tell you that you're the only man who has touched me."

"Linnet, I—"

"Don't give me that look. I can tell you now because I plain do not care any longer what you believe of me."

"But I love you. I just told you that I loved you."

"And that's supposed to make everything all right? Why didn't you say that the night you gave me Miranda? Why couldn't you have said it the day you found me after Cord had taken me away?"

"I didn't know then. You must forgive me."

"Oh, I must forgive you!" she said sarcastically. "You always accused me of wanting Cord and now, years later, you walk into my life and accuse me of sleeping with the Squire. The Squire!" she gasped.

"Linnet, please." He took her arm. "Miranda is my daughter."

She jerked away from him. "By what right is she your daughter? Were you there when I went through a sixteen-hour labor bringing her into the world, when I lay in a fever for two weeks after her birth, or were you just there for one afternoon's fun when you proved to yourself what kind of woman I really was?"

Their eyes locked for a moment and Devon knew the truth in her words. His voice was very quiet when he spoke. "I never realized before what I was like, how I've treated you. And it's worse for me because I know the thoughts I've had about you. You're right. I can't ask you to forgive me, but can we start again? Can I make things up to you?"

Her eyes flashed at him, her mouth hard. "What a clever little idea, start again, erase all the past. It can't be done. I could never trust you again, never love you again. You could never change. The first time I said, 'Hello,' to another man, you'd be accusing me of everything you could think of. I'm sure that someday you'd wonder if Miranda was your child or some other man's. Cord has blue eyes."

He looked as if he'd been struck, and he stepped away from her. "Then there's nothing I can do or say?"

"Nothing."

"Then someday someone else will be a father to my daughter?"

"*My* daughter. You have no claim on her."

He stepped very close to her, put his hand to her cheek, the warm, hard palm against the smooth, soft skin. "I love you, Lynna. Doesn't that mean anything? I've never said it to anyone else before."

She stared at him coldly. "Once it would have meant the world to me, but it comes too late now."

He moved away from her. "Do you want me to go away from here and leave you alone?"

"Yes," she said quietly. "Let me find the pieces of myself and make a new life for Miranda and me. I think I can do it now, now that I'm rid of you."

He nodded, his long-lashed eyes blinking rapidly. "If you ever need me," he whispered, but he choked, then turned and left her.

Miranda was frightened when she heard her mother's voice, so angry and loud. She held the kitten over her arm and looked up from under the porch. Her mother was shouting at a tall man, the man Aunt Nettie knew. Miranda's eyes teared as her mother's anger grew and grew. She didn't like the sound and wanted it to stop.

The tears rolled down her little cheeks and she opened her mouth to let the sound escape, but the kitten suddenly leaped from her arm and scampered out from under the far side of the porch. Miranda closed her mouth and sniffed as she watched the little black and white kitten chase a big, blue butterfly. Miranda dropped to her hands and knees and crawled from under the porch, following the kitten. She pushed herself up and ran across the clover toward the kitten and the butterfly, the fear her mother's anger had given her forgotten.

The door to the schoolhouse was open, and Miranda forgot the kitten as she climbed the three stairs, one at a time. She knew the schoolhouse, knew it had something to do with her mother and the games of the older children. She tripped on the rough floor and sat down heavily. She started to cry and then realized there was no one there to hear her, so she stopped and stood and walked toward the big desk at the back of the room. She peered behind the chair and saw a snug little cave, warm and secret and she climbed inside. She sat down and looked about her, liked the little place and lay down on her side and went to sleep.

"See, I told you ain't nobody here," the boy said. "Now you gonna do it or you too afraid?"

"I ain't afraid!"

"Ssh. Somebody's comin! Let's get out of here."

The two boys ran from the schoolhouse to the edge of the woods. "See, there ain't nobody."

"Well, just the same, there could 'a been. Hey! What'd you do with the lantern?"

The boy looked at his right hand as if amazed that the lantern wasn't there. "I guess I left it inside."

"You gotta go back and get it."

"Not me. I ain't goin' in there at night."

"When my pa finds out I took one of his lanterns, I'm gonna tell him it was you what done it."

"Me? You're a liar then."

The boys jumped simultaneously toward one another and rolled together in their fighting.

The kitten saw the open door to the schoolhouse and padded softly inside. On the floor sat the lantern, its little blaze flickering, up and down, orange and yellow, moving, enticing the kitten. It watched the flame a moment, head to one side, and then stuck out one white-tipped paw toward the heat, but the kitten soon realized it would take some strategy to control this foe. Quietly, it jumped onto one of the school benches, studied the flickering light, getting to know its erratic movements and then pounced, its little body upsetting the lantern, spilling its contents on the floor.

The fire burned the kitten's left leg and it screamed and ran outside into the cool night air. The clover helped to ease the pain and the kitten sat down to lick the wound, glad the hair was only singed. Repaired and its dignity regained once again, the kitten walked away from the schoolhouse, its tail in the air, never once looking back.

The boys continued to wrestle, not really serious, until one of them saw the flames.

"Look! The school's on fire."

The other boy paused with his fist drawn back as he looked at the fire beginning to show through the side window. "You did it," he said as his arm dropped. "You left the lantern in there."

"But it was you that give it to me."

"Whatever happens, both of us is gonna get skinned."

"You know it! Look, it's just the schoolhouse, ain't like it was somebody's house or there was somebody inside. If it burns down we get out of school for a long time, maybe even forever."

The other boy looked on in wonder. "You're

right. The school burns down, won't be no more school. We better get out of here 'fore somebody comes and we get blamed for what was only a accident."

The Squire was the first person to see the glow of the flames and he rang the bell on the end of his porch, the bell that was sounded only in times of emergency.

"What's up? Injuns again?" Butch Gather waddled toward the Squire's house.

"The schoolhouse is on fire! Let's get a bucket brigade going."

"Hmph!" Butch muttered as he wheezed after the Squire. "Why not let it burn? Then there wouldn't be no more trouble with that school-teacher."

The flames already covered one side of the building, long skinny tongues of orange slithering out the window, trying to reach the roof. It seemed that many people of Spring Lick thought as Butch did and were reluctant to help. They didn't want school to take their children away from work anymore, and no one regretted seeing it burn. It was only the anger and the orders of the Squire that made any of them scurry away after their buckets.

The front door of the school burst open, and a sheer wall of flame showed inside, and many people smiled because they knew they wouldn't be able to save much of the building.

Linnet came running through the night toward the blaze. She ran to the Squire and put her hands on his arm, stopping him from passing the bucket of water. "Miranda. I can't find Miranda," she yelled over the noise.

He pushed her away. "There isn't time now to look for her. We'll find her later. Get in line and get a bucket."

Linnet looked toward the blaze, the dancing lights showing her red and swollen face. The school meant nothing to her while Miranda was everything. She turned and walked away from the people who tried to douse the fire.

Nettie came running across the field, her two daughters behind her. "Oh, Linnet," she said. "I'm sorry about the school. I know you were proud of it. It looks like it's too far gone to save."

"Yes," Linnet said absently, her eyes searching the oddly illuminated night.

"At least Miranda got out," Rebekah said.

Both Nettie and Linnet turned to her.

"I didn't mean nothin'." The ten-year-old girl stepped back from the intense scrutiny of the adults.

Linnet grabbed the girl's shoulders. "What did you mean about Miranda?" she demanded.

"Ain't you got her?" Rebekah stammered. "I mean I seen her in the schoolhouse just a while ago."

Nettie pried Linnet's fingers from Rebekah's arm. "Now, Rebekah, I want you to tell us exactly what you're talkin' about."

"I was goin' to the spring and I saw Miranda

goin' into the schoolhouse. The door was open so I thought Mrs. Tyler was in there."

Linnet turned, picked up her skirts and began to run back to the fire. The people had stopped throwing water on the building, but stood ringed around the blaze, ready to stop any flying sparks. Only the back of the cabin remained whole.

Linnet ran straight toward the flames, not pausing for a second, not noticing the brilliant heat.

"Linnet!" the Squire yelled and grabbed her waist. She began to kick and claw at him, writhing, doubling as she fought against him, more animal than human.

"My God, Linnet! What's wrong with you?" He couldn't believe anyone so tiny could have so much strength. He held her with both arms about her waist and the pain as her heels struck his shins was no little matter. They were too close to the searing heat of the fire.

"It's Miranda," Nettie yelled at the Squire over the roar. "Linnet thinks Miranda is in there."

He understood and he frowned, but if the child was in there, she couldn't be alive any longer, not with the front of the cabin a wall of flame. "Linnet!" He tried to get her attention but could not. She still kicked, and his hands were raw and bloody from her nails. "Linnet! You can't save her. Listen to me! She is in God's hands now."

Later it was said that the scream Linnet gave was more horrible than anything anyone had imagined before. It was a long, hollow wail of agony and pain, and of hopelessness. It sounded above the fire, above the shouts of others, above the sounds of the dark, bleak night, and not a person or creature hearing it did not stop and shudder.

Devon seemed to appear instantly and from nowhere. "What is it?" he demanded of the Squire.

"Miranda," the man said, a limp, senseless Linnet in his bleeding arms. He motioned his head toward the fire.

Devon did not lose a second. He tore the shirt from his body, wet it in a bucket, rolled it into a lump and put it to his face. He then ran straight into the flames. Only Nettie reacted enough to scream "No!" at him but he didn't hear her.

The child lay huddled on the floor, her face wrapped in her long skirts, the desk over her head having given her some brief protection from the fire. She slept, drugged by the smoke and the heat. Devon took the little body and wrapped her completely in his shirt and she did not waken.

Quickly, he looked about him. There was as yet no fire in the back of the cabin, but the solid log wall offered no means of escape. The windows on either side were both aflame and too small for him to carry his daughter through. The only exit was the front, the way he had entered, and already he felt the skin on his back and arms as it pulled and burned.

He held the unconscious baby to his chest, holding her firmly into a tight little knot, sure that her body was protected by his. He took a breath of the smoke-filled air, put his face against the lump that was Miranda and ran straight through to the outside, his moccasined feet little protected from the burning, red-hot floor.

The Squire shook Linnet to make her look up as Devon held the bundle out to her.

"I think she's all right," he said huskily.

Linnet didn't look at him but greedily snatched her daughter from Devon's grasp. She pulled back the shirt, the skirts covering the child's face. Miranda lay perfectly still for one long, breathless moment and then gave a little cough, her eyes opening slightly and then going back to sleep.

Linnet began to cry. Great huge globules of tears of relief tore their way through her body. She clutched Miranda to her, rocking her, holding her, aware of nothing but that her daughter was well and alive and in her arms.

Nettie and the Squire hovered over her, both of them relieved that the child was unhurt. No one noticed the tall, dark man slip away past the crowd, the fire and the noise. He walked steadily to his horse, breathing lightly, his mind concentrating on the single objective of reaching his horse. He came very close to making it. He fell, face forward, his hand clutching the reins.

"Ma." Rebekah tugged her mother's skirt.

"Not now, Becky," Nettie said. "Let's help Mrs. Tyler get Miranda to her cabin."

"Ma, it's that man."

"What man?" Nettie demanded of her daughter.

"That man that saved Miranda. He just fell down."

Linnet lifted her eyes from her sleeping daughter. "Devon?" she asked quietly.

"I guess so. He's the new man just come to town and the one that run through the fire. He was goin' to his horse, and I saw him fall down."

"Did he get back up?" Nettie asked.

"No, he was just layin' there when I left."

"Show me," Linnet said, Miranda clutched tightly to her breast.

Rebekah led her mother and her teacher through the woods to an old sycamore tree.

"How'd you ever find him?" Nettie asked.

"I followed him. He sure walks quiet. See! There he is."

The women paused for a moment because even at a distance, with only the light of the moon, they could see the horror that had once been Devon's smooth, clean back. Nettie took Miranda as Linnet walked forward. He was unconscious, the reins in one blistered hand. Most of the beautiful black hair was burned from the back of his head, and his back, shoulders and upper arms were a mass of large, oozing, hideous blisters.

His heavy pants had protected the lower half of his body somewhat but they were burned away in patches, showing red, raw skin beneath. The soles of his moccasins were gone and his feet were burned.

"Devon," she whispered as she touched the side of his face, the cheek unhurt and still beautiful. "Devon, can you hear me?"

"Linnet." Nettie put her hand on her friend's arm. "He can't hear you. Linnet, you're gonna have to face it sometime, but he can't live long with a burn like that."

"Can't live long?" she asked stupidly.

"Yes. Look at him. There's places where there ain't even skin left on him."

Linnet touched his ear. Devon's beautiful, smooth skin, she thought. "He can't die, Nettie, not after saving Miranda."

"It's not a matter of wishin', it's a matter of what happens. I ain't never heard of nobody livin' after a burn like that."

"Well, I have."

The women turned to look up at the Squire.

"When I was a young'un, a woman was burned worse than that and she lived. In fact, she still is livin'."

"Could she help?" Linnet asked. "Could she help with Devon?"

The Squire didn't like the tone of Linnet's

voice. "Phetna doesn't like people much and won't come near if she doesn't have to. She—"

Linnet stood. "You will get this woman for me," she said. "I would like for you to leave now and return as soon as possible. I will pay her whatever she wants for coming but she must come."

The Squire frowned, but he did as he was told.

When he was gone, Linnet took Miranda from Nettie. "Go to my cabin and get some blankets. We'll put them under him, and I think that will be the best way to carry him," she said to Rebekah. "Nettie, go get four men and come back quickly."

"Yes, Linnet." She smiled. "I'll do that."

Chapter Sixteen

"LORD, WHAT DO YOU DO WITH HIM? TO THINK he used to be a good-lookin' man," Butch Gather said as he stared down across the great bulk of his stomach at the blistered body of Devon Macalister. "Don't seem no use to try and help him. We ought to just leave him where he is. It'd be the merciful thing to do."

"That is wholly your opinion, Mr. Gather," Linnet said firmly. "And I might add that I do not share your opinion. Now if you men would please help me, I'd like to take him to my cabin."

Butch and Mooner Yarnall exchanged looks, eyebrows raised. Butch spoke again. "Now I don't know if that's right, takin' him to your cabin and all, you and him not bein' married." He gave a sly smile, little eyes glistening over enormous cheeks. "Course we all know what he's been to you." The fat man looked from one person to another to make sure they shared in his secret. "Other towns might allow such goin's, on but we're decent people here in Spring Lick and we don't hold with such things."

Linnet's eyes flashed brilliant glass splinters of red light that included each of the four men. "Decency is something I doubt this town even understands. Whatever you think you know or whatever you think you have a right to judge, now is not the time. Either you help him or I'll move him myself."

Butch smiled. "If you're aimin' to scare us, you ain't succeedin'. Anyhow, I'd like to know how come the schoolhouse got burned down just now. Maybe you and him set it so's you'd have more time to . . ." His little pig eyes swept her slight form, "—to do what you obviously done so much before."

"As for me," Mooner stepped forward, "I don't know as I like a schoolteacher what flaunts her lover afore ever'body. Look at her now, demandin' us to take him to her cabin so's they can keep on where they left off."

The woods were dark, the still-burning building heard in the distance, and Linnet could feel the menace of the men. Devon needed help, and they were not going to allow her to help him.

"You know, Butch, I think she's been askin' for it since she come here." Mooner took another step forward and Linnet held her ground, not allowing herself to give way to the fear she was beginning to feel. Devon's welfare was more important than some overexcited men.

"Yeah," Butch said, walking close to her. "I been thinkin' the same thing."

"What's goin' on here?" Nettie's voice broke the ugly spell. Her arms were full of blankets, and she looked with hatred from one man to the next. "I sent you men out here to help, and looks to me like you're causin' more trouble."

Neither Butch nor Mooner moved, the other two men looking defiant.

"Why should we help her?" Butch demanded. "What kind of woman is she anyhow? What's she been teachin' our kids when she's no better'n a bought woman? You know who that man is?" He rolled his little head in the direction of Devon's unconscious body.

"I know very well who he is," Nettie answered. "And I know a lot more, too, only not about Linnet. I know about that woman out in the holler."

The four men stared, then looked away.

"He who is without sin may cast the first stone," Nettie quoted. "Now we need some help gettin' him onto these here blankets and up to Linnet's cabin."

Butch stepped away from Linnet and sneered down at Devon. "I ain't helpin' him. For all I know he's the one set the school on fire."

"With his own daughter inside!" Linnet fairly screamed.

Butch chuckled. "You just told us what we only guessed at before. As for me, I ain't doin' no extra work when I know there ain't no need to it. You can just look at him and see he's a dead man."

Nettie answered before Linnet could speak. "I see no such thing, and as for him settin' the school on fire, I think you ought to count your lanterns and find out where all your children were about the time the fire started."

"You accusin' my young'uns of that fire?" he sneered at Nettie.

"Probably. I wouldn't put it past 'em to set it a'purpose. Now I'm tired of you talkin' while a sick man's needin' help. If you ain't gonna help, then get out of here."

Linnet knelt by Devon's side, relieved that the men were gone. "Do you think we can carry him, Nettie?" she asked quietly.

"Yes. I sent Rebekah for Ottis and Vaida. We'll be able to move him, don't you worry. Let's get him on top of these blankets first."

Gazing down at Devon, Linnet began to wonder at her own folly. The blisters on his body were increasing in number and already some of them had broken and the thin yellow water was making little rivulets across the tortured skin. What did one do with such severe burns? She had no idea and was afraid that whatever she tried would be wrong. If only the Squire would return with Phetna, the woman who knew how to treat burns. Should she try to wash the burned area or would the soap cause an infection? All the blisters were full of water. Should she try to make Devon drink something?

He had not moved nor made any sound when Nettie, her husband, her two daughters and Linnet slowly carried him to Linnet's cabin. His breathing was shallow and strained, his eyes closed and she wondered if he were even aware of what had happened to him.

"Devon," she whispered. "Can you hear me?" He was still lifeless. The sound of a horse outside caught her attention.

"I don't need you no more," Linnet heard a high, querulous voice say.

"I'll introduce you," the Squire answered.

"Don't need you," the woman's voice said. "She ain't likely to mistake me for another. You go on. I got work to do."

Linnet watched the door as she heard the Squire ride away and she saw the door swing open. The face that appeared had once been a woman's but now it was mutilated almost beyond recognition. Onc eyelid was drawn across the eye so that little of the piercing iris could be seen. One cheek was corded, striated, pitted with thick white scars. Half of her lips were gone. The other side of her face wasn't so badly scarred, but the ear was gone and most of her hair.

"I'm Phetna," said the high voice. "I hear tell you got a burned man in here."

Linnet was silent.

"I'll help unless you're too weak to stand the sight of me," the woman sneered.

Linnet didn't blink. "If you'll help make Devon well, I don't care if you are a two-headed devil sent from Hell."

The woman blinked, then threw back her head and gave a shrill cackle, her neck showing more of the thick, corded scars. "I ain't got two heads, but you can decide later if I'm from Satan's place." She stepped inside the cabin. "What you willin' to do to help this man?"

"Anything," Linnet said quietly.

"Hmph! Lots of young girls say that, but we'll find out whether you mean it or not. Takin' care of a burned man ain't no sweet task."

"I'll do anything I can," Linnet repeated.

"All right," Phetna nodded, "let's get to work. First get me as much light in here as you can. I can't see too good, even at best."

Linnet built up the fire, lit each of her precious candles and turned the lantern to its highest. Phetna pulled back the linen sheet Linnet had spread over Devon's back, and Linnet saw the woman's hands. Her left hand had only a thumb and the first two fingers, the right one had healed together so that all four fingers were fused into one curved appendage.

"First thing we gotta do is let the air get to him. Ain't nothin' like the Lord's own air for healin' a burn; and then we gotta wash him. I'll tell you what to do, and you'll have to do it." She

stared steadily at Linnet and held up the mutilated hands very close before the young woman's face. "Can't do much with these." She
seemed to be daring Linnet to show some sign of
revulsion, challenging her, as if she wanted her
to draw back.

Linnet ignored the hands thrust in her face.
"Tell me what to do."

Phetna dropped the hands to her sides, ready
once again to think of her patient. "Heat some
water. You got some soap?"

"Yes, and if more is needed I can borrow
some."

Phetna snorted. "That's surprisin' in this
town."

Linnet had already filled the kettle and took
the crock of soft soap from the wall shelves.

"This your young'un?" Phetna asked quietly,
her voice suddenly not so gratingly high-pitched.

"Yes. Her name is Miranda."

Phetna turned away from the sleeping child.
"You better send her away in the mornin'.
Young'uns don't much like the sight of me," she
said through clenched teeth.

Linnet was just as firm. "I do not rear my child
in that way. I will not allow her to judge a person
by her outside characteristics."

"It won't be so easy when she starts cryin' at
the sight of me."

"I believe the water is hot now," Linnet said.
"Will you show me what to do?" Linnet cut
Devon's pants from his body and inspected the

burns on his legs, so much less than his back, arms and feet.

"You better get used to him 'cause there ain't gonna be a thumbprint of a place on his body you ain't gonna know in the next week."

"Week? Do you think he'll be well in a week?"

"Not well," Phetna answered, "but beginnin' to heal. We'll know in three days what's gonna happen, one way or t'other. Now take that cloth and begin washin' him, real slow and real gentle. We don't wanta break any more of them blisters than we have to. That water's the Lord's way of coolin' the skin."

It took Linnet hours to slowly wash all of Devon's long body, being painstakingly careful not to hurt him more than he had been already.

"Should we feed him?" she asked.

"Not yet," Phetna answered. "He's too weak yet to hold it down. You got him all washed?"

"Yes," Linnet sighed and sat back on her heels as she wrung out the cloth.

"All right, then, go to the spring, get some fresh water, heat it and start all over again." Phetna watched the young woman closely, but Linnet didn't flinch. She took two buckets and went out the door as Phetna knelt over the young man stretched nude on the corn shuck mattress.

"You awake, boy?" she asked fiercely. A sound came from Devon, and she knew he heard her. "I know it hurts bad but we're gonna try to fix it.

You just concentrate on breathin' and stayin' alive. That girl's gonna wash you some more, and it'll feel cool and good to you. You just 'member to breathe and don't give up hope. The pain'll stop after a while, and all you'll have left is memories."

Linnet took a handful of moss and scoured the inside of the buckets before filling them. For the first time she wanted to cry. The whole day had been horrible, with Devon's accusations, their fight, Miranda nearly dying, and now Devon lying in her cabin, his body a mass of hideous blisters. She filled the buckets and carried them back to the cabin. Whatever she still felt or didn't feel for Devon didn't matter anymore. What did matter was that she worked to save him.

She looked up at the clear, dark sky and offered a silent prayer for Devon's recovery. Her shoulders ached and the buckets pulled the tendons in her arms, but she didn't care. There was something more important than tired shoulders.

Phetna sat in a chair near the table, a plate of stew and bread before her. She barely acknowledged Linnet's presence.

Linnet knelt and began washing Devon's back again. The blisters were oozing constantly.

"He your man?" Phetna asked, her mouth full.

"He's . . . he's not my husband, no, but I have known him a long time."

"What's your husband gonna think when he

comes home and finds a naked man on your bed?"

"I'm not married."

Phetna cackled. "World ain't changed much in the last years. I thought Squire said you was the schoolteacher."

"I was." Linnet did not want to talk about it more. Phetna would find out sooner or later.

"What's his name?" the woman asked, pushing away the empty plate.

Linnet touched Devon's ear lovingly. "Devon Slade Macalister," she said.

"Slade Macalister!" Phetna said, disbelief in her voice.

Linnet smiled as she toyed with a black curl of Devon's hair. "Slade's for his father. I remember the day he discovered he was named after his father. Everyone said he loved his father so much, that he was so upset when he was killed." She returned to the washing.

"Slade was killed?" Phetna asked quietly.

"Yes. By a bear." Linnet didn't see Phetna's grimace of pain. "Agnes said Devon looked like his father."

"Both of the boys did," Phetna said.

Linnet looked up at the woman, realizing for the first time what she meant. "You knew Devon's father? You knew the twins?"

"Yes," Phetna said as she moved from the table to a chair near the sleeping Miranda. "I come out here with Slade and the others and the boys' mother."

"Georgina," Linnet said, dipping the cloth in warm water.

"I reckon she had a name besides Mrs. Macalister, but I never was allowed to use it," Phetna said contemptuously. "Where's the other boy, the one like her? I heard she went back to her fancy folk in the East, took one boy and left the other."

"Yes, she did, but I never met the brother."

Phetna was silent for a moment, then smiled at Linnet's back. "This boy the baby's father?"

Linnet turned and smiled at her, already not seeing the grotesqueness of her face. "Yes."

"If he's anythin' like Slade, I can understand why you'd take him without a preacher."

"Agnes said—"

"Agnes Emerson?" Phetna interrupted.

"Yes. Do you know her?"

"I know 'em all. I was a mite older'n them, about Slade's age but we all lived together in North Caroliny, come out here together, built our homes together."

Linnet frowned at her. "Why would you leave Sweetbriar and come here?"

Phetna understood immediately and grinned. "I'm an old, ugly woman, and he's dead now, so I guess the sayin' of it don't matter none. I was in love with Slade Macalister, had been most of my life, and when he went north and married that . . . that woman, I thought I'd go crazy. I come west with him just hopin' somethin' would happen, and when it did and she left him to go back east, he still wouldn't have me. I guess I was a sore loser. I run off with the first man'd have me and come here."

"You live with your husband now?"

Phetna turned away and Linnet could see the white scars in her neck stand out and turn purple. "He died in the fire, but then it was him started it, a'purpose, when he drunk too much corn. He meant to kill me, burn the evil out of me, he said, but the wind caught the fire and he died and I didn't. There have been times when I wished—"

"His back seems to be burned the worst." Linnet cut into Phetna's memories, guessing that they could lead her to a time best forgotten.

Phetna knelt by the bed and studied the burns. "They look bad but they could be worse. I've seen 'em burned all the way to the bone, the skin black and fallin' off. There ain't no hope for 'em then. You best get some sleep now. In the mornin' he's gonna need more washin', and soon we'll start to feed him."

"I don't need to sleep. These blisters are already beginning to run again."

"And they'll be cryin' for days, and you'll need to wash 'em, but now you're gonna sleep. You gonna cooperate or fight me?"

Linnet gave a weary smile and pulled a mattress from where it rested against the wall. Nettie had brought it earlier. "You take the mattress, and I'll make a pallet on the floor."

"No," Phetna said sternly. "I'll stay here in the chair. One of us has to watch him."

"Then I'll—" Phetna's look stopped her. "All right, you can sleep tomorrow." Linnet put the mattress very close to Devon and stretched out. She was asleep instantly.

Chapter Seventeen

WHEN LINNET AWOKE SUNLIGHT FILTERED IN through the oiled paper over the windows and it was a moment before she remembered the events of the past night. Phetna's face looked worse in the daylight, the taut, misplaced skin giving her a grotesque look, and Linnet realized why she lived so far from other people. The inhabitants of Spring Lick would never be so generous as to include someone who did not fit with their idea of what a person should be. Miranda still slept peacefully, the effects of the smoke still drugging her somewhat.

She turned her head to Devon and smiled at his innocent nakedness, the smooth firm buttocks lighter than the rest of him. The blisters on his back were encrusted again, and she stood, picked up the buckets and quietly went outside for fresh water.

"Linnet."

She looked up to smile at the Squire. "Good morning."

He smiled back. "I don't know if it is so good. It feels like we're in for some rain. How is . . . he?"

"Devon is holding his own." She looked down at her skirt. "I don't really know. Phetna says we'll know in a few days, whether he'll . . . whether he'll be all right or not."

"You are getting along with Phetna? I know she can be cantankerous at times."

Linnet frowned. "I find her to be pleasant. We talked a good deal."

"The people of Spring Lick don't really care for her, they . . ."

Linnet glared at him, her distaste obvious.

"It's not me, of course, although I will admit her face isn't something I'd like to look at every day, but the people of the town have some beliefs about her. There was another fire a few years back, a whole family burned, but we got them out. Phetna came but the family still died."

Linnet lifted one eyebrow. "You mean they blamed Phetna for the deaths?"

"I don't know if they blamed her or not, but they were pretty unhappy about her. It's her ways as well as her looks. She kept ordering everyone to help her. If she'd just asked—"

"Asked!" Linnet said angrily. "As I asked four

of the men to carry Devon to my cabin? I asked and they refused."

"Refused!" the Squire exclaimed. "Who were they? Who refused to help you?"

"It doesn't matter now. Nettie's family helped me, but I just don't want to hear any more about Phetna. She has been good to me and helped me with Devon."

The Squire took the full buckets of water from her, and they began walking. "I'm sorry to have upset you, Linnet. I just wanted to prepare you if you find her difficult to deal with."

"Quite the contrary," Linnet snapped. "Now I must go, his burns need washing."

The Squire opened the door for her and then stopped at the sight of Devon's nude form. His face drained of color.

Linnet could hardly control her smile. "Phetna says we must let the burns get air."

"Yes, I am sure she's right." He could not bring himself to look at the scarred woman. "But couldn't you cover, ah, part of him?"

Phetna gave her cracked laugh, causing the Squire to turn toward her, and even prepared for the sight, he still felt his stomach roll over.

Linnet saw his look and took the buckets from him. "I have work to do," she said coldly; "so if you'd excuse me."

The Squire couldn't let his problem alone. "Linnet, I really think you should cover him somewhat. Think of Miranda."

Linnet met his eyes. "Devon's welfare is much

more important than Miranda's delicate sensibilities, if she has any at her age. I will not rear a fragile flower who is upset at the sight of a sick man's bare behind. Now, please, I must wash him."

The Squire glared at her, turned and slammed the door behind him.

Phetna's sustained cackle and the slamming door woke Miranda. The baby rolled over and looked about her, somewhat dazed by the transformation of her home.

Linnet saw Phetna's immediate reaction to Miranda—she turned her face away, not wanting the child to see her. Linnet took a deep breath and knew it was now or never. "Phetna, I need to tend to Devon. Would you please take care of Miranda? She will need to be taken to the outhouse right away, if she isn't already wet."

"No, I can't," Phetna said, desperation in her voice.

Linnet kept washing, going slowly and tenderly around the blisters on Devon's back. "I can't do this and take her, too, and I have enough of a mess to clean up now."

"But I can't take her outside. They're outside."

Linnet turned to her. "I am sure you mean the people of Spring Lick and I am just as sure that you are right, but there are more important things than a person's scarred face."

Phetna blinked, the one eyelid pulling tightly. "What about her, your young'un?" She still refused to look at the little girl.

"Miranda," Linnet called and held out her arms. "Come here. Miranda, I'm afraid, has been in the care of several other people in her short life. Until she was a year old she didn't know who her mother was. I came to Kentucky with several wagons and when there was sickness, which there always seemed to be, I acted as nurse while someone else cared for Miranda. In Spring Lick Nettie has always cared for her while I taught school. Miranda is one of those people who never meets a stranger. Miranda." She turned the baby to face Phetna. "This is—I don't know your last name."

"Been so long, I forgot it myself." She reluctantly looked at the smooth, perfect face of the baby.

"Miranda, this is Aunt Phetna. She's come to stay with us. Will you go to her now, and she'll take you outside?" Much to Linnet's chagrin, Miranda did not like Phetna's face. It scared her, as when some of the boys made faces at her, and she turned back to her mother and began to whimper.

"I told you not to do that. I don't know how you can stand to look at me but there's no reason for you to make that child look." She stopped talking when Linnet put Miranda in Phetna's bony lap.

"Miranda, look at me." The child looked at her mother, afraid to again look at Phetna. "Now, Miranda, Aunt Phetna looks different, but there's nothing to be afraid of." Linnet touched

her own eye. "See, eye. Now, Miranda's eye."
She took the child's hand and Miranda touched
her own eye.

"Where's Mama's eye?" Miranda smiled and
kicked her bare feet. She liked the game. "Now
Miranda's eye." The child touched her own eye.
"Now Aunt Phetna's eye."

Phetna was startled when the child stuck a
little finger into the scarred eye.

"See, Miranda," Linnet said. "Mama's nose,
Miranda's nose, Aunt Phetna's nose." The baby
laughed and Linnet turned to Phetna. "It may
take a few minutes, but she'll get over her
shyness. Why don't you let her touch your face
and let her see you're not trying to frighten her?"

Phetna was overwhelmed by all of it. Not
since she had been burned, twelve years before,
had she let anyone touch her face. The truth
was, she hardly even touched her own body,
refusing to acknowledge the missing ear, the
heavy cords across her cheek and neck, the
scarred lips. Miranda was too young yet to form
opinions of what was really hideous. Phetna
took the child outside, and Linnet was alone
with Devon.

She washed him tenderly and, as she came
close to his face, she bent and kissed his warm
cheek. "You'll get well, won't you, Devon? Soon
you'll be back on your feet and we'll be arguing,
as always." She continued washing him, talking
to him, encouraging him to get well. She was
free with her endearments because she knew he

couldn't hear her, and the helpless man beneath her fingers was far removed from the Devon of the day before, the man she said she could no longer love.

Phetna came back into the cabin, Miranda holding her webbed hand, and Linnet could see the rain beginning behind them. Phetna's mutilated face was further distorted into a smile. "I think we're in for a downpour. It'll be hard on Squire ridin' in it."

"Why does the Squire have to go out today?"

"We have to start feedin' him today." She nodded toward Devon. "And I got all the rose hips at my cabin. We need to make him drink rose hip tea. I brung a bag with me when I come, but Squire's horse bucked and we lost it, and the fool horse trampled the bag into the ground. Squire said he'd go back for more today, but so far I ain't seen him."

Linnet was on her feet at once. "I'll go to him and see where he is." She grabbed her shawl, threw it over her head and left the cabin. The rain was cold and she was immediately soaked, but she hurried ahead to the Squire's house. Although she pounded on the door, no one answered.

She didn't like the idea of going to Jule Yarnall, but she felt she must in order to find out where the Squire had gone.

Jule's face was a smirk of I-told-you-so when she opened the door to Linnet's knock. She did not invite her in but left the younger woman standing in the rain.

"What do you want, as if I didn't know?"

"Do you know where the Squire is?"

"He left first thing this mornin' to go huntin' with my man. I 'spect right now he's holed up somewheres out of the rain. What you want with him?"

"He said nothing about going to Phetna's?" Linnet asked, swallowing her pride.

"What's he wanta go to that ol' witch's house fer? We don't like havin' her kind around Spring Lick. That woman's evil."

"Evil?" Linnet asked incredulously, water streaming down her face. "She is a kind woman, only scarred. There's nothing evil about her."

"You wouldn't think so, not your kind. But I warn you, she better be gone right soon or . . . well, she just better be gone, you mind my words."

Linnet turned on her heel and left the woman standing in the doorway.

"You mark my words," Jule called behind her.

Linnet stepped into the warmth of her own cabin. "I can't find him. Jule said he went hunting. Do you think he forgot?"

Phetna snorted. "It ain't whether he forgot but whether he wants to 'member. The way he looked last time he saw Slade's boy, I don't reckon he was rushin' to get somethin' to help make him well."

"You're right." Linnet held her hands toward the glowing fire. "How far away is your cabin?"

"You ain't thinkin' of goin' there alone, are you?"

"How far is your cabin?" Linnet persisted.

"Look, you been in Kentucky long enough to know the dangers. This ain't the East. The Indians don't attack whole settlements much anymore like they done when I was a girl, but why do you think people still live so close together? Indians just love a lone farm or even better, a young girl walkin' somewheres all alone. You know what the Indians would do if they caught you?"

"Yes, I do," Linnet said quietly. "I know exactly what they would do. Can I get rose hips anywhere else at this time of year?"

"No." Phetna shook her head. "It's too early yet for June roses."

"Then it seems the supply is at your cabin; yet they are needed here."

Phetna stared at her. "You said you was willin' to do anythin' for the boy, but I didn't think it included riskin' your life."

"Why is it so unsafe for me, yet you live there alone and you are a woman?"

Phetna threw back her head and laughed, the shrill, broken sound that fitted her looks so well. "There's a mite of difference between me and you. The Indians stay away from me mainly, but eight years ago they brung one of the chief's sons to me. He'd been burned, and they stood guard while I tended him. He got well, and ever since the Indians have brung me presents. There's hardly a day goes by I don't find somethin' to eat layin' on my doorstep. Ever' once in a while they bring me somebody else to look at, and sometimes the chief's boy comes by. That's the reason I can stay there, but you—you'd be fair game for some young brave."

Linnet shook her wet shawl in front of the fire, the flames hissing. "I don't really think I have a choice. The rose hips are something Devon needs, they are at your cabin, and I am the only person who can get them."

Phetna knew it was useless to argue. "You always so stubborn?"

Linnet considered the question seriously for a moment. "I guess I am. Sometimes there are things that must be done, and if others thwart you, you have to take a stand. I guess I get it from my father." She smiled. "Now tell me how to get to your cabin."

She listened carefully to Phetna's description of the seven-mile journey, seven miles there and seven back. She would have to hurry since the rain would slow her down. The rain was pelting the earth in hard torrents when she went outside and, as she shut the door, she did not hear Devon's attempt to talk, to tell her, "No," his attempt to stop her from her dangerous journey.

The mud of the narrow trail was up to her ankles, covering her shoe tops, running down inside the leather, covering her feet, squishy

and gritty between her toes. The water ran down
her face, wet her wool shawl until the musty
smell of it floated around her. Her long, thick
hair was heavy with water and weighted her
head down, pulling on her neck.

It was a great relief when she saw the little
cabin ahead. Gratefully, she pushed open the
heavy oak door and sat before the cold, empty
fireplace. She was breathing heavily, her leg
muscles pulled and tight from the long arduous
journey, the constant fight against the sucking
action of the mud that made each step a burden,
a fight to accomplish. She took the pins from her
hair and let the heavy mass fall about her
shoulders, wringing it out with her hands onto
the stone hearth.

She was caught unawares when a hand
clutched the wet hair and jerked her head back
fiercely and a cold, sharp, steel knife blade
caressed her throat.

"What you do here?"

"Please," she whispered against the sharp
steel. "I came for medicine. Phetna is helping
me with a burned man, and I came for medicine."

He released her, shoving her forward until she
caught herself with her hands against the rough
stones of the fireplace. She turned to look at
him. He was a young Indian dressed in fringed
buckskins, his thick black hair falling past his
shoulders.

"I must get the medicine now and return to him."

The young Indian watched her as she stood on a chair and began pulling the long stems from the ceiling rafters. He seemed perplexed as to what to do with her.

"To which tribe do you belong?" she asked, her voice shaking. The man certainly didn't seem to be a menacing warrior, and she had a feeling he had come into the cabin only to escape the rain.

He threw back his shoulders. "I am Shawnee," he said with pride.

Linnet smiled and felt safe once again. "The man who is burned is also part Shawnee. His name is Devon Macalister." The Indian's face registered no recognition, and Linnet wondered if Devon had another name among the Shawnee.

He studied her. "How you get back to white man's town?"

"I will walk since I don't have a horse."

"Yellow Hand will take you to white man's town." He seemed to think this was a great honor for Linnet.

She smiled at him. "That's very kind of you. Would you please hold this bag for me while I fill it?"

"Man does not do such work." He looked at her in contempt.

"Oh. I didn't know. I thought maybe since it was for one of your tribesmen you might help."

He seemed confused for a moment and then resignedly held the linen bag open while she dropped the rose hips into it. She smiled at him, but he ignored her. He was little more than a boy really, she thought.

The rain hammered on the roof, and the two young people inside were isolated from the noise of the approaching horses. The door burst open, and the Squire and Mooner Yarnall burst in, both armed with Kentucky rifles.

Linnet and Yellow Hand froze with unexpected shock.

"Linnet, move away from him slowly," the Squire said, his voice low and cautious.

"Nonsense!" she said and stepped down from the chair, her body carefully placed between the white men and the Indian. "Please let me introduce Yellow Hand, he is—"

"He's an Injun, and the only good Injun is a dead one," Mooner said, his upper lip curled.

"Yellow Hand is a friend of a friend of mine."

"I told you she warn't fit to live with decent folk," Mooner said, his rifle raised.

Yellow Hand pushed Linnet aside. "I hide behind no woman," he said, staring straight at the rifle aimed at his head.

Mooner jerked on the trigger but the rifle did not fire. "Damn powder! Got wet in this confounded rain. I woulda had me a dead Injun that time."

Linnet stepped before Yellow Hand again and looked at the Squire. "Are you going to allow this? He nearly killed an innocent man. You stood there and would have allowed him to kill an innocent person!"

"Now, Linnet, Mooner has his reasons for his feelings about Indians."

"Well, I do, too!" She turned to face the young man. "You said you'd give me a ride back to Spring Lick. Will you still do so?"

He nodded to her curtly.

She put her hand on his arm. "I know you are proud, and brave, but it would not be an honor to be killed by such a white man as he."

He considered her words and then nodded again, seeming to agree with her.

She turned back to the Squire and Mooner. "Since it is obvious that I do not need your protection, would you please leave now?"

"Linnet, we can't leave you in the care of some Indian."

"Then I suggest you ride back with us, since I am riding with Yellow Hand."

"Linnet, please," the Squire said, "you can ride with me."

She looked at Mooner, who eyed Yellow Hand eagerly. "No, I have my escort." Linnet was careful to keep her body between the young Indian and Mooner at all times. She rode behind the Shawnee on his horse, her arms tight around his waist, the big bag of rose hips carefully held against her body.

The rain and the far distance of Yellow Hand's head above her own made it difficult for her to talk to him. About a mile outside Spring Lick he kicked his horse to an opposite path and Linnet looked to see the Squire and Mooner work hard to keep up with them, but the young Indian was familiar with the trail and was more accustomed to the rain which blinded the two white men.

Within minutes he led them to higher ground, where they looked down on the confused and lost men. Linnet put her hand over her mouth to keep from laughing at their bewilderment, their struggle to fight the rain. When she looked at Yellow Hand, she saw that the corners of his mouth twitched also, and what could have been a deadly encounter turned into a harmless bit of fun.

Chapter Eighteen

"LORD-A-MERCY, GIRL, WHAT YOU BEEN DOIN' to cause so much commotion?" Phetna greeted a wet and shivering Linnet. "Squire's been here givin' orders, shoutin' and cursin' so much the young'un took to cryin', and it took me a while to calm her down." Phetna looked adoringly at Miranda, who sat on a stool by the fire, concentrating on getting food onto her spoon and into her mouth.

"How is he?" Linnet went to Devon, leaving puddles of water behind her.

"'Bout the same; leastways he ain't causin' the trouble you are. You gonna tell me what you done, somethin' 'bout runnin' off with an Injun and bringin' a massacre down on Spring Lick?"

"Posh! I truly cannot understand how these people get so upset over something so minor."

"Indians ain't 'minor,' and if you'd lived here as long as me you'd know that."

"I am not unaware of the dangers of Indians; after all, my parents were killed by Indians. I saw my own mother—" She stopped. "I must put on some dry clothes first," she said as she began to unfasten the front of her dress.

"Yellow Hand is little more than a boy and he was calmly helping me collect the rose hips."

Linnet had her back to Devon, facing Phetna, and did not see him laboriously turn his head to face the women. Phetna wondered if it was the mention of Yellow Hand or Linnet's declaration that she was going to remove her clothes that made him go to such efforts. She saw his open eyes for the first time and, with a strange tightening of her skin, she saw Slade Macalister, just as she remembered him, unchanged even after twenty years. It took a few seconds to remember he was Slade's son.

She watched him interestedly, but he had eyes only for Linnet, now down to a wet, clinging camisole and petticoats. Phetna's eyes lit with amusement. Just like Slade, she thought. It would take more than a body burned raw, excruciating pain and his life hanging by a thread to keep him from watching a pretty girl undress.

"Well, ain't you gonna tell me?" Phetna persisted, trying not to show the laughter that bubbled inside her as she surreptitiously watched Devon.

Linnet peeled the wet petticoats from her body and began rubbing herself briskly with the coarse linen towel. She wore the short camisole top and the underpants that came to just above her knees. "There was a young boy, a Shawnee, in your cabin. I'm sure he only went inside to get out of the rain. I think he was as frightened of me as I was of him." She untied the strings of the camisole and pulled it over her head, then stepped out of the underpants.

"Turn around and I'll dry your back. You think Miranda's gettin' enough to eat?"

Linnet turned, her nude body facing Devon, her head turned toward her daughter. She smiled at Miranda and the girl smiled back while Phetna rubbed Linnet's back. When Linnet turned her head again to look toward Devon, he lay still, eyes closed, breath shallow and even. She took the towel from Phetna, walked across the room and began to dress in dry clothes.

When Phetna looked again at Devon, he seemed to be sleeping, but she was sure she saw a hint of a smile on his lips. "Ain't nothin' gonna kill a boy what still looks at women," she muttered and breathed easier because she hadn't liked the idea of one of Slade's sons dying while under her care.

Linnet knelt by Devon, touched his hair, ran her finger along his ear. "His color looks better, doesn't it, Phetna? Or am I just imagining it?"

Phetna's face twisted into some semblance of

a grin. "I think he's gonna be just fine. In fact, I'm right sure of it."

"You are!" Linnet was exhilarated but just as quickly deflated again. "I'll only believe it when I see for sure myself, when I know he's Devon and not just a rag doll."

"Oh, he ain't just a rag doll. I'm about as sure of that as anythin' in my life." Phetna stood. "Enough of this jawin'. We got us a lot of work to do now. You feelin' strong, girl?"

"I'm as strong as usual, I guess. What must we do?"

"We gotta lift that boy up and get him to settin' up, 'cause he's gotta start drinkin' some of my tea. And do you realize he ain't had a relief a' nature since he got burned?"

In spite of herself, Linnet blushed, and Phetna enjoyed her red face greatly. "I told you carin' for a burned man ain't no sweet job. Now you get them pillows and put 'em on that bench like I showed you."

It took the two women a long, strenuous time to lift Devon and put him on the bench. They couldn't touch his burns, and since his feet were hurt badly, he could give them little help, and they both could see the lines of strain in his face; and how the raw, fragile skin pulled and seemed as if it might break apart. They draped a mattress across the table, and Devon was able to lean forward, his ribs heaving after the exertion. There were tears in Linnet's eyes as she felt his pain with him.

It took her a few minutes and a silent lecture to get over her embarrassment at helping Devon relieve himself. Phetna didn't help any and seemed to thoroughly enjoy Linnet's confusion.

When the tea was ready, Phetna added a bit of salt to the brew, explaining that all the water that left Devon was salty (Linnet refused to ask how she knew this) and needed to be replaced. Devon struggled to drink the tea, not wanting it, choking on it.

"You got to make him drink," Phetna said. "It's the same with all of 'em. They just wanta die and can't nothin' convince 'em they ain't goin' to."

"But he won't drink any more," Linnet said in frustration. "How can I make him?"

"I don't know, people use all different ways—hold their noses, threaten 'em, cry, kiss 'em—you been doin' a lot of that lately—anythin' to make 'em drink. This is the easy part. You gotta make him start eatin' pretty soon."

"How can I do anything when he can't hear me? He's been unconscious since the fire."

"Ha! He hears as good as you, and I 'spect a sight better'n me."

Linnet was astonished. "Then why doesn't he say something?"

"Pain, girl, burnin', horrible pain! No need to talk when all you can do is feel your body on fire."

"Devon," she said softly in his ear. "You have to drink the tea. We want you to get well. Miranda wants to meet you. She thinks you're just some big stuffed doll, not real at all. When you get well you can carve the head of a doll for her, and I'll make the body. Would you do that for your daughter?"

Something Linnet said was right because Devon finally made an effort to drink.

By the third day Devon's burns stopped oozing, and the blisters began to shrivel. It was on the third day, while an exhausted Linnet was forcing more tea down Devon's throat, that he said his first words to her.

"Kiss me," he rasped.

"What?" She set the tin mug down on the table. Phetna and Miranda were outside, and they were alone in the cabin.

"Kiss me," Devon repeated, and he turned his head to look into her eyes.

How good it was to see the brilliant blue eyes again!

"I won't drink unless you kiss me."

"Devon! What are you saying? I don't hear your voice for three whole days, your back is burned beyond recognition, and now you make absurd requests of me."

"Not fight, Lynna, please." His head sagged and his eyes closed once again.

"No, my love, I'm sorry. I'll kiss you." She kissed his cheek, his temple, his eyelids, all as she'd done many times in the last few days. Had he been aware of those kisses, as Phetna said he was, or was he unconscious, as Linnet believed?

By the fourth day he seemed to be stronger, and although he rarely said anything, Linnet was aware that he was awake and knew when she touched him, and there were certain times in the day when she thought her embarrassment would devour her.

"Looks like he's gonna make it now," Phetna said the afternoon of the fourth day.

"I wish I could be as sure as you. Why doesn't he talk?"

"Lord help us, but give him a couple more days. All burned people are alike, first they hurt too much to complain and then they get well just enough to tell you everythin' that's wrong with 'em. It's then they try your patience, but once they're well enough to start complainin', you know they're all right."

"At this point I'd like to hear a complaint. This silence is deafening."

"I'll remind you of them words later."

Linnet picked up the wooden buckets. "I'm going to the spring."

"Why don't you stay a while, walk around, pick some flowers," Phetna called after her. "He ain't goin' nowheres, and you need a change."

The spring air smelled good, especially after the stuffy cabin, and rather than going straight to the spring she went to a quiet place under some elm trees, the ground covered with clover, honey bees everywhere. She felt almost guilty at leaving Devon alone, at being able to escape when he must stay indoors while the birds sang and the flowers moved in the soft breeze.

"Linnet."

She closed her eyes for a second against the unwanted intrusion. She hadn't seen the Squire since the day she and Yellow Hand had stood atop the hill in the rain and laughed at the Squire and Mooner. "Yes." She forced herself to smile. "How are you?" He didn't look well at all, as if he hadn't been sleeping very well or very much.

He sat down beside her, fell almost. "I guess I should ask how you are. I haven't seen much of you lately. I guess you stay with him all the time now."

"I stay with 'him' because Devon is burned and needs me. I really shouldn't be here now since he needs to be fed again soon."

"Fed? You feed him? A grown man?"

"Squire, he nearly died, saving my daughter I might add. He is weak and can do nothing for himself. I would do as much for anyone who saved Miranda."

"Would you, Linnet, I wonder, or is it that you still love him and want to help him?"

"I don't guess there's an answer for that since I doubt if anyone but Miranda's father would have run into a flaming building."

The Squire looked away from her. "I guess you are right. I didn't see any hope of rescuing her that night, but if she'd been my own child, maybe then . . . who can say?"

Linnet was silent.

"You look tired," he continued.

"So do you."

Linnet was suddenly angry. "What is it you want to know? The exact details of the night I spent with Devon Macalister, or is it now that so intrigues you? Do you want a report of every time I touch him? What exactly do you want? He is a very sick man."

The Squire was quiet. "You know, I've learned a lot about you in the last few weeks. I've learned how you don't even make an effort to get along with people, that you even seem to delight in causing gossip, in doing everything you can to make yourself different. It isn't enough that you're English, that your ways are already different, but you work at standing apart."

Linnet's eyes flashed, her mouth set in a firm, hard line. "In England I had what may be called an unusual upbringing. I was taught to accept people for what they were, not what someone else told me about a person. When I first came to this town the people were willing to accept me, but only if I became exactly like them. Jule and Ova wanted me to hate Nettie and her daughters, wanted me to constantly say vicious things about people who were absent, but I couldn't do that."

"But it was your sneering at them that has caused so many problems."

227

"I'm very sorry I sneer, I certainly don't mean to, but I cannot understand why you would want me to join them."

"It's not that I want you to join them." He took her hand and held it between his. "I thought that when I paid your way to Kentucky, gave you this job in spite of the fact that you had an illegitimate child, that you'd want to repay me."

She jerked away from him. "Did you think you were buying a mistress? Or did you want me to help your prestige? It could look good on your record and help you become governor if you took in penniless, downfallen women and saved their souls. But here I am ruining everything. It's not going to look good to your constituents if the woman you 'rescued' and made a teacher has her lover living with her, is it? You were willing to forgive me my sins as long as you had hope that I'd become your mistress, but things are changing now."

"You'll regret this, Linnet. I'm going to become governor of this state, and no two-bit whore like you is going to stop me."

"Don't worry, I won't. As soon as Devon is well enough to travel, I'll leave this place, even if I have to crawl out."

"And go where?" he snapped. "Back to that town, Sweetbriar, you revere? You going to spread the word that Squire Talbot isn't good enough to become governor?"

She gave him a cold look. "I doubt very much

if I'll so much as mention you. Now I must return to Devon." She turned and left.

Linnet was so angry when she entered the cabin that she slammed the door behind her, her eyes wild and unfocused. She didn't notice that for the first time Devon was sitting up by himself, a quilt about the lower half of his body.

"You get caught in a storm or you plannin' to start one all by yourself?" Phetna asked, but Linnet ignored her, still too angry to see or hear.

"Miranda, honey," the older woman said, "why don't we go outside and see if any of them peas come up yet." She held her scarred hand out to the child.

Miranda took one look at her mother, who was not at all like the mother she knew, and gladly went outside with Phetna.

Neither Devon nor Linnet spoke when they were alone, Linnet staring at some point beyond the back wall, Devon watching her. "Lynna," he said quietly, his voice hoarse from lack of use. "Lynna," he said again when she didn't move.

She turned and saw him for the first time. "Devon! You're sitting!"

He grinned. "Thought you'd never notice. Come sit by me, I need somethin' to lean on."

She sat down beside him on the bench, and he lifted the quilt across his legs and spread it over her as he moved nearer to her. She could feel the warmth of his bare skin through her skirt and petticoats. Suddenly he was no longer a sick, helpless nonentity, but a man, warm, vital and very much alive. She started to move away from him.

"Please don't," he said and she stayed where she was. "Tell me, what made you so angry?"

She couldn't look up at him. "I had, I guess you could say, an argument with the Squire." She didn't see him smile.

"A love quarrel?" he asked.

"I don't love—" She looked at him, then smiled. "I have never loved the man. He gave me a job, nothing more."

Devon was quiet for a moment. "It upset you about Yellow Hand, didn't it?"

"Yes, that and other things, too, such as when the men refused to help carry you here. How can two towns be so different, Devon? How can Sweetbriar be so different from this . . . this place?"

"I don't know and I don't think I'd like to know. It's a good thing nobody shot Yellow Hand, or this town'd be nothin' but some heaps of smolderin' wood."

"I was right about him!"

"Lynna, you have to understand somethin'. The Indian way of life ain't the same as a white man's. You can't go around thinkin' all Indians are good, honorable people that you can trust with the protection of your pretty little body." Lord! But he wished he weren't so weak. Even talking was making him feel as if he'd been the ground part of a stampede.

"But he was a Shawnee."

Devon opened his mouth to speak and then closed it again. Sometimes talking to Linnet was like trying to reason with a tree. "I don't think I wanta talk no more. You wanta help me to the mattress?" It looked to him to be miles away.

"No, Devon, you have to eat. I've boiled a chicken and made a strong broth. I'm going to feed you some of it." She threw back the quilt and went to the fire to fill a mug with the broth.

Devon sat there dejectedly. He couldn't lean back and he couldn't fall forward, and the strain of sitting was too much for him. He'd felt good when he first sat, careful to keep his feet off the floor, but now he just wanted to rest, to sleep, to not think or talk and especially not to eat.

Linnet stood in front of him with another mug of something steaming. Those two women had done nothing but feed him for what seemed like months now. Didn't they know that he hurt, that the skin on his back was much too small and that it was going to tear apart at any moment? Didn't they know how tired he was, how he couldn't stand, couldn't even go to the outhouse by himself? Didn't they know he was a man? All they cared about was crammin' food down his throat. Suddenly he was mad.

"Damn it, Linnet! I don't want anythin' to—" He stopped because she was looking at him so strangely. She carefully set the mug down, then began to laugh, laugh in such a way as he'd never seen an adult do before. Her mouth opened wide, and her whole body began to shake. He stared in fascination as her legs turned rubbery and she collapsed on the floor, her laughter filling the air, her legs helplessly entangled in the long skirt. She held her stomach, tears rolling down her face.

"Linnet, why are you laughing? All I said was I didn't want to eat any more and you wouldn't even let me finish that."

But Linnet couldn't explain; she had no extra breath. Damn it, Linnet! Sweet, musical words. He was going to get well! He was going to be Devon again. Nothing else could have convinced her that he was going to recover.

Devon just stared at her and began to find her laughter infectious. He grinned. "You are the beatinest woman. I don't guess I'll ever understand you."

Phetna returned with Miranda and looked at the two of them, Devon smiling and Linnet rolling on the floor in a mass of skirts, her face covered with tears.

"She's gone plumb crazy," Devon said.

Miranda didn't care why her mother was so happy, only that she was. She ran and jumped on top of her and the two of them rolled together, Linnet tickling her daughter mercilessly, the child kicking and screaming with delight.

"Here, boy, drink this 'fore it gets cold," Phetna said.

Devon watched his daughter and Linnet with

interest, never really having seen her so abandoned before, and drank all of the hot, thick broth.

Finally Linnet lay back on the wooden floor, her sides heaving and exhausted from the romp. Miranda still wanted to play, but she held her away. "I'm afraid I'm too tired for more, Miranda." Finally the child subsided beside her mother, content to lie close to her.

"You two plan to stay there all night?" Phetna asked from her lofty position above them. "That boy o' yourn needs some help gettin' back to bed and I'm afraid I'm too feeble to give him much help."

"I doubt that," Linnet said as she sat up and looked at Devon.

He gave her a very solemn look and turned the mug upside down to show it was completely empty.

She smiled at him. "Please don't do anything else. I'm sure my stomach will be sore tomorrow as it is."

Devon was very serious. "I'll rub it for you."

Linnet's face turned red and she distinctly heard Phetna snicker. She stood before him. "Put your arm around my shoulders and I'll support you. Just be careful of your feet."

As he stood, the quilt fell away and he made a grab for it, then let it fall. He grinned at her wickedly. "I forgot there ain't nothin' about me you ain't seen—and handled—many times."

"Devon!" Linnet felt her entire body turn red, even her ears and her toes. She gave a furtive look to Miranda.

"I thought you said you didn't raise no young'un who'd—what'd you say?—get upset at the sight of a man's bare behind."

Linnet couldn't answer, and when Devon stretched out, face down on the mattress, she tossed a sheet over him, not looking at him. She grabbed a piece of cloth from across the top of her sewing basket.

"What you doin', girl?" Phetna asked, her voice betraying her laughter.

"I think the serpent has just appeared in the Garden of Eden, and Adam will now get his fig leaf." She held up the cut and burned pants that Devon had worn the night of the fire. "They'll have to do until I can make new ones." She still avoided Devon's eyes.

Chapter Nineteen

BUTCH GATHER LEANED BACK IN THE CHAIR, his hands clasped over his enormous stomach. "If you ask me, we got a real problem on our hands. Now I don't wanta be the one casts the first stone, but there's more people in this than just me. I mean, we got young kids involved in this. I can't help thinkin' about what sins she musta done been tellin' our young'uns.

"As for me, I'm wanting to do somethin' about this. You all know me, I ain't one to set when there's a job to be done."

The other people in the store agreed with him.

"And then there's the burned woman," Jule said. "I know you all remember the time she let the Willises die. It always did seem funny to me. They was doin' all right 'til she come. And somethin' else bothers me, and that's the way that woman looks. Now I ask you, could any normal person live through a fire like that? Could anybody what didn't have a line with Satan last through a fire like that?"

They were silent, staring at Jule and she began to become excited at the attention directed toward her.

"Now this is the way I figure it: none of us can stand bein' near the burned woman, and rightly so, bein' good Christians, yet we never knew why we didn't like her. But then there was somethin' inside us told us to stay away from her and I think it was our knowin', inside like, what's good and what's bad.

"And 'member when that English girl come to Spring Lick? Oh, we tried, all of us did, but none of us could like her. And why, I ask you? What was there about her that caused all of us Christians to stay away from her?"

She paused, and her body began to shake with the pleasure of having everyone listen to her. "There's somethin' born into Christians that makes 'em know evil, feel it, and all of us knew somethin' was wrong from the start."

They all stood quietly, and Jule looked from one to the other.

Butch spoke again. "Jule said it for all of us, and now what're we gonna do about it?"

No one spoke for a moment, and then Ova seemed to have an idea. "You know who I feel for in all this? That young'un. That poor little girl. They got her bewitched, are trainin' her to follow in their ways."

"Ova's right!" Jule said. "What we oughta do is take that little girl away from them witches and raise her ourselves. It'd be a fight all her life to keep the devil out of her, but it'd be our duty."

"Mmm," Butch murmured. "You ladies are right. Now all we gotta do is decide what to do with 'em, the two women and the man." His little eyes gleamed as he had some thoughts on what to do with the younger woman.

"Lynna, come sit beside me."

"Devon, I have work to do."

"What if I told you my back hurt a lot and I think you could ease the pain?"

She put her knitting in her lap. "Does it and can I?"

"Lord! I can't remember what it's like not to be in pain and, yes, you could help me."

They were alone in the cabin and, although she knew it was a ruse, she went to sit beside him and studied the wounds that were gradually beginning to heal.

"Could you eat something?"

He rolled his eyes at her. "Please, no more food." He whispered something she couldn't hear, and so she leaned closer to his mouth. He kissed her ear and she began to pull away, but her threw one arm around her waist. "Don't go away, Lynna, please. I just been thinkin' and I wanta talk to you."

"About what?" she asked stiffly.

He pulled her closer beside him, his face

buried in her neck, his arm about her waist, one leg thrown over her thighs. She struggled to get away from him but even as weak as he was she couldn't match his strength.

"I been thinkin' about that night we made Miranda."

She pushed against him earnestly, all the time realizing she didn't want to leave him.

"Just let me talk to you, Lynna, what harm can there be in that? Remember the night we spent together? No, don't move away. I promise not to do anything but talk. What can I do when I'm burned like this?"

She lay still under his arm, telling herself to move away from him, unable to make her body obey her mind's commands.

"You know where I'd like to be?" he whispered in her ear. "I'd like to be on a mountain top, in a little cabin with you. There'd be a stack of firewood and lots of food and you know what the first thing I'd do would be?"

She didn't answer.

"I'd burn all your clothes, every stitch. I'd watch you walkin', and look at your skin, at the way you bounce in the right places, the way you're all soft and jiggly. Then when I'd watched you for hours, maybe days, I'd pick you up and put you on the bed."

He looked at her, her eyes closed, her mouth parted, soft and warm, the edges of her little teeth showing. "I'd kneel at your feet and enclose them in my hands, your tiny little feet, run my fingers between your toes. I'd look at the color of you, your cream-white skin next to mine, oak and walnut or maybe you're pine since you're so soft and I'm so . . ." He chuckled low in his throat.

"I'd run my hands over your ankles and onto your calves, the little calves that I've watched so many times, watched when you lift your skirts and run, throwin' one foot in. Your knees, the tiny bones, the little carvings, and then your thighs, ah yes, your thighs. How I'd like to touch them, love them, the firm outside and the inside! The inside where you're so soft, like a jewel box that holds something so precious.

"Then my fingertips would touch your hip bones and my thumbs? What would my thumbs do? They would entwine themselves in the soft mat of silk, the dark curls pulling at them, teasing them. I'd touch the hole in your belly and by then my mouth wouldn't be able to wait any longer. I'd run my teeth along that little hole, nipping you, touching you with my tongue.

"At your waist I'd squeeze so hard my hands would overlap and I'd make you open your eyes. They'd be the color of the whiskey the traders bring me from England, kind of gold but deeper than that and they'd look at me, Lynna, they'd shine only for me."

His teeth ran along her neck. "I'd touch your ribs, so little, like a bird's really, and then, mmm, your breasts. The sweetness of them. I'd go slow, real slow, touching only the fat part at the sides, running each of my fingers one by one over the soft juiciness of them, and slowly, so slowly I might make you cry, I'd touch the little pink tips.

"Lynna," he whispered. "Lynna." He touched his lips to hers, softly, but she put her hands in his hair and pulled him roughly to her, crushing their mouths together, drinking, dying of thirst, choking, drowning.

She rolled next to him, both on their sides and her body arched to his and she clutched his firm buttocks and pulled him closer to her, painfully, her body crying for his. His hand twisted in her hair, pulling her head back to a breaking curve and their passion was a fierce, red-orange thing.

The door to the cabin slammed open, hitting the wall, causing a break in the spell. Linnet turned, her breath still held, not functioning as she saw no one there and knew that the wind had blown it open.

She became a person again and ran to close it but stood a moment with her face in the cool spring air, calming herself, wondering at such an emotion that she had experienced only once before.

Devon unbuttoned his pants and adjusted himself to relieve the pressure he felt, then turned on his stomach, not looking at Linnet, surprised by the violence of his own feelings.

Linnet ran from the cabin, wanting to be in the air to clear her head.

"Linnet!"

She heard Nettie's voice and she was all at once very happy to see her friend. "Nettie, I haven't seen you in such a long time." They clasped hands.

"How is he?" Nettie asked.

"He's . . . he's . . ." Linnet bent her head in embarrassment.

"I take it he's recovering all right," Nettie said, eyes twinkling.

Linnet had to laugh. "I believe you could say he was more than recovered."

"Good. Let's walk a bit. I got a pot of indigo settin' in the barn, but it'll let me rest a minute. Linnet, I'm worried about this town."

"What do you mean?"

"It's just too quiet, and this mornin' ever'body was over at Butch's store for the longest time. Rebekah said she saw some people comin' and they was smilin'. People in this town smile, and I worry."

"I'm sure they were discussing what a disgrace I am to the community, how I taught their children immoral ways, as if I ever taught them anything."

"No, I think it's more than that, and it's not knowin' that scares me. Rebekah wanted to spy on them, and I told her no, but I'm thinkin' about lettin' her more and more."

"Nettie! Please don't make Rebekah do something like that. I'm sure that as soon as I leave—"

"Leave!" Nettie cut in. "You ain't meanin' to leave, are you?"

Linnet looked at her in surprise. "Yes, I will go away. I'll go back to Sweetbriar."

"With your man," Nettie stated flatly.

Linnet smiled. "Yes, with my man. He's not perfect, Nettie, it seems we've never gotten along well, that we've always fought, but there are also so many things I love about him." She looked ahead dreamily to the edge of the woods. "He always helps people. He complains about it but he always helps them and he accepts people for what they are, whether they're white, Indian, rich or poor. He never lets wealth or color influence him. And he's brave. He risked his life to save me and he didn't even know my name. And on the trail back—"

Nettie's laugh cut her off. "Sounds to me like he's about ready to leave this earth to join the angels, he's so good."

"Oh no!" Linnet was quick to keep her friend from thinking that. "He's very human. Half the time he's angry with me, he snaps at Gaylon and Doll all the time and—"

"Linnet!" Nettie laughed and her friend joined her.

"I guess I do go on. I'm afraid I've been in Kentucky too long. A year ago I would never have told anyone what I felt about anything.

Nanny always said it was better to keep things inside, then the world couldn't hurt you since they didn't know your secrets."

Nettie patted her friend's arm. "You got to stay in Spring Lick long enough to tell me about Nanny and about all the time you lived in England, but right now I got to turn that wool. Maybe you'll help me spin it."

"I will if I can," Linnet answered honestly, their eyes locked together.

"I'm still gonna have Rebekah keep watch, and if I hear anythin', I'll let you know."

"I'm not worried. The people here are gossips, no more."

"You got more faith in 'em than I have." Nettie turned toward her house and the friends parted.

Linnet looked at her own cabin and when she saw Phetna and Miranda enter, she followed.

"Here, boy," Phetna was saying, "A girl brought these to you, said they was on your horse." The scarred woman held out a beaded pair of moccasins. "They'll protect your feet some."

Devon gave a brilliant smile to Phetna, and Linnet was amused to see her turn away, almost as if she were a young, blushing girl.

"I thank you kindly, Miss Phetna."

"Not Miss—," Phetna began but stopped.

Linnet walked past both of them and began peeling potatoes. "Phetna knew your father, Devon," she said, hardly able to look into his eyes, remembering too clearly his words and lips near hers an hour ago.

"I heard somethin' like that, but my memory of . . . of most things," he arched one eyebrow at Linnet and she looked away, "is hazy. You knew him in North Carolina?"

Phetna sat down in a chair and stared at Devon. "You shore look like him. I wouldn't aknowed you wasn't him if somebody hadn't told me."

"Cord looks like him too," Linnet said as she handed Miranda a piece of raw potato. "They move differently and they're built differently, but there's a resemblance."

"Who's Cord?"

When Linnet looked up and saw Devon's face, she realized what she had said. To her it had been something she had known so long that she had forgotten that Devon had no idea Cord was his half-brother. "I . . . I'm sorry, I shouldn't have said that." She stood and dumped the potato peelings in the slop jar that she kept for Nettie's pigs.

"Linnet!" His voice was low. "I want you to explain what you just said."

She sat down on the bench and told them Cord's story, the story of how Cord and Devon were brothers. When she finished, Devon's eyes were closed.

"What a fool," he said quietly.

"Slade?" Phetna asked, obviously ready to do battle in defense of Slade's good name.

"No, Cord was the fool." He opened his eyes. "My pa woulda loved him, woulda taken him in if he'd known Cord was his. Pa always hated the loss of Kevin, my twin brother. There wasn't a wagon train or even a man on horseback who rode east who didn't take a letter back to Kevin and his ma."

Linnet noticed how he did not claim ownership of his own mother.

"Pa used to say that they was gonna come back to him someday. Cord coulda helped Pa."

Linnet watched him and heard the love he held for his father in his voice. Devon was only interested in what Cord could have done for Slade.

"Cord woulda been different if he had shared my pa."

Linnet smiled. "Speaking of fathers, do you realize you're one yourself?"

Devon looked down at Miranda as she sat on the floor playing with the black and white kitten. "It's hard for me to think of. She's just so little and . . . Miranda, can I see the kitten?"

Miranda looked up, startled to hear her name from the man who slept on her mother's bed and got so much attention. She stood and looked at him, two pairs of blue eyes studying each other. He held out his hand to her, and she looked at it but backed away to hide against Phetna's skirt. But she smiled at her father.

"I like her, Linnet. She's pretty."

"I'm glad you like her," Linnet said sarcastically. "I'd hate to have to return her to where she came from."

Phetna snorted, half laughed, and Devon grinned at her. "Ain't she the sharpest tongued woman you ever met?"

Phetna smiled at him. "Seems like there's been some times when she ain't said some of the things she should of." She looked pointedly at Miranda.

Linnet was embarrassed and changed the subject. "Devon, when are you going to make the doll head for Miranda? You seem to have enough strength now."

He gave her a look that made her hurriedly look down at her apron full of string beans. "Soon's you take me to get a piece of wood."

"You'll have to tell me what to get, and I'll find something for you."

"Huh! You'd probably bring back a chunk of oak or a piece of dried hickory."

Linnet didn't understand what would be wrong with either item and her consternation showed.

"See," he said to Phetna, then turned back to Linnet. "I'm so sick of bein' inside, I'm gonna start carvin' the walls—with my teeth! Why don't we go outside for a while?"

"Now? But we can't."

"Why not?"

"Your feet, they're still raw, and I have to cook and—"

"You two just go on," Phetna said. "Me and Miranda'll take care of what needs doin' here."

Linnet opened her mouth to protest.

"Why, Lynna, you look like you're scared to be alone with me," Devon said, a smirk in his voice. "What can I do when I'm so helpless?"

Linnet refused to blush again. "Of course we can go. I'm not afraid of you in the least, Devon Macalister."

They walked together, Devon slowly and painfully to the front porch, where he picked up the little hand saw. He paused and touched the hair at her temple. "Nor am I afraid of you, Linnet . . . Macalister."

She walked past him but she smiled when her back was to him.

"Wait a minute," he said. "I can't go so fast."

She turned and saw the pain on his face as he tried to walk on his burned feet. She took his arm, and he used her for support. "Devon, you shouldn't have come outside, shouldn't have tried to walk yet."

He smiled down at her, a bit crookedly but a smile just the same. "A spring day spent outside with the pretty woman I love will help me more than anythin' else. You wouldn't begrudge me that pleasure, would you?"

She touched his shoulder with the top of her head. "No, Devon, I can't deny you anything."

"Oh, no! This may prove to be a very pleasant day."

"Stop it right now or I'll push you down onto your sore back."

"My back? I remember a night I spent on my back while a little English girl—"

"Devon!"

He laughed but said no more. When they finally reached the patch of clover, Devon sat down gratefully, and Linnet removed his moccasins and saw that his feet had cracked and bled in several places. The sight brought tears to her eyes.

"Come here, you silly girl and stop lookin' like that. Now go over to that poplar tree and saw me off a branch."

It was not easy getting a piece of wood to Devon's exact specifications, and she began to see the artist side of him and the amount of time and thought he put into one of his carvings.

"Mind you, this is gonna be pretty crude since I don't have my carvin' tools here."

She lifted her eyebrows but said nothing as she sat down beside him. It was good just to see him well and moving about.

When the wood was in his hands, he took out his knife and began to carve and talk. "I had a long time to think while I was layin' there, Lynna, and I thought about all the things you said to me the mornin' of the fire."

"Devon, I—"

"Don't stop me. You had your say, and now I get mine. In my whole life I never treated nobody like I treated you, and I'm sorry, for more reasons'n one. I guess I've always had strong feelin's for you, else I wouldn'ta taken on Spotted Wolf. I just knew I couldn't let somebody die who worried about other people like you done when your own life was about to end. I can't say I was in love with you but I sure felt somethin'. Then when you washed up so pretty, I guess I felt like you betrayed me. Maybe I felt kinda noble rescuin' that ugly little thing, but then when you wasn't ugly, I felt like you'd laughed at me. I guess I can't say what I feel so good."

"Your Thomas Jefferson couldn't do so well."

Devon gave her a puzzled blink, having never heard of Jefferson. "Well, I guess that means you understand me. I'm . . . real sorry for what I done to you. I know it can't help matters much now, not after you sayin' you could never have any feelin' for me again, but I want you to know I am sorry, and I want you to be real happy with your Squire."

"My—!" she began, then stopped and started again, her voice sad. "I'm sure I will be, since he is a fighter."

"A fighter!" Devon stopped carving. "He wouldn't know how to fight a four-year-old. He's lived soft all his life."

"And you haven't? Haven't you always had everything you've ever wanted in your life?"

"Damn you! How can you say that when the woman I want more than anythin' else wants somebody else?"

"Of course you've never asked her to marry you, have you? You may have said you'd marry her when you found out she had borne your child, but you've not asked her since she's had time to think and realize that she can't seem to stop herself from loving you."

Linnet's eyes twinkled as she watched Devon. At first he stared unbelievingly, and then when he began to understand her words, he relaxed and gave her a slow smile. "Then you think maybe if I asked her now, she might consider marryin' me?"

"I dare say she would consider the proposal seriously."

He smiled wider at her. "Then where are my moccasins?"

She frowned in puzzlement. "They're behind you, but you don't need them now."

"I sure do," he said as he turned and picked one up. "I got to go ask Phetna to marry me. I never dreamed that she'd accept, but now that you've opened my eyes, I—"

"Phetna," Linnet exclaimed. "Phetna!" She was incredulous but before she could say another word, Devon lunged at her and pulled her to him, crushing her against his chest. "Devon," she managed to gasp.

He loosened his hold on her, but not much. "Lynna, will you marry me and live with me and spend every night with me?"

She pushed away from him and looked up into his happy, sparkling blue eyes. "What kind of proposal is this? Spend every night with you? No gentleman would ever mention such a thing as . . . as night time activities to a lady."

He was very serious and slightly puzzled. "I ain't no gentleman and it's been a long time."

She laughed, her face against his smooth, bare chest. "I would rather have your honesty than all the sweet-smelling, lace-attired gentlemen in the world. I hope you always desire me, Devon."

He pulled her head back, tired of talk, and kissed her sweet, eager mouth, both of them totally unaware of the two men who watched them from the woods.

It took Linnet a while to make Devon understand that she wanted her wedding night to be more than a quick tumble in some clover, and although he did point out they'd already had one wedding night, nevertheless, he did let her win the argument. It was two very happy, laughing people who returned to Linnet's cabin, but the sights and sounds inside the cabin broke their joyous mood.

Chapter Twenty

MIRANDA WAS SCREAMING, HER LITTLE BODY covered in great globs of mud, and when she saw her mother, she kicked against Nettie to be released and ran to Linnet. Linnet soothed her and began trembling herself when she felt her child's fear.

"What's been goin' on here?" Devon demanded angrily.

"They started," Nettie said. "Them young'uns threw mud at Phetna and the baby, callin' 'em witches." She leaned over and dabbed at the blood that ran down Phetna's face from a gash on the side of her forehead.

Devon went to kneel by the woman and took the cloth from Nettie. "Looks like more'n mud to me." Phetna sat quietly while Devon tended to her wound.

Gradually, Linnet calmed Miranda, and the

cabin was quiet. Phetna turned her hideous, mutilated face to Devon, her eyes bright with tears. "You woulda been my boy," she said quietly.

He looked at her a moment, then grinned and returned to cleaning her wound. "It's a good thing you weren't my ma 'cause I got a feelin' you woulda tanned my hide ever' time I needed it, and if you'd done that, I still wouldn't be able to sit down."

Phetna laughed her high, shrill cackle. "I guess it was a good thing then."

It was hours before the cabin returned to order. Nettie went home, and so Devon helped Linnet bathe Miranda, and the child took advantage of her father's inexperience and managed to drench both him and half the cabin. The wound on Phetna's head had to be sewn, and she would allow no one but Devon to do it. Exhausted, Phetna and Miranda finally fell asleep.

Sometime in the night Linnet heard Devon slowly make his way outside. When he didn't return right away, she went to find him and saw that he sat on the edge of the porch, his head in his hands.

She tried to keep her voice light. "It seems you've conquered three females today."

He ignored her jest. "Somethin's gotta be done, Linnet. There's too many of 'em, and I'm too weak to fight 'em alone."

She sat beside him. "You're not alone, I'm here."

He looked at her in the moonlight. "You've had to fight too many battles already. For once you're gonna have somebody take care of you. We're gonna leave this place. Tomorrow we're goin' home."

"Home," Linnet said quietly. "Sweetbriar."

"Yes, we're goin' home to Sweetbriar and we're takin' Phetna with us. That suit you?"

She felt so good, warm and happy. "Perfectly. That suits me perfectly."

"Now get back inside 'fore I forget you're my intended and all them stupid reasons you give me this afternoon for not makin' love to you and I take you right here on the front porch."

She hesitated but then stood and went inside. At the door she looked back but he was already deep in thought again.

The Squire poured another drink, his hand shaking uncontrollably. It seemed that there was nothing in his line of vision but colors: red, orange, yellow, figures of black. The little bitch had made him the brunt of a joke. Everyone was laughing at him!

He turned and looked at the Indian man tied and thrown in a corner of his cabin. So, she thought the Squire was something to joke about with her lover, did she? Just how did he earn the title, yes title, of *the* Squire if he were such a weak object?

He refilled his pewter mug. The whiskey no longer burned his throat. In fact, he seemed almost immune to its effects except that his anger grew more and more strong. He remembered Boston and saving her. Where would she be now if it hadn't been for him? And what had she ever done to thank him properly?

He remembered the way she kissed Macalister, not just with her lips but with her whole body. He slammed the mug down. Well, by God, she was going to kiss him like that someday. He turned to the Indian and saw the black eyes burning with hatred, and the idea of someone else feeling the same emotion as he felt made him smile.

What had that Indian been doing, spying on the young white couple? Was he perhaps just wanting to watch what seemed likely to happen? But it must have been more since the Indian's concentration had been so intense that he'd not even heard the Squire's rather heavy footsteps behind him, hadn't heard the whistle of the gun handle as the Squire brought it down on the Indian's head.

He lifted the mug in salute to the Indian. "What were you wanting out there, boy? You don't look like one of those young bucks that have to steal to prove they're men. No, there's something else on your mind." He drained the last of the whiskey. "I can tell you I have other things on my mind. First of all, there's a woman I'd like to pay back in kind. I'd like to give her some of what she's given me. It doesn't make one feel like a man to be used by a woman.

"Rattlesnakes! That's what all women are. They lie and use you, take forever. Well, this one," he tried to get more whiskey from the empty bottle, "this one ain't gonna win." He was unaware that he had slipped into the Kentucky slur. "No siree bob, this one ain't gonna win. She's gonna repay me for all I done for her and she ain't gonna laugh at me no more. All I gotta do is get Macalister outta the way."

Even drunk, he saw the way the Indian's eyes lit at the name. He considered this knowledge for a moment. "So, you know Macalister, do you? That figures, him bein' an Injun an' all. You talk English, Injun?"

The tied and gagged man nodded curtly.

"Where will it all end? Injuns what speak English. Next the government'll set up schools and teach the animals to read and write. I'm gonna take that gag off you, boy, but you try doin' anythin' and I'll happily kick your teeth and most of your face down your throat."

He untied the man's gag. "Now, what's your name?"

"Crazy Bear," the Indian said.

"All right, Crazy Bear, you and me are gonna have a long talk."

When Linnet woke, the first thing she saw was Devon's empty bed. She sighed. She had liked it better when he was immobile, before he had walked with her to the clover patch, before he had gone to sit on the porch last night. She put her hands behind her head and stared at the ceiling. Phetna and Miranda still slept, the horrible events of the evening before causing their exhaustion.

Today, she thought, today they would all leave this ugly town. Devon would take them back to Sweetbriar. Nettie was her only regret at leaving Spring Lick, but then there were so many friends at home, just thinking of them made her feel good.

"Where's the boy?"

Linnet looked across to Phetna stretched out on another borrowed mattress on the floor. "I don't know. Now that you've given him the moccasins, I'm afraid he'll be walking everywhere." She tried not to let her resentment seep into her voice but did not wholly succeed.

Phetna smiled. "You better learn now you can't keep a Macalister in some bottle just waitin' for you to give him leave to go where he wants."

"I guess not." She smiled back. "It's just that I've grown used to knowing where he is. Last night he sat on the porch for hours, worrying. At least I guess it was hours. I never heard him return."

Phetna sat up. "That's a man's duty in life, takin' care of his womenfolk. Now I got to get up and start cookin' us somethin' to eat."

Linnet smiled dreamily. "We can't cook too much because we are going home today." She didn't see Phetna's bleak expression.

257

"You all goin' back to Sweetbriar?"

Linnet turned onto her stomach and looked up at Phetna. *"We* are going, all of us. Devon especially said he wanted you to go with us."

Phetna sat down on the bench. "He don't want an old woman like me."

Linnet stood and began folding the quilt. "Devon knows exactly what he wants, and we don't have time to argue with him because we have a lot of packing to do."

Phetna seemed to realize what Linnet was saying. "I don't guess I ever wanted to go anywheres worse'n I wanta go to Sweetbriar. I got things at my cabin I need to gather up."

"Of course," Linnet said. "There's very little to do here really, so Miranda and Devon can help me. Why don't you go and pack and we'll meet you there as soon as you're ready?"

Phetna made an expression that looked like a grin. "I'm just gonna do that. You don't need me here?"

"No, the sooner everything, both here and at your cabin is done, the sooner we can leave."

"I'm for that." Before Linnet could blink, Phetna was out of the cabin door and Linnet knew exactly how the woman felt, because she felt the same way.

Linnet knew Devon needed time alone, which he hadn't had for nearly a week, and she also knew how much he hated being kept indoors for so long, but when he hadn't returned by noon, she began to worry. She went to the woods, calmly walking around, expecting any moment to find him asleep under a tree. She planned the scolding she would give him and she thought how he'd pull her into his arms and wouldn't let her talk anymore.

When she returned to the cabin she was further alarmed to see he had not returned. Absentmindedly, she gave Miranda her dinner, Linnet too nervous to eat. The few things she and her daughter owned were packed. She refused to take anything that was not essential.

When a knock sounded, she opened the door to the Squire and they stood staring at one another for a moment. He looked over her head to the neat bundles on the floor and pushed past her into the little cabin.

"So, you're leaving."

"Yes," she said, all at once realizing that she had totally forgotten him.

"I take it you had no intention of even letting me know of your plans."

"I . . ." She put her chin in the air and met his eyes. "My conduct has been unforgivable and I apologize. It seems that everything has happened so quickly that I haven't had time to think."

"Huh!" he snorted. "I guess you mean about your old lover comin' back into your life and sweeping you off your feet again. You know, I pity you young girls. No matter what a man does to you, if you have the idea you love him, you'll keep on believing in him no matter what else he does to you."

"I have no idea what you're talking about."

"You don't? Well, look about you. You're all packed and ready to go, yet where's your young swain?" He smiled when she didn't answer. "You see, Linnet, just as he left you once, so he's done it again. He had no intention of marrying you. Why should he? Why should he saddle himself with a wife and child when the whole world's at his feet? He's young, good-looking and the women like him, so why should he give up something like that?"

"I don't want to hear any more of this. Would you please leave?"

He sat down on the bench in front of the table and leaned back. "You're throwing me out of my own cabin? Might I remind you that everything you supposedly own is mine? I even paid for Miranda's birth." His eyes turned cold. "Now that he's gone and left you, just what do you plan to do? You gonna follow him back to Sweetbriar? Chase him like the common woman you've become?"

"I won't hear any more of your insults. It's true I don't know where Devon is, but I will not believe the snide remarks you have made about him."

"Believe them or not, they're true. This morning he came to my house and traded me this for

some supplies, enough to get him back to Sweetbriar."

Linnet looked at Devon's knife that the Squire
held. "I don't believe you."

"You should ask Nettie if Macalister's horse is
still with them. It isn't, because he took it with
him and several people in Spring Lick saw him
riding away on it."

"I don't believe you!" It was all she could say,
over and over.

He laughed. "That's your right. Now I got to
go. You think over what I said and ask yourself if
you want to raise Miranda with a father like
that." He paused at the door. "By the way, did he
get what he wanted from you?" His eyes carefully went over every part of her body, but she stood
straight and did not answer him, and he closed
the door behind him, laughing.

"I don't believe it," Linnet said. "Whatever
problems Devon may have, he is not a liar."

Nettie put a generous scoop of the precious tea
in the pot. "I don't know the man so I can't say.
All I know is, his horse was gone this mornin'."

"He wouldn't steal away in the night like that,
I just know he wouldn't."

And I know how much you'd like to believe in
him, Nettie thought. "What are you gonna do
now, now that he's gone?"

"I . . . I don't know. I have to go to Phetna,
she's been expecting me all day." She looked out

the open door toward the setting sun. "It's getting late and I don't know what to do."

Rebekah ran into the room, breathless. "I found out, Mama, I found out."

"All right, sit down," Nettie said, "and tell us."

Linnet looked from mother to daughter in wonder. "Nettie, you didn't . . . ," she began.

"I shore did," Nettie said and smiled fondly at Rebekah. "This child has a special talent for listenin', through cracks in the chinkin'."

Linnet didn't like the idea but she wanted desperately to know what had made Devon leave Spring Lick so suddenly.

"I heard the Squire talkin' to Mrs. Yarnall. They was havin' a fight, leastways a argument. Mrs. Yarnall said she wanted somethin' to be done about Miss Tyler and Mr. Macalister, and the Squire said that somethin' already had been." She looked from one woman to another to make sure they were hearing her every word.

"What did he say?" Nettie prodded.

"The Squire said he sold Mr. Macalister to the Injuns."

"To the—!" Nettie gaped, wide-eyed.

Linnet appeared to be very calm. "What else did he say, Rebekah?"

"That's about all. He said he saw this Indian in the woods and he knocked him over the head and tied him up. He said the Indian was watchin' Miss Tyler and Mr. Macalister kissin'!" The girl looked at her teacher in wonder.

"What else?" Linnet ignored the girl's curiosity.

"He said when he got the Indian back to the house he found out the Indian had been chasin' Mr. Macalister all over everywhere, said the Indian wanted to kill Mr. Macalister but he didn't have no horse or gun to take him back to his men."

"So the Squire made it possible for the Indian to take Devon," Linnet finished.

"Yes, ma'am."

"Well." Nettie let out her pent-up breath. "I guess there's nothin' we can do then."

"We can go after him," Linnet said, her eyes staring.

"You and me?" Nettie asked. "Two women alone in the woods? Ain't nobody else in this town gonna help you, and my Ottis won't be back for another week. Who you gonna get to help you?"

"I don't know." Linnet stood. "I don't know yet what I'm going to do, but I can't let them have Devon." She paused at the door and looked back at Rebekah. "Did you by any chance hear the name of the Indian?"

"Ah . . . oh yes, it was Crazy Bear."

Nettie at first thought Linnet was going to faint. The color drained from her face, her eyes immediately became glassy, and her knees seemed to weaken. "Linnet, are you all right?"

She shook her head to clear it. "I must go. I must go and find him."

Nettie started to protest, but then Linnet was gone and she turned back to the bread she had to knead.

"You think she's gonna go after that Indian that took Mr. Macalister?"

"No, of course not," Nettie told her daughter. "She'll have time to think it over and see how impossible it is. No woman can go alone through the woods, and even Linnet knows that."

"I would!" Rebekah said. "I'd go after him. I wouldn't let no Indian have my man!"

"Hush," Nettie said sternly. "You don't know what you're talkin' about. There's just some things a woman can't do, and get on a horse and ride through the night after a bunch of Indians is one of 'em. And even if Linnet sometimes doesn't seem to know her place in the world, she at least has enough sense to . . ." She stopped and stared at the bread.

"What's the matter, Mama?"

Nettie wiped her hands on her apron. "Linnet doesn't have any sense at all when it comes to that man and she'd do just what she said. She's gonna go after him, and I know it as well as I know my own name. Rebekah, you finish up that bread and set it to rise."

"Ah, Ma, I wanta go see you talk to Miss Tyler."

"It's more likely Miss Tyler is gonna talk to me."

Chapter Twenty-one

LINNET'S CABIN DOOR WAS OPEN AND SHE SAT quietly at the table, absently watching Miranda play with her kitten. She didn't hear Nettie enter.

"Well, where you gonna get horses?"

Linnet looked up and they understood each other. "I'm going to steal one from the Squire."

In spite of herself, Nettie smiled. "You think you could get two horses?"

"No," Linnet said seriously. "This is my own problem, and you can't go with me."

"I'd like to know why not," Nettie said indignantly.

Linnet looked at her, very calm. "You'd be a hindrance. I'd be worried about you all the time, and you can neither ride well nor shoot."

Nettie looked startled for a moment and then

laughed. "You shore do lay it on the line, don't you?"

"I have to. This is a serious undertaking. Crazy Bear hates Devon and he hates me. If I don't free him, then we will both forfeit our lives."

"Lord!" Nettie sat down in the chair. "I don't know how you can sit there and talk about dyin' so easy."

"I'm sure my calmness is only a facade. Devon's life is at stake, and there's a chance I can save him, a small chance, I know, but as long as there is a sliver of hope, I plan to take it."

Nettie sighed. "All right, I can't go but I can take care of Miranda."

"No, I'm taking her to Phetna. These people may harm her if I leave her here. They'd be afraid to go to Phetna's."

Nettie looked at her friend in admiration. "I ain't never seen nobody with a cooler head than you. What can I do to help?"

"You can help me steal a horse."

Nettie smiled, mostly to herself. "I'll be glad to, more glad than you know."

They waited until full dark before slipping through the blackness to the Squire's corral. Nettie held Miranda at some distance while Linnet slipped between the split rails. Nettie couldn't see her once she was inside the pen and she began to worry that something was wrong. The horses walked about quietly, undisturbed at

Linnet's presence. Once she could have sworn she saw the brightness of Linnet's hair underneath one of the horses' bellies, but she told herself that she had to be wrong. After what seemed to be hours, Linnet led a horse through the gate.

"What took you so long?" Nettie whispered.

"Saddle," was Linnet's curt reply. "I must go now. Good-bye . . . friend."

They hugged one another.

"Good luck, Linnet, I wish you all the luck in the world and please, please be careful."

She swung into the saddle on the tall, black horse.

"You sure you can handle this animal?" Nettie asked as she lifted Miranda up to her mother.

"Certainly."

"I'm gonna miss your funny way of talkin'," Nettie said as she wiped her eyes with the back of her hand, but Linnet was already reining the horse away, her mind on the journey ahead.

"Where's the boy?" were Phetna's first words when she saw Linnet and a sleeping Miranda.

"The Squire—" she choked on the name, "turned him over to the care of Crazy Bear."

"Crazy Bear? Ain't he the one killed your folks?"

"The very same, but he'll take no more of my family." She handed Miranda to Phetna.

"You ain't thinkin' of goin' after him, are you?"

"I am going after him, yes."

"Alone? I thought you had some sense, but you ain't."

"Please, I've already been through this with Nettie."

Phetna was silent a moment before she spoke. "All right, you're gonna go after him but you ain't goin' alone."

"You can't go with me, Phetna. You're too—"

"Don't even say it. It ain't me what's gonna go with you but Yellow Hand."

"Yellow Hand? Is he here?"

"No, he ain't but he will be. I got a signal in case I need help. You just get on down here, and Yellow Hand'll be here in no time."

Inside the cabin, Phetna took a hollowed deer horn from the mantel and went outside and blew it, several times in each direction and the women began to wait. Phetna prepared packages of food, cornmeal and jerky, while Linnet wrote in the flyleaf of Phetna's Bible. She made out her will, making Phetna the child's guardian.

"If I'm not back in two weeks, you can—"

"Hush!" Phetna cut her off. "I'll take care of the young'un till you get back and I ain't gonna think of it no other way. Here now, eat this and don't talk so much."

Linnet carefully unwrapped Devon's four carvings. "I brought them in case—"

"'Cause you ain't goin' back to Spring Lick.

Now shut up and eat, then I got somethin' I wanta give you, might come in useful."

Neither woman heard Yellow Hand's arrival. He just seemed to all at once be standing inside the cabin. "I am here," he said quietly.

Linnet told him what had happened to Devon, and the young man listened carefully. "I do not ask you to go with me," she said softly. "I will go alone."

The boy puffed out his chest. "How you find him? How you read trail?"

"I . . ."

"Woman not trained to do this. You can ride horse?"

"Yes."

"Then we go now. Too much time lost already." His words were hardly out before Linnet was outside and on her horse.

Phetna came to them and handed her a rifle, powder and shot. "You can use this?"

"Yes."

"Then go with the Lord's blessin' and come back safe, all of you."

When they were gone, Phetna sat down in the rocker and watched the sleeping Miranda. Somehow, it seemed hopeless, the two young people setting out after somebody as wily as Crazy Bear. Phetna sighed and remembered how this was to have been the day when they were all to go to Sweetbriar.

She closed her eyes and leaned her head back.

Sweetbriar and the days of her youth, the time before the fire. She could remember the face of each person in Sweetbriar.

"I wonder if Doll's as ugly as he always was?" she murmured. Now Doll'd be the one to help find Slade's boy, Doll and Gaylon and Lyttle, they'd all be able to help. She smiled as she thought of the formidable sight of Agnes Emerson behind a six-foot-long rifle. Warn't no Indian gonna threaten her.

Suddenly Phetna sat bolt upright. Sweetbriar. The word rang in her head. She looked down at her lap and stuck out her legs. "A mite rusty," she said aloud, "but they'll make it."

She began to throw provisions into a bag. For once she thought of something good about her face. At least nobody, white or red, would harm her while she made the trip. No siree, nobody'd bother her. She smiled as she thought of leaping out at Doll Stark and watching him jump. Lord! She hadn't felt so good in twelve years, not since before the fire.

"Come on, Miranda." She lifted the sleeping child. "We got work to do."

Phetna was gone, and the three masked people who later stole through the night and burned the little cabin never knew it was empty. "The Lord's will be done," said a woman's voice, but she never noticed the doubt in the other two pairs of eyes.

* * *

Linnet followed Yellow Hand quietly and she never gave him any cause to doubt her or sneer in disgust at the softness of white women. She seemed indefatigable, almost as if she were not human in her drive to pursue Crazy Bear and the man he held captive. They stopped once to sleep by the side of a stream, and he watched her, saw that she slept lightly, as if she resented the time spent in the necessity of sleep.

The terrain was rough, the underbrush thick. Once they had to go through swampland and later stop and pull leeches from the horses' legs. Linnet's arms were scratched, there were mosquito bites along her cheek, yet she seemed not to notice any discomfort.

"We're getting closer to them?"

They were the first words either had spoken in twenty-four hours.

"Yes," he answered. "Crazy Bear is careless. He does not hide his trail. He thinks no one follows him."

"No." Her eyes looked into the distance. "He has no reason to think he would be pursued."

"Come, no more talk now."

They rode hard for two more days, Linnet's dress becoming torn and ragged, her hair dirty and full of matted grasses and twigs, yet her eyes burned feverishly bright as she looked ahead, expecting any moment to see Crazy Bear's men and Devon.

Yellow Hand made them stop to eat a small

amount of the jerky and some wild strawberries. They sat facing one another, the rifle loaded and by Linnet's side when she saw a slight movement by Yellow Hand's leg and saw a cottonmouth prepare to strike. Instantly she grabbed the rifle and fired, her years of training and practice with a rifle making her perfectly accurate.

Yellow Hand stared at her and then at the dead snake by his leg. He lifted it before looking back at her. "You have saved my life," he said quietly, "but you have killed us both. Come, we must hide for a while. They may not find us."

Linnet understood what he meant, that they were really close to Crazy Bear and his men. It seemed only seconds before their peaceful camp was surrounded by men and Linnet's mind was swiftly taken back to the time her parents had been slaughtered and she had been led away by these same men.

She was pressed against Yellow Hand under a clump of blackberry bushes. The sharp thorns pushed into her skin. Suddenly her mind was very clear. Crazy Bear would find them and he would kill them, just as he'd probably already killed Devon. She could not save herself from the man but she could save Yellow Hand.

She kicked against the boy and rolled down the little incline and landed at the feet of Crazy Bear.

The Indian grinned, bent, and pulled her to her feet by her hair. He turned to the others and said something, pulling Linnet's head back until it threatened to snap away from her body. The four other Indians grinned as Crazy Bear threw Linnet across his pony's back and mounted behind her.

They rode for hours, the pony's backbone hammering into Linnet's middle. When they stopped, Crazy Bear pushed her from the little horse, and she had every intention of landing on her feet, but her knees gave way and she fell into a heap on the ground.

A sharp stick and a woman's shrill voice made her look up. A horrible sense of *déjà vu* overcame her as she saw the same woman who had hit her before when she'd been in Crazy Bear's camp. It didn't seem like nearly three years ago. In fact, it seemed as if she'd never left the dirty camp. She looked at each of the faces watching her, expecting to see a pair of blue eyes, but there were none.

Crazy Bear pulled her hair, and she stood in front of him. He said something to the women in his own language, and they giggled in unison and approached Linnet slowly, their eyes menacing. They stopped when a man, old, his thin body hanging with fatless flesh, ran into the camp. He seemed to be very excited and kept pointing at Linnet and then to something in his hand, waving his arms in the direction where Linnet had been captured.

Crazy Bear grabbed the object held by the old man and shoved it in front of Linnet's face. She recognized it as a pouch which had hung at Yellow Hand's side. She gasped, thinking they had caught the boy. Crazy Bear slapped her face hard, and she struggled to remain standing.

He gave some orders to the women, who knocked her to the ground and tied her hands with coarse, cutting rawhide. Then they bent her legs back and tied her hands and feet together, causing her body to form a painful, twisting loop. The women lifted her, and as they swung her to and fro in the air, hands loosely holding her, she heard horses near her. A sharp bark of an order from Crazy Bear, and the women tossed her into a dark and empty hut, the fall stunning her. When she regained her breath, she saw she was once again in the same sort of low hovel that she had been in after her parents had been killed, but this time there was no hope of rescue from a blue-eyed half-Indian.

Chapter Twenty-two

"HELLO, TAR BABY."

Linnet couldn't move, her legs bent behind her, tied to her hands, but she knew that voice, knew it well and the tears that filled her throat choked her. The joy of knowing he was alive! Not for long maybe, but alive.

"Can you turn over?"

It wasn't easy, and Linnet reminded herself of a fish flopping about on dry land, but she would have died rather than give up hope of facing her Devon. It took a moment to see him. "Devon! What have they done to you?"

He tried to smile but his lips wouldn't slide across his dry teeth. "They've enjoyed themselves. Why are you here? You should be safe with Miranda. Come closer."

She scooted across the floor so that she was touching him.

"Kiss me," he said hoarsely. "I need you."

She didn't question him but found his kiss to be more searching than anything else, and when she felt the inside of his mouth, dry, almost cracked, she knew he needed moisture from her more than anything else. He broke away and his eyes brightened for a moment.

"An old Indian trick?" she asked.

"No. Macalister alone. Linnet, why are you here? You shouldn't be."

"You said that. Devon, I have a knife."

He almost jumped as he looked at her, his body tied into a backward circle just as hers was.

"It's strapped to the inside of my thigh, only I don't know how to get it."

He seemed to have trouble thinking correctly or swiftly. "Fast. We must move fast. Can you move up?"

"How can you get it?"

"With my teeth," he answered.

Linnet managed to move upward, her muscles aching and crying for rest. Devon pulled her skirt and petticoats up with his teeth, high above her waist to expose the drawstring of the linen underpants. The string was knotted, and he could not unfasten it.

"Damn it, Linnet! Why'd you have to make a knot?"

She smiled through the darkness at his words. With a powerful wrench with his teeth, he tore the string and a great deal of linen away. The knife Phetna had given her was strapped inside her thighs, the hilt of it having rubbed a raw, chafed mark on the soft opposite thigh.

Devon looked at her body, ivory, gleaming in the dark for a moment before lowering his head and removing the knife from its sheath. He seemed to take much longer than he needed to remove the knife.

Linnet realized how tired she was—or was it only tiredness? She rolled to her stomach so he could cut the rawhide that bound her feet to her hands. How good it was to stretch out straight once again!

Devon dropped the knife from his teeth and rested the side of his face against the cold dirt floor, too tired to cut the binding on her hands. After a moment, "Lynna, can you cut mine away?"

She frowned at his tone. He was hurt, and his joviality was a supreme effort for him.

"Quick, Lynna, quick."

"Yes, Devon." Her hands still tied behind her, she felt for the knife. He did not stir when she moved to his back and tried to work the knife blade under the rawhide leather attaching his hands to his feet. She tried to calm her frantic thoughts when she cut the rope, because Devon did not move from his cramped and unnatural backward position.

"I'm afraid my body's been this way too long. Can you get my hands loose?"

It wasn't easy to conquer her fear and control

her hands as she tried to saw the rawhide apart with the little knife. The cords were so tight that she could hardly find a place to slip the blade under.

"Don't worry about hurting me," Devon whispered. "Cut my hand off and I wouldn't know it. Just do it fast."

She felt the blade tip touch him once but he didn't flinch or move and she knew he was telling the truth when he said his hands were numb.

When he was free he moved his arms slowly, awkwardly. "Give me the knife. Linnet, listen to me," he said in her ear as he sawed at the rawhide across her wrists. "I've been here a long time and I'm . . . not well. Promise me somethin'. If I fall somewhere, leave me. Go on by yourself and leave me. I don't want you recaptured by Crazy Bear. Do you understand me?"

"Perfectly," she said quietly.

"Then I have your promise?"

Linnet pulled her arms forward and rubbed her wrists. "No. Now let me have the knife and I'll cut this off our feet."

"Lynna, please."

"Devon, do not waste my time." She cut the bindings, and as she felt his feet they seemed to be wet, and she realized it was blood. She had no time to cry and made herself do what had to be done. "Can you walk?" she asked when they were free.

"Not if you can carry me."

Linnet held her breath as she cut away the side of the little hut and peered into the fading daylight to see if anyone was about. Crazy Bear's people were lazy and didn't post guards always, and now that he was away, searching for Yellow Hand, his people were even more lax.

"It's clear," she said and offered him her hand. He took it, and she helped to support him to stand in a crouch, his face a mask hiding all his thoughts and feelings. He nodded, and she led the way outside the hut and into the woods. At her first look at Devon in the daylight, she saw that his half-healed burns were raw again. She didn't ask what Crazy Bear had done to him.

His eyes were hard, and without saying a word, he cautioned her and told her to lead ahead. They walked slowly for an hour, and Linnet knew he could go on for only a little while longer. If only I could carry him, she thought as they came to the bank of a river. The water's surface was covered with several logs, notched and ready for building. Linnet's mind wandered, and she wondered what catastrophe had caused some settlers to lose all the logs they had so carefully prepared for their cabin, when a thought struck her. She couldn't carry Devon but the water could.

"Devon, if I got you into the water could you hold on to a log?"

He nodded, his eyes glazed.

She supported him as much as her slight frame could as he walked to the river's edge. She saw by the way he drew in his breath that the coolness of the water hurt him at first. He was bare from the waist up, wearing only the heavy linsey-woolsey pants and no shoes. Yet as he went more deeply into the water, the chill numbed him and cleaned the wounds. The buoyancy of the water helped to take the pressure off his cut feet and he felt better.

"Smart. Smart, Lynna," he said as he let the water lift him.

"My governess made me study about what to do with raw, bleeding men in the Kentucky wilderness."

He put his arm across a log and looked at her, one eyebrow lifted, not sure if she joked or was serious. "Don't talk anymore. They'll look for us soon," he said and put his cheek against the rough bark, resting for the first time in four days.

They floated silently for hours as the sun set and the night spread about them. There were times when Devon seemed to sleep, and Linnet kept watch over him, ready to hold him if he should slip.

"Someday I'm gonna take care of you," he whispered once when she thought he was asleep.

"I'd like that," she said as she touched his ear.

They heard horses along the bank, softly padding, almost inaudible. Devon's arm came down from the log and pulled Linnet's head under him, beneath his chest, between him and the log. She did not breathe for fear of making a sound. Long after the horses were no longer heard, Devon still held her beneath him, her neck cramped and hurting. He released her slowly, and she kicked backward to take her place beside him. She looked at him in question.

"Your hair," he said, "too bright," and rested against the log's bark.

When the sun came up, Linnet began to realize they would have to stop somewhere, rest and eat. "Devon?" she asked softly.

He opened his eyes, clear and bright, the blue sparkling. "I thought it was a dream," he said, smiling, perfect white teeth against his dark skin. "I thought if I opened my eyes you wouldn't be here, and I'd know I made it all up."

She put her hand in the soft, curling thickness of his black hair. "You'd be right, too, because you're not even going to be able to get rid of me in your sleep from now on."

He grinned broader. "When we get out of this, let's make more Mirandas."

She gave him a look of disgust. "Don't you think of anything else?"

"It's been—"

"Don't tell me—a long time."

He smiled at her and didn't answer.

"Devon," she said seriously. "I don't know what to do now. You need to be dry and to rest, and we both need food."

He lifted his head and stared about him. "We're not far enough yet from Crazy Bear. Can you hang on and just drift for a while longer?"

"Yes, if you can."

"Yes," he said as he closed his eyes again.

In the afternoon it rained, and Linnet was glad because her neck and hands were beginning to get sunburned. Devon's dark skin seemed impervious to the sun, and she was glad the exposed sores were starting to heal. At sundown, when the rain stopped, Devon helped Linnet paddle the log to shore. She could not believe how weak she had become from lack of food and twenty-four hours of floating, drifting down a river on a log.

Devon sank to a soft bed of dried leaves. "Go find us something to eat, woman," he said as he closed his eyes.

Linnet stood over him and glared down as he opened one eye in amusement. "You will pay for this, Devon Macalister," she said, but he closed the eye and smiled peacefully as she slowly walked into the woods.

The Kentucky wilderness was a haven of wild game, wild fruits and nuts. She filled her skirt with fat, ripe blackberries and took them back to Devon. He ate slowly, sucking on each berry while Linnet gobbled them.

She stopped and stared at him. "How long has it been since you ate?"

He shrugged slightly. "A few days. I lost track of time." He looked at her and his expression was tender and loving. "I didn't expect to see you there, Lynna. You shouldn't have come."

"Once I lost you because I thought there was no hope for us and I certainly wasn't going to let it happen again. Besides, the Squire said you'd run away and left me."

He didn't speak and became very interested in a blackberry.

"I know it was he who . . . I know what he did."

"I reckoned you did," Devon said as he put the berry in his mouth. "Now let's get away from this river and get some sleep. Tomorrow we'll start walkin'."

"But how can we? Your feet are so awful."

He reached across the space separating them and took a handful of her wet skirt and petticoats. "If I remember rightly, you got on enough clothes to make a hundred pairs of moccasins and maybe a couple of shirts, too."

"Yes, of course." She stood, lifted her skirt and untied the drawstring to the top petticoat.

Devon watched her intently but said nothing.

She tore the cloth into strips and bound his feet, trying not to look at the awful mess they had become. When he stood again, she looked away from the stoic expression he adopted. There were times when Devon seemed very remote and very much a Shawnee. They did not walk far, and he constantly showed her how not to leave a trail.

They finally stopped and slept under the sheltered overhang of a washed out gully. Linnet removed the bandages from his feet and then slept peacefully, wrapped tightly in his arms.

Something tickled her nose and she scratched it before opening her eye. Devon kissed her slack, sleep-softened mouth and her arms slid about his neck.

"No, my sweet little bird, not here. We must travel."

He looked up at the overhanging trees. "I don't feel safe here. We're being followed and he's close to us."

"He?" Linnet's eyes were wide.

"I don't know who. Let's go quickly and quietly." Devon's feet had begun to scab and she knew the reapplied bandages would not be good for them.

They walked slowly, and very weakly, Devon more used to the semi-fast than Linnet. She felt dizzy and merely followed him, not questioning or even really aware of where they were. Sometimes he stopped and seemed to almost sniff the air.

"Devon—," she began, but his stern look silenced her.

He was very aware of her noisy footsteps, while Devon, much heavier, could hardly be heard, he stepped so lightly and carefully across the forest floor. They stopped once for more blackberries, but Devon always seemed to be watching for something, preoccupied, while Linnet, with shaking hands, tried to eat as much as possible.

"Come," he said, very softly so that she barely heard him, and she looked with regret at the vines heavy with ripe fruit.

At dusk she looked at Devon's scarred back, and then the earth seemed to spin round and round, and she felt so heavy and then so light. Her knees gave way, and she fell to the ground.

"Linnet!" Devon held her head in his arms. "Linnet," he said again, and she opened her eyes in surprise.

She started to sit up but he held her firmly. "I fell?"

"Yes," he said, frowning slightly. "I'm afraid I've pushed you too far. See those rocks over there?"

She lifted slightly and nodded.

"Can you make it over there?"

"Of course." She tried again to sit, but he held her and his eyes flashed angrily.

"Linnet! I'm tired of your 'of courses,'" he mocked her crisp accent. "I guess I forget that you're an Easterner and not bred to this life. You should have had enough sense to tell me you couldn't go on. Now stop tryin' to do everything in the world by yourself and get over between those rocks. I'm gonna make a roof over our heads."

"But what about you, Devon? You're the one

285

who's hurt." She touched his scabbed arm. "And you haven't had any more food than I."

"When we get through all this, I'm gonna take you to meet my great-grandfather. He was so afraid that my white blood would make me too soft that he nearly killed me when he put me through the Rites of Manhood. The fire and Crazy Bear ain't nothin' compared to the things that old man thought up."

"But it couldn't be! You had no scars before this."

He smiled down at her. "It's nice to know you been lookin'."

She looked away. "I think I'll go to the rocks now."

"Tell me, are all English girls like you?"

"Not in the least. I'm afraid I have dishonored the entire English people. If my father had known the things I've done since meeting you, I'm sure he'd refuse to acknowledge me as his daughter." She sat back against one of the boulders and watched Devon break off thin branches from the trees for the roof.

"Lynna," he said softly, "tell me about your family. Why'd you leave England and all that money you had?"

Quietly, she told him of her childhood of luxury, of having everything within her grasp. But when her father's mines failed, he walked away without a backward glance, almost as if he looked forward to a new life in a new land.

"You havin' all them servants—is that what's made you so bossy?"

She ignored his comment.

"You ain't gonna have no big house and people to wait on you if you stay with me," he said almost threateningly. "My mother—"

"All rich people are not cut from the same cloth, nor are all Indians nor, I hope, are all vain store clerks! If I'd wanted riches I could have married one of my suitors in England. And perhaps your mother had other reasons for leaving besides her hunger for silk gowns. Perhaps she was worried that her sons would grow up to be pursued by Indians, that her husband would risk being killed by a bear or her friends disfigured in fires." She turned away, trying to control her anger.

"Maybe," Devon whispered, his hands busy with building the shelter.

It was a long while before Linnet spoke again. "What about whoever was following us?"

"Not was, still is, by my figurin'. He's been followin' us since we left the river. If it was Crazy Bear's man he'd a' made his move by now, but he ain't, just keeps followin' us, so I guess he's just curious."

"How can you hear him? I listened and heard nothing."

He looked at her as if she had suddenly sprouted three new heads. "Lord! He makes more noise than a buffalo. He must be a big man, heavy. Walks stiff-legged, probably a white man."

She looked at him in wonder and then her eyes scanned the forest. "Where is he now?" she asked quietly.

"He went off a while ago, just after you fell down, reckon to get some food or maybe he got tired of watchin'. Anyways I don't think I wanta leave you alone out here."

"Me? But I have nothing to steal."

He looked at her in amusement, and she felt her cheeks grow hot. "I reckon it's my fault," he said as he carefully placed tree branches across the top of the rocks. "I shoulda had you by my side for the last three years teachin' you just what it is you got to steal."

She looked up at him and smiled, suddenly happy.

"You stay right here, and I'm gonna get us somethin' to eat. I'll be within earshot so if you move one foot from there I'll know it and I'll know if anybody comes, too. You understand me?"

"Yes."

He slipped into the woods, his dark skin and pants blending with the deep, rich green of the Kentucky woods. Linnet didn't remember even closing her eyes, but all she knew was that she opened them to Devon's kiss.

"Here." He dumped several kinds of berries in

her lap. "I got a couple of rabbits, but I don't wanta light a fire out here at night."

She ate the berries greedily, and even in the darkness she could sense Dévon's tiredness. He stretched out, his long body barely fitting in the little shelter, and pulled Linnet into his arms. She lay awake a moment, listening to his quiet breathing, smelling the rich earthiness of him. A remembrance of a ball she had attended when she was fourteen floated before her. She had worn a white satin gown with an overskirt of yellow silk, a rose of the same yellow in her hair. She remembered all the slim, handsome young men bowing politely before her. "Miss Linnet, may I have this dance?" The words echoed through her mind, and she snuggled closer to Devon.

"Lynna."

"Yes?" she whispered, her lips close to his.

"You've told me no before, but I wanta make love to you now. Would you say no to me again?"

She didn't answer him but pulled his face down to hers. She was hungry for him and her fear, the long journey with Yellow Hand, seeing Devon hurt and in pain, all these things lent a fierceness to her passion, a longing and desperation.

"Sssh, love," he calmed her and kissed her temples, and Linnet could feel her own tears as they rolled down her cheeks.

Devon understood the tears and he wished

he could promise her they were useless, but he couldn't. He joked with her, teased her, but he never let her know the danger he knew they could be in. Crazy Bear was a lazy man, and Devon doubted if he'd follow them this far, but he wasn't sure. They shouldn't have stopped now, at least not on the ground, in a tree maybe, but he couldn't let her know how close to death they could be. Whether she knew it or not, Linnet was near exhaustion, and as yet he was still too weak to carry her.

"I love you, Lynna, remember that, I love you."

"Yes, Devon, yes." But Linnet no longer cared for words of love or for any emotion but the weight and feel of the man above her. Her hands ran down his sides, fingertips on his ribs. Her mind turned about in a whirlpool as he touched her. She wanted to scream with the pleasure, the joy of him. She arched her body to meet him, drawing him closer, nearer. She did cry out once, and he heard it and should have silenced her, but his own ecstasy was too sharp, too exquisite, to stop.

He hovered above her, looking at her, her face and hair pale in the moonlight. She smiled like a cat, dreamy, languid. He moved slightly, and her eyes flew open and her legs locked around him.

"No! Don't leave me." She couldn't get enough of him. He had left her before.

"Never, love, never. I'll not move all night if you don't want me to. I'll not crush you?"

She just closed her eyes and smiled that little cat smile again. "I'll manage to bear the pain," she whispered and soon slept, contented, her mind not even aware of the concept of danger.

Chapter Twenty-three

IT WAS VERY EARLY MORNING WHEN DEVON'S tenseness woke her. He rolled from her, his eyes searching the grayness around them as he silently drew on his pants. One look of warning was enough to keep Linnet from either moving or speaking. Devon vanished into the half-light, and she turned to her stomach, watched and listened, but hearing or seeing nothing. The sun began to lighten the day, the birds called to one another, but Linnet still saw nothing. She began to relax and felt herself falling asleep.

"So we meet again."

Linnet opened her eyes but she didn't look up because she knew the voice and dreaded it.

"I reckon Mac heard me comin'," he said.

She turned her head and looked up at the brilliant, white form of Cord Macalister. She pulled her petticoats closer about her, the covering that Devon had draped over her nude body.

"You don't have to look at me like that." He smiled, and Linnet felt herself warming to him in spite of herself. Cord's handsomeness had that effect on most women.

"Why are you here?" she managed to ask from her undignified position.

"I saw you floatin' down the river, looked like you needed help."

"Then it looked wrong," came Devon's quiet voice.

She hadn't heard him approach, and from the surprise on Cord's face, neither had he. Something strange passed across Cord's eyes for a moment, and then he smiled lazily.

"Mac, it's good to see you again. At least it's better'n last time." He made a noise that was meant to be a laugh.

Linnet couldn't read Devon's face, as his eyes turned hard and brittle, his wide-legged stance unforgiving.

"I brung some birds," Cord continued. "Thought you could use 'em."

Devon nodded his head once, and Linnet knew he thought of her more than himself.

The five birds, skewered and dripping into the fire, Linnet considered the most beautiful sight in the world. Cord grinned at her as she pulled away one leg, black, crusty skin on the outside, pink, hot, and succulent on the inside. Cord helped himself to an entire bird, but Devon remained immobile, watching Cord, wary, untrusting. Linnet could say nothing. This conflict was between two brothers, and she had no right to interfere.

Cord licked a finger, studying the half-eaten bird. "Now, Mac, this ain't no way to greet your long-lost brother." He watched Devon, saw he showed no sign of surprise. "You tell him?"

"Yes," Linnet answered. "Devon, would you like something to eat?"

He ignored her.

Cord chuckled. "Seems the boy's afraid he takes his eyes off me, I just might run off with you—again," he added, his eyes sparkling as they left her face and flickered briefly on her body, one shoulder exposed by a torn sleeve. "What he don't seem to know is that I come to make my peace with him. I had a long while to think on what happened and I decided women are easier to come by than brothers, and if it's all the same to him, I'd like to start over again."

Linnet looked at Devon, his face unreadable. She knew well how hard it was to forgive someone for what seemed unforgivable. She stood and held her hand out to him. "Walk with me?"

He stood silently, seeming reluctant to leave Cord, to let the man out of his sight. They were some distance from the little camp before he spoke. "Linnet, if you think you're gonna talk me into—"

"I have no intention of talking to you at all,"

she interrupted. "I just wanted a little privacy. I think we have nearly three years of wasted time to make up for. I thought you might like to kiss me."

He grinned crookedly. "I dare say I might like to," he mocked her accent. He grabbed her in his arms and twirled her around, then held her close, not noticing that he supported her entire weight, her feet completely away from the forest floor.

"I'm glad it's past," she said into his neck.

"You mean the bad times?"

"Yes." Her teeth nipped his neck, her tongue savoring the smooth skin.

"Lord, Linnet!" He bent and put his arm beneath her knees and lifted her. "I never want to let you go. I never want you to be out of my sight."

She smiled, unnaturally happy, too happy. "I never thought we could have gotten over all the bad times, did you?"

He brought his lips down on hers, his mouth open, swallowing her, pulling her from herself. Suddenly he broke away and she saw anger in his eyes. "I know what you're tryin' to do, Linnet Blanche Tyler."

She looked at him in astonishment. "I don't know what—"

"Oh yes you do, and stop tryin' to look innocent. You're about as innocent as . . . as, well, I don't know what, but I do know what you're doin', and you can stop it."

She snuggled against him, nuzzling his shoulder. "Whatever do you mean?"

He pulled her face back to look at him. "Now I know some men let their wives tell them what to do, but I'm not one of 'em, and you can start gettin' used to the idea right now. You mighta spent your life in school, but I ain't exactly dumb and I can see through your little tricks."

"Devon, I have no idea what you're speaking of. Could you possibly explain it to me?"

"You're tryin' to get me to talk about how mean I was to you and how you forgave me. Now you want me to forgive Cord, after all he's done to me."

"And what would be so wrong with that?"

"First of all, I ain't the forgivin' kind. When somebody does me dirt, I don't forget it in a hurry."

"That's a fine thing to say! What if I felt that way about you?"

He grinned. "You were influenced by wantin' to be in my bed."

"Devon!" She looked shocked.

"But I ain't got no feelin's like that towards Cord. He wants my forgivin' he's gotta prove himself before I say he's my brother."

She looked away and found it almost impossible to be disdainful of a man who held her in his arms high above the ground. "I think you're totally unfair."

"And I think you're totally too bossy." He nibbled her ear. "You think we made another young'un last night? I didn't even know I was so strong as to give you a baby after only one night."

She gave him a look of disgust. "I am finding different facets of your personality that I do not like."

He looked puzzled for a moment. "Sometimes I think I'm glad I don't understand everythin' you say. You know I almost forgot how to read?"

"No!"

He grinned, since she had looked back at him. "Come on, let's go back. I'm gettin' hungry."

"Then you'll speak to Cord?"

"Maybe," he said noncommittally. "Let's go." He set her down, and she followed him, watching his back, the burns still raw.

Cord watched them approach, waiting quietly for some sign from Devon. The two men stared at one another, so different yet, the same fire in both pairs of eyes.

"You seen anythin' of Crazy Bear?" Devon asked as he sat down on the thick leaves, his back against the cool rocks, and reached for one of the birds on the skewer.

Cord relaxed. "Nothin'. Was he the one burned you?"

"No." Devon ate the meat slowly so as not to hurt his fasting stomach. "That happened back in Spring Lick."

Linnet knew Cord was curious and that Devon would say no more. "Devon ran inside a burning building and saved my daughter."

Cord looked from one to the other. "Daughter, heh? I reckon that makes me an uncle."

Linnet tried not to blush but she couldn't help it. She reached for another piece of bird.

"Don't eat no more of that," Devon said.

"But I'm hungry."

"Linnet!" His eyes narrowed at her. "You been too long without food and you can't stuff yourself."

She knew he was right and she wanted more to eat, but she lay back against the rock and closed her eyes. How good it was to have someone else make decisions. The insects hummed, and she fell asleep, not even waking when Devon pulled her down so her head rested on his lap. He stroked her forehead and watched her, aware of how tired she was, how she needed someone to look out for her.

"Looks to me like she's plumb done in," Cord said quietly. "You two been through a lot?"

Devon nodded. "Crazy Bear held me for a while, removed some skin, and then Linnet here"—he looked down at her in admiration—"come to get me. Rode for days."

"How'd she track you?"

"Yellow Hand came with her. I don't know how she got caught and he didn't."

"Yellow Hand?" Cord lifted his eyebrows and looked down at the sleeping Linnet. "It's hard to believe that boy'd help any whites after what happened to his ma."

Devon touched her hair, his arm across her

shoulders protectively. "Linnet has a way with her."

"That she does." Cord grinned. "I'm gonna go outside and keep watch, just in case Crazy Bear gets any ideas."

Devon nodded and watched the big man walk away. He touched the side of Linnet's face, his thumb caressing her eyebrow, and thought of how good it was to be near her, that they were safe. He leaned his head back against the rock and slept.

Only the forest knew of the four Indians who stalked the two men and the woman. Only the forest saw and heard.

Chapter Twenty-four

THERE WAS NO SOUND TO WAKE OR WARN HIM. One moment he was asleep, the next the cold steel blade of a knife pressed against his throat, and Devon opened his eyes to meet Crazy Bear's, the fierce, fanatical gleam showing his triumph at catching his prey. The knife pierced the skin of his neck, and a stream of thick, hot blood ran from the wound.

Linnet woke, feeling Devon's body grow tight, rigid. She did not move, sensing the danger. Only her head turned slightly, and a huge lump came into her throat when she saw the blood on Devon's neck. She felt his hand tighten on her shoulder and she was silent.

Devon spoke quietly to the Indian, words she did not understand, but Crazy Bear's eyes burned brighter and he grabbed Linnet's hair and pulled her away from Devon.

"No, Devon, no!" Linnet screamed as he lunged for her.

His rib deflected the knife blade that would have slipped deeply into his side. Crazy Bear hit the man who'd stabbed Devon, and the man fell to the ground. Crazy Bear did not want to lose Devon yet, he wanted the pleasure of his own method of killing his prisoners. Devon talked to the Indian, quiet and low, but the words seemed to make the dark eyes more and more ugly, more feverish. She thought she even saw the man laugh once. Their hands were bound tightly with pieces of rawhide.

"Lynna, I . . ."

She looked into his eyes and saw more pain there than she'd ever seen when he'd been burned. His eyes were awful, insane. "Devon, please don't blame yourself."

Crazy Bear's sharp cuff to her ribs sent her gasping to her knees and she saw three men holding Devon as he struggled to protect her. The Indians pulled them from the rocks into the sunlight, and Linnet screamed at the sight of Cord, his throat deeply cut from side to side. He stared up at them, unseeing. She turned away, head down, eyes closed, as the Indians pulled her past him. Her tears came unbidden when she heard Devon whisper, "Brother," as he passed the dead man who had been Cord Macalister.

Crazy Bear threw her into a saddle and mounted behind her, his greasy arm tight about her waist and cutting off her breath. She dared not look at Devon, fearful of seeing in his eyes knowledge of what she knew would happen to them. Please, Lord, she prayed, let it be over quickly. She thought of Miranda and Phetna, of how the child would grow up without ever seeing her mother again. And Devon, at least she'd had one more night with him. She lifted her head and looked out across the forest. Her father had always been a brave man, all the Tylers were, and she would not disgrace them now as she met her own death. Soon it would all be over, and she would join Devon in another world, a world without danger or sorrow. Her chin came up, and she held herself high. She would not disgrace her ancestors or the man she loved by any show of cowardice.

Devon watched her, and his stomach rolled over at the thought of what Crazy Bear would do to his lovely Linnet. He had tried to bargain with the man to get him to forget her and just take him, but the Indian would not. Would that he'd never seen her again rather than lead her into this. Her little chin in the air made his stomach further contract, and he looked away from her.

It was night when they reached Crazy Bear's new camp, and instead of putting the prisoners in one of the huts, he tied them to two poles, set about a yard apart. Two men guarded them, war clubs across their brown arms, while the other men began to talk, laugh and pass several jugs of homebrewed whiskey. Only once did Linnet try to talk to Devon, and the hurt in his voice when he answered made her stop any other words.

They stood all night, while the women poked both of them with sharp little sticks and the men sat and watched.

"Will it be in the morning?" Linnet whispered, her voice ragged as she breathed deeply, trying to calm herself against the hundreds of little painful places on her body.

"Yes," he said, his voice very low. "Lynna, I . . . I want to tell you that . . ."

She twisted against the bindings, trying to see him. "Please don't say anything. I knew what might happen when I left Spring Lick."

He looked ahead to the trees and prayed to the gods of his great-grandfather. He prayed for strength to endure, not the pain but the loss of Linnet, the ability to endure the pain she would feel.

A shot echoing through the dense woods brought every head up. Devon looked and saw a pattern of shadows where it should not be. There was something familiar about the shape, the way the long, thin shadow, the arm, moved slowly, languidly. He blinked his blurry eyes. No! It couldn't be!

The four Indian men were on their feet, their bows and arrows, their hand weapons a poor defense against the Kentucky long rifles.

"What is it?" Linnet asked, and Crazy Bear's eyes silenced her.

Another shot sounded, and one of the renegades went down, a gaping hole in his chest. Linnet closed her eyes, trying to bury her face in her neck, anything to block out the horror that was beginning to happen around her. She didn't see Crazy Bear raise his arm with the sharp steel axe as he aimed at Devon's head. Nor did she see the man who attacked him with a pitchfork.

Devon twisted toward her. "Linnet! Look! Look up!" he called.

There was noise all around them, screams, people yelling, and she didn't want to look.

"Linnet!"

His commands brought her head up in time to see Agnes Emerson lean into the recoil of a six-foot rifle. In wonder, Linnet looked all around her. They were all there! All of Sweetbriar was swarming over the Indian camp—Esther and Doll, Wilma and Floyd, Lyttle and Agnes, Phetna, Gaylon, Corinne, Yellow Hand with them, and others she didn't know. She began to cry, great wrenching sobs that tore through her. Sweetbriar! Beautiful, wonderful Sweetbriar! They had come when she most needed them, when they most needed their help.

"You all right?" Wilma Tucker cut Linnet's bindings.

Linnet couldn't talk, she could only cry, and Wilma cheerfully pulled her friend into her arms.

"What we gonna do with 'em?" Agnes' voice boomed.

Linnet looked up from Wilma's shoulder to see a blur that was Devon as he lifted her from the ground. She felt his tears on her neck as he held her, and she hugged him tightly, trying to take some of the trembling from him. "I'm all right, Devon, please, I'm all right."

"Looks like you two quit feudin', at least for a time."

Linnet turned toward the unmistakable voice of Doll as he stood by Gaylon. Devon lifted his head, and his grip on Linnet loosened. She smiled at him, then released him and ran to clutch Doll, her exuberance nearly knocking him from his feet. The laughter began to come as everyone hugged everyone else.

Corinne held Linnet to her. "You ain't mad at me no more for lyin' to you?"

"No," Linnet said truthfully. "It's turned out all right, and that's what matters."

Corinne sniffed and looked away as Worth Jamieson proudly introduced his new little wife.

"What's the matter, boy, you 'fraid you gonna lose her again?"

Linnet turned to see Devon hovering near her.

"Don't blame 'im none," Gaylon continued. "If I found me a little gal dressed like that runnin' loose in the woods, I'd be afraid of losin' her, too."

Linnet looked down at her ragged dress. The

skirt was torn up to her thigh on one side, one shoulder and half the neck were torn away at the top.

"You two old men ain't changed none, always buttin' in where you ain't needed," Devon drawled.

"Ain't needed!" Doll exploded. "Why, when we found you two you was—"

"You young'uns stop it right now!" Agnes commanded. "In case nobody's noticed, we're standin' amongst somethin' not so pretty." Her words made everyone look at the carnage about them.

"Cord," Linnet said. "They killed—"

"We know." Esther patted her arm. "He went quick though, and we done buried 'im."

"All right," Agnes said. "Let's get to buryin' these. Esther, you and Corrine take Lynna and Mac somewheres and let 'em rest." She eyed Devon. "And don't you give me no trouble. Your back's so ugly it makes me hurt just to see it."

"You should see his feet!" Linnet said, then stopped when she met silence from everyone until Doll began to laugh.

"Go on, Corrine, take 'em somewheres, and don't you start no fights between 'em like you done before," Doll told his daughter.

"Ah, Pa," Corrine said, "I'm done married to Jonathan now." She turned to Linnet. "I got me a little boy."

Linnet almost told her of her own daughter

but didn't. Devon refused to move more than a foot from Linnet and held her hand constantly. She needed the reassurance, fearful that she'd wake and find herself tied to a pole as Crazy Bear danced around her.

The others returned quickly, and Agnes pointed to a tall, thin blond man Linnet didn't know. "That's Lester Sawrey. He's come to Sweetbriar since you been there." Lester seemed to be a man of importance.

Lyttle went with Jonathan to the horses, several miles away, and all the people sat together around a fire, and when the supplies were brought, they began to eat.

"How is Lincoln?" Linnet asked Esther of the child she had helped deliver.

"Lord!" Agnes said. "Esther's already had another one since you left. If Mac don't come back and keep Doll at the store, she's gonna get wore out havin' kids."

Esther hid her face, but Doll grinned from ear to ear.

"How'd you know?" Devon asked as he looked from one person to the other.

"Phetna," Doll said as he motioned his head back to the woman. "There I was just settin' on my front porch, mindin' my own business, whittlin' and workin' like I'm always a doin'." His eyes danced with merriment. "When this here woman sticks her ugly face up and grins at me. It didn't take me but a minute to know it was

Phetna. She always was so ugly she could turn a man's hair white with just one look, and she ain't changed a bit."

He paused and looked at his audience. "Later somebody told me she'd been in a fire and was burned, so I looked real hard and you know, they're right. She ain't quite so ugly as I 'membered."

Everyone, and loudest of all, Phetna, laughed and Linnet knew how good the woman felt to be part of a group of people again. They spent the day talking, the men preparing crude shelters for the night and remembering the days they had spent together in Sweetbriar.

Linnet remembered Cord and thought how he would have been glad when Devon called him brother. Agnes understood her sorrow and talked to her about Cord, how he worried about getting old, how maybe it was better this way. Linnet didn't believe a word of what she said, but at least she had good memories of him.

Strangely enough, the people asked very few questions about Linnet, and she wondered how much Phetna had told them. She felt the blood rise in her face when she thought of all Phetna could have told them. The sun was setting and the long day was finally coming to an end. Linnet stretched and was glad it was over, that they were finally safe, but she cast one wistful look at Devon. Only last night she had spent the night in his arms. How long would it be again before she got to spend another night with him?

The Squire's words about Devon haunted her. Would he still want to marry her after all they'd been through? He'd gotten what he wanted from her so why should he marry her? When Devon met her eyes, she looked away.

"I reckon it's time," Doll said as he exchanged looks with Agnes.

"I reckon you're right."

The others in the circle sighed in resignation and avoided Devon's and Linnet's eyes. Slowly, they rose to their feet.

"No," Agnes said, "you two just stay there. This is somethin' we gotta do whether we like it or not."

The people walked into the woods and Devon took Linnet's hand. "What do you think they'd say if I crawled into your sleepin' roll tonight?"

She jerked her hand away. "Please don't. I had enough of that in Spring Lick."

"I got 'im," Gaylon said and they looked up to see the man holding a long rifle aimed at Devon's head.

"Gaylon!" Linnet exclaimed and started to rise but she felt something behind her and looked at Agnes aiming a rifle at her.

"Just what the hell's goin' on?" Devon asked and started to stand, but Jonathan grinned and pushed him back down, with more force than was needed.

"Doll, you're the talker, you tell 'em," Lyttle said.

"Well now, Sweetbriar was a real peaceful

town until Mac here brung home this little English girl." He grinned at Devon's frown. "Since then things been turned upside down. Mac's gone half the time, either chasin' her or tryin' to get away from her, and when he's in Sweetbriar, he's so ornery, can't nobody live near him. Now this happens. Phetna comes tearin' into Sweetbriar on a mule with this god-awful story that we can't hardly believe but she swears is true. What's more, she's got this young'un in the saddle what she says belongs to you two."

Linnet bent her head, not able to look at any of them.

"Now that just ain't right," Agnes said. "It ain't right for you two to be moonin' after one another and causin' two towns so much trouble, but when you two start makin' babies and still ain't married, then that's goin' against the Lord, and we figure we gotta do somethin' about it."

"And just what're you plannin' to do?" Linnet could hear the anger and hostility in Devon's voice.

"We decided to take matters into our own hands," Doll continued. "We decided we can help undo some of what's been done."

"How's that?" Devon snapped.

"Lester, here, if you remember, is a preacher and he's gonna marry you two. And if you don't agree, I reckon we're gonna have to do somethin' about it."

Linnet looked at the familiar faces holding

rifles, pitchforks, scythes, and couldn't help wondering how much Doll really meant.

"You ain't sayin' nothin' you're gonna back up, old man," Devon said, anger saturating his voice, his every movement. "I don't like anybody tellin' me what I'm gonna do, especially who I'm gonna marry. I'll make up my own mind whenever I want, and I don't need anybody tellin' me when that's gonna be."

"Shoot him," Linnet said quietly, and everyone looked at her, her eyes flashing the red Jessie and Lonnie liked to tease her about. "You heard me, shoot him. You cannot imagine what I've been through since I met this man, and for the last week he's been swearing he loves me and wants to marry me and now I find he's been using me for his own purposes."

"Linnet!" Devon said as he grabbed her hand. "That ain't true. You know what you're sayin' ain't true."

"All I know is that you're refusing to marry me."

"It's not that. It's just that I don't like being forced."

"And I'm forcing you? I believe I have shown an incredible amount of both patience and tolerance in regard to you."

He stared at her, then began to laugh, hugged her and held her to him, her arms pinned immobile against his chest. "I think you're doin' it again, ain't you?"

She smiled against his shoulder. "I have no idea what you mean."

He held her away from him. "I think it's gonna take a long time to teach you that men are the head of the household."

"Household?" she asked, wide-eyed.

Devon turned to look up the rifle barrel to Doll. "Go get Lester. I'm ready."

Doll grinned and lowered his rifle. "'Bout time, I'd say!"

The wedding was quiet, mostly with the sounds of the forest around them, and a few sniffs from some of the women, although Linnet did think she saw a tear glisten in Gaylon's eye. Corinne and Esther made wreaths of flowers to cover Linnet's torn dress, and she held a bouquet in her shaking hands. Once the decision was made, Devon seemed not to be bothered with the seriousness of marriage, although Linnet found his hands to be suddenly cold.

"You can kiss her now."

Devon held Linnet's shoulders and kissed her hard, and she was startled because of the intense relief he showed at the ceremony's ending. As Lyttle turned her around to kiss her cheek, she had a brief thought of quiet evenings before a fire as Devon told his thoughts during their unusual wedding.

They ate again as they sat around the fire, and neither Devon nor Linnet looked at one another, both suddenly shy. Two hours after the ceremony, Lyttle and Jonathan showed them a shelter they had made that day. It was a short distance from the camp of the others.

"We figured you been through enough for one day so we'll leave you alone," Lyttle said. "But I'll warn you to be expectin' a shivaree when we get back home."

Devon smiled and pulled the blanket aside to admit Linnet. They still didn't look at one another as their eyes adjusted to the darkness.

"I'm sorry about all this," Devon began. "I don't just mean this thing with Crazy Bear, but all of it. I'll try to make it up and be good to you."

Linnet looked at him very, very seriously. "Does this mean you'll always be a perfect husband and not get angry at the least little thing I do and—"

A quick flash of anger crossed Devon's face. "Damn it, Linnet! I'm—" He broke off when he saw the laughter in her eyes. "You are the beatinest woman."

Linnet's joyous, triumphant laughter filled the air inside and out of the crude grass shelter.

"Shut up, Doll," Agnes said to the man's laughing remark, but neither Devon nor Linnet heard any sounds for a long, long time.

Tapestry

HISTORICAL ROMANCES

Breathtaking New Tales

of love and adventure set against history's most exciting time and places. Featuring two novels by the finest authors in the field of romantic fiction—<u>every month</u>.

Next Month From Tapestry Romances

DAWNFIRE
by Lynn Erikson

MONTANA BRIDES
by DeAnn Patrick